MAID OF HONOUR

The Anne Boleyn Chronicles
Book One

Rozsa Gaston

SAPERE
BOOKS

MAID OF
HONOUR

Published by Sapere Books.

24 Trafalgar Road, Ilkley, LS29 8HH

saperebooks.com

ISBN: 978-0-85495-721-7

For Ava Gaston,
who encouraged me every step of the way

ACKNOWLEDGEMENTS

Thank you to my eagle-eyed editor Amy Durant at Sapere Books, without whom this series on Anne Boleyn's time before joining the Tudor court would not have been born.

A deep debt of gratitude goes to Dagmar Eichberger, art historian and world-renowned expert on Margaret of Austria, whose insights were invaluable on Margaret's use of carefully selected artwork to strengthen her authority as ruler of the Netherlands.

Thanks also to Sarah Gristwood, who fired my interest in Margaret of Austria with her opening chapter in her book *Game of Queens.*

Additional thanks go to my team of manuscript readers, Michèle Callard, Keira Morgan, Cynthia Louise Moore, and Sasha Pinto-Jayawardena, Kim Huther of Wordsmith Proofreading, and noted European medieval and Renaissance historian, Susan Abernethy. With your help, may Anne Boleyn's time at Margaret of Austria's court come alive for the legions of readers who fan the flame of her legend.

I am indebted to Hervé Passot and Laurence Delsaut of the Departmental Archives of the North in Lille, France for providing original documents to aid me in my research.

Thanks also to Anne Boleyn experts Sylvia Barbara Soberton, author of *The Forgotten Years of Anne Boleyn,* and to Natalie Grueninger, whose *On the Tudor Trail* blog fired my imagination.

My deep appreciation to Bronxville Library in Bronxville, New York, for their unflagging help in obtaining works from larger libraries to aid me in my research.

LIST OF CHARACTERS

MAIDS OF HONOUR
Anne Boleyn
Barbe Lallemand
Agnes de Middelbourg
Isabelle de Longueval
Veronique de Hallewijn
Françoise de Bréderode
Jeanne de Rosimbos
Claude de Saillant
Étiennette de la Baume

ROYALS
Margaret of Austria — Archduchess of Austria, Dowager Duchess of Savoy, Governor of the Netherlands, Dowager Princess of Spain

Maximilian I of Austria — Archduke of Austria and Holy Roman Emperor, and Margaret's father

Charles of Habsburg — Duke of Burgundy, and Margaret's nephew

Lenore, Isabella, and Mary of Habsburg — Charles's sisters and Margaret's nieces.

Henry VIII of England — King of England and Anne Boleyn's future husband

OTHER NOTABLES
Thomas Boleyn — Anne Boleyn's father, English diplomat and career courtier to Henry VIII

Elisabeth Culemborg, Countess of Hoogstraten — Lady Margaret's head lady-in-waiting and *mère des filles* (mother of the maids)

Madame de Verneuil — lady-in-waiting and deputy *mère des filles*

Monsieur Semmonet — French tutor

Charles Brandon — Henry VIII's Master of the Horse and closest companion

Mercurino di Gattinara — Piedmontese statesman and jurist in Margaret of Austria's service

William de Croy, Lord of Chièvres — Tutor and chief advisor to Charles of Habsburg

Charles of Egmond, Duke of Guelders — Dutch nobleman who refused to recognise the legal transfer of his duchy sold by his father to Margaret's grandfather, Charles the Rash, in 1473

Desiderius Erasmus — Catholic theologian from Rotterdam

"*Groigne qui groigne, vive Bourgogne.*"
Grumble those who may, long live Burgundy.
— a favourite motto of Margaret of Austria

"*Ainsi sera, groigne qui groigne.*"
Let them grumble, this is how it's going to be.
— motto of Anne Boleyn, briefly adopted in 1530

ONE

The Burgundian-Habsburg Netherlands, 1512

Margaret scrutinised the painting on the wall. The new ambassador from England would arrive shortly. She would bathe him in Burgundian splendour from the moment he set foot in her palace. The discriminating expression on Philip the Good's face would do nicely. With a careful finger, she straightened the portrait of her great-grandfather, then stepped back, satisfied. Whoever the English king had sent didn't matter. What mattered was that he would return to England and report back on the glories of the Burgundian Low Countries to stoke his sovereign's interest.

At age twenty-one, King Henry VIII of England was reputed to be an eager and energetic pup. Margaret guessed he was as anxious to gain membership to the circle of Europe's most important princes as she was to gain his alliance against France. She sat at her desk and picked up the young English king's letter again. He was pressing for the betrothal agreement between his sister Mary and her nephew to be formalised. Henry Tudor had planned the engagement in 1507, but with his death, his son wished to reconfirm it and hoped for a firm answer from Lady Margaret's father, Emperor Maximilian, to be delivered to the new ambassador he was sending to the Court of Savoy now.

Margaret set down the letter and chuckled. A firm answer from Maximilian was a tall order, indeed. She looked up to see her steward appear at the door. "Madame, the ambassador from London has arrived," he announced.

"Remind me of his name."

"Thomas Boleyn, Madame. At your service," a cultured voice rang out, its French only slightly accented. Brushing past the steward, a trim, mid-sized man in travelling clothes entered the room. He bowed, fluid and practised.

Margaret studied him before rising. Perhaps in his mid-thirties, close to her in age, he wore his reddish-blond beard clipped short. Assessing his sharp eyes and tightly controlled expression, she guessed young Henry had sent someone reasonably intelligent. "Welcome to the Court of Savoy, Monsieur Boleyn." She came around from behind her desk and held out a hand.

The Englishman bowed then kissed it. "Madame, I am honoured to meet you. My king sends his highest regards and asks you to accept my credentials." Thomas Boleyn offered a leather pouch with King Henry's seal upon it.

Margaret dropped the pouch on her desk. She would read it later. "Your first credential is that your French is good."

"Thank you, Madame. I've studied for years, and French is often spoken at our queen's court."

Margaret chuckled. "It is I who taught your queen to speak it."

"I have heard, Madame. Was it in Spain, not too many years ago?"

"You have done your homework, Monsieur, but it was long ago, indeed." Fourteen years — at age thirty-three, it seemed a lifetime past.

"*Tempus fugit*, Madame."

"Time does indeed fly. If your Latin is as good as your French, we are off to a good start. Come, let us take some refreshment while you fill me in on your king."

As they left the room, Margaret caught Boleyn's lingering glance at the portrait of Philip the Good, his eyes taking in the refined visage of Burgundy's most glorious duke. She allowed herself a faint smirk. Let him admire her great-grandfather's legacy. Burgundy had once been a mighty duchy under his steady hand. How different it might have been had his son, Charles the Rash, not been so reckless. Charles's portrait was safely tucked away upstairs, out of sight. There was no need to remind visitors to the Court of Savoy of the man who had ended Burgundy's chance to become a great kingdom.

"I'll bet you one of my Spanish coursers against one of your hobbies," Margaret challenged the following day. What fun it was to disport with Boleyn. He was clever and quick — and just a little brazen, too. The evening before he had won at cards, beating her with a bluff even she hadn't seen through.

"Madame, I would hate to divest you of a fine courser, but we are counting on the emperor to give us an answer within ten days," Thomas Boleyn countered.

"It will be at least twenty. You may depend on it and decide now on the hobby you will give me when he finally answers." Her father hated to be pinned down, so she would, no doubt, win her bet.

"There is no contest between one of your Spanish stallions and an Irish hobby, my lady. I am entirely advantaged by such an unfair bet," Boleyn protested.

Margaret laughed. "Of course there's no contest. I'll enjoy seeing what one of your Irish hobbies looks like."

Boleyn extended his hand with a grin. "May the best man win."

Margaret gave his hand a firm shake. "I intend to."

Boleyn dipped his head. "I don't doubt it, Madame."

Ten days later, Margaret stared at her father's letter. Against all expectations, the emperor had responded promptly. His message was clear — the marriage was paramount. He trusted her to handle the negotiations. She read the letter aloud to Boleyn, who listened with a small smile on his face.

"Well, Monsieur Boleyn," she said, folding the letter, "it seems I've lost our wager."

"You've won where it counts," he replied. "Strengthening the alliance is worth far more than a courser."

"You're right," Margaret agreed. For Maximilian of Austria, no alliance was stronger than a marriage one. As much as he had complained of his own father, Frederick III as a weak ruler, it had been he, as Holy Roman Emperor, who had arranged the matrimonial masterstroke that had delivered Burgundy into Habsburg hands. The agreement between Frederick III and Charles the Rash to marry their children had resulted in Maximilian wedding Margaret's mother, Mary of Burgundy in 1477, bringing Europe's richest duchy under the aegis of the Holy Roman Empire. To France's detriment, Europe's balance of power had been permanently altered.

"No agreement can guarantee what lies ahead," Boleyn said thoughtfully.

"As well I know, Monsieur."

"I'm sure you do, Madame. I was a lad of fourteen when I heard my parents say you were dropped like a hot oatcake from the throne of France."

"I'm glad I never sat on it," Margaret huffed.

"I wondered that such a young princess could bounce back from such a defeat."

"Yet here I am." Margaret smiled stoutly as she squelched the memory of those two years in limbo. After being raised at the French court from age three as the future king's betrothed, she had been thrown over at age eleven. Forced to remain in France until Charles VIII of France and her father negotiated the return of her dowry lands, she had spent the next two years waiting to return to her homeland.

"Governing your own realm instead of sitting next to that smallish king," Boleyn added.

"I would have towered over him had we wed," Margaret jested.

"Not in height, alone, Madame. You would have run circles around the man."

"Better that Anne of Brittany did. I would not have had the patience to manage him." *Nor the desire*, she thought, recalling how small and gnomish Charles VIII had been.

"But now I must manage my king's impatience while we wait to see if this agreement comes to pass." Laughter twinkled in Boleyn's eyes.

"You must keep his attention on this plan," Margaret counselled. "After all, it was his idea in the first place."

"His wish since the day he ascended the throne has been to take a seat at the table of Europe's princes," Boleyn summed up.

"Then advise him to sit at my table and not at the French king's."

"Right you are, Madame. And with English wool spun into Flemish cloth, your table is solid oak, indeed."

"Remind him of that. He need only look to history to recall how flimsy French promises are." Margaret squeezed shut her eyes to blot out those childhood years spent on shifting sand. Mentored by Anne of France to become the future queen, at least she had been raised to rule. As for the French, she would never trust them again.

"Promises between princes are like gossamer webs," Boleyn remarked.

"If spun well enough, they are inescapable," Margaret parried.

"That is true, but your role is paramount, Madame. You are the linchpin of Europe's players."

"Tell your king if he wishes to play, he must join my wheel," Margaret said.

Boleyn cleared his throat, a smile playing at the corners of his mouth. "I will use other words to convey your message."

"You will know what words to use. And once you have passed this agreement to him, he will find reason to come to the Continent."

"Once I describe your court to him, he will be spoiling to replicate it himself."

"Do you think so?" Margaret chuckled. That was precisely her intention. "Be sure to remind him that his great aunt Margaret of York was my godmother."

"He is well aware of it, Madame. The king was close to his mother. He resembles his York ancestors far more than his father's side."

"And who does his sister Mary resemble?"

"Her mother, praise God. She has flowered into a great beauty."

"My nephew will be pleased." In truth, he would be terrified, but she wouldn't draw in too many details until he was older. At age thirteen, he would likely turn red and go mute at mention of a beautiful sixteen-year-old he was contracted to marry.

"But not as pleased as my king," Boleyn countered.

"Nor the emperor," Margaret agreed. Maximilian would be overjoyed on the day England joined matrimonial forces with the Holy Roman Empire. Such a union would deliver the death blow to France's aspirations to dominate Europe. Finally, both she and her father would be avenged for the wrongs committed against them by the French.

Tingling with anticipation, she met Thomas Boleyn's eyes. If only the wedding could take place tomorrow. "Now, where do I deliver the courser you have won from me?"

Boleyn paused. "Would Madame keep her courser and allow me another prize?"

Margaret appraised him coolly. Boleyn was turning out to be a good bit of fun. "What do you have in mind?'

"I have a daughter whose French is passable but not yet good. Could I send her to you?"

"How old is she?"

"Almost thirteen, Madame. A bright apple in need of some polish."

Margaret considered, then smiled. "Send her to me. I will make her one of my maids of honour."

"You are too kind, Madame."

Margaret's smile grew sharper. "Only when it suits me, Monsieur."

A few weeks later Boleyn's daughter arrived. The slight girl entered Margaret's room and curtseyed. She looked to be no more than ten years of age, although Thomas had said she was older.

"Lady Margaret, I am honoured to meet you," the child said in halting French.

"So, you are the daughter of Thomas Boleyn?" Margaret asked. The girl was dark-haired with olive-toned skin, not at all like her father, with his reddish complexion. Yet she shared his sharp chin and large dark brown eyes, with the same spark of intellect in them.

"Yes, Madame. I am Anne Boleyn," the girl replied.

"Your father is my favourite diplomat," Margaret remarked.

"He is my favourite, too," Anne responded.

Margaret chuckled. "Bless you, *ma petite*, of course he is. And if you are anything like him, you will do very well here at my court."

"I will try my best, Madame," Anne replied.

"You will now go with Lady Elisabeth, who is in charge of my maids of honour. You must listen closely to her and to her deputy, Madame de Verneuil, and follow their advice in everything."

"I will do my best, Madame."

Margaret signalled to her head lady-in-waiting, who stood in the doorway, a second woman behind her. The first stepped forward and put a hand on Anne's shoulder.

"Come, child. Madame de Verneuil and I will show you to your lodgings and explain your duties."

"Thank you, Madame," Anne answered, curtseying to her and then to Madame de Verneuil. "And thank you, Lady Margaret, for hosting me."

"You are welcome, little one. Now go and get settled before my flock of demoiselles descends on you. Do not listen to anything they say but only to your seniors."

Margaret waved a hand, bidding Anne goodbye. Thomas had sent a small, dark gem. She would see to it that this tiny treasure was polished to a high lustre at the Court of Savoy.

TWO

Anne's father's words echoed in her head, about how Lady Margaret ruled the Netherlands with a firm hand as regent, aunt to a boy destined for greatness. Her mother had added that the young prince might even win the title of Holy Roman Emperor someday. They had both turned to Anne with eager eyes that fired her. She would try her best at Lady Margaret's court.

Meanwhile, her sister had hung like a shadow behind her, passed over and forgotten. Anne had been chosen over Mary to go, ostensibly because her French was better. For two years she had applied herself to the lessons their tutor had given them while Mary dawdled and looked out the window. But Anne knew the real reason she had been picked was that her parents could see that she shared their driving ambition.

"Are you tired, *ma petite*?" Lady Elisabeth's voice broke into her thoughts.

"No, Madame. Only excited to begin my stay here," Anne replied in her best French.

Lady Elisabeth's eyes widened as she pursed her lips. "Lady Margaret has arranged for Monsieur Semmonet to be your French tutor. You will begin with him tomorrow morning. Then Madame de Verneuil will introduce you to the archduke and the princesses."

"Oh, Madame, I look forward to meeting them," Anne enthused, wondering if she had said something wrong.

"They are housed across the street at the palace of Lady Margaret's godmother, Margaret of Burgundy."

"Shall I take lessons with them?" Anne asked. Margaret of Burgundy — wasn't she the same as Margaret of York, the one her mother had mentioned? The woman who had sheltered the pretender, Perkin Warbeck, and been a thorn in Henry Tudor's side?

"We shall see. Your French will need to improve first."

"How old is the archduke, Madame?"

"Thirteen."

A thrill shot through her. "I'll be thirteen soon!"

Lady Elisabeth smiled. "So, you are twelve? You look younger. We'll fatten you up here."

Remaining silent, Anne followed her escort, traversing a large gallery hung with yellow and blue damask drapes and lined with portraits. Among them were those of her own sovereign, King Henry, and his queen, Katherine of Aragon. The portraits' subjects seemed to watch her as she passed, their eyes unnervingly lifelike, the details finer than in any painting she had ever seen before.

They climbed a broad staircase then hurried down a long hallway until they reached a large room filled with beds. Light streamed through tall windows and a sunbeam shone on one bed where Anne's trunks sat waiting.

"This will be yours, shared with another demoiselle," Lady Elisabeth explained.

"Who is she, Madame?"

"She arrives from Bremen next month. You will meet her then." Lady Elisabeth gestured towards a cupboard. "The ladies' maids will help you to unpack your things."

Anne was to serve Lady Margaret at the Court of Savoy, but she would also be served by her host's considerable staff. It was an improvement on her position back home. "What are my duties, Madame?"

"You are to attend to your studies, and to support the archduchess in all things," Lady Elisabeth answered simply.

Anne nodded, wishing she knew more about her host. Her father had meant to tell her all about Lady Margaret, but a sudden summons from the king had left him with time for only a brief farewell and a parting piece of advice — 'Master your French.'

Tingling, she imagined his pride on reading a letter from her, written in perfect French. Perhaps he would write back, to congratulate her.

"So, this is the new girl?" a voice sang out. Across the room an older demoiselle approached.

"This is Anne Boleyn from England," Lady Elisabeth said. "Her father was the English ambassador here last year."

"Hello, I'm Barbe. Welcome to Lady Margaret's court," the girl said, a smile lighting her broad face. Tall and sturdy, her hair was between blonde and light brown and her eyes were blue-grey.

"Thank you," Anne said. "My French is not so good."

Barbe laughed lightly. "Not to worry. It will improve fast, as most of us don't speak any English."

Anne relaxed. The older girl's open expression told her she was in good hands.

"I will leave you now and see you at the midday meal. Barbe will show you around and introduce you to the others," Lady Elisabeth directed.

Anne nodded, her senses dancing. Already, her life was more exciting than it had been back at Hever. Following the lead of the older girl, she left the room, drinking in all that she saw.

*

"Do you like dogs?" Barbe asked, stepping into the inner garden of the Court of Savoy.

"Oh yes! Especially boy dogs!" Anne's eyes darted around, searching for them.

The older girl laughed, the sound bright in the warm spring air. "Why boys?"

"They like me better than the girls."

"So, the *salopes* don't like you?" Barbe threw out a French word Anne didn't know; she could tell it wasn't meant favourably.

"I'm too much like them," Anne quipped.

The older girl gave her an assessing glance. "Is it the same with people?"

Anne sucked in her breath. "I hope not."

"You'll do well here if you manage to be like the others," Barbe advised, her tone light but her meaning unmistakable.

Anne nodded. "I'll try..." *to be as much like the ones I admire*, she finished silently.

Up ahead, a pair of small dogs burst into view, their high-pitched yaps echoing off the garden walls. "Here come the dogs now. Let's see if you are right."

Anne knelt, offering her hand, fingers curled. The larger white one sniffed then wagged its tail. The smaller, reddish-brown one held back, yapping furiously and flashing its teeth.

Anne stroked the white dog's ears, enjoying the softness beneath her fingers. In a minute, the dog's eyes closed, a groan of pleasure escaping it.

Barbe chuckled. "I see what you mean."

"The other one's a girl, is she not?"

"Yes. Babou here is a boy."

"I could tell."

"You'll have to win over Mignonne, too, if you wish to please Madame. Part of our job is to keep the dogs away from her when she's working. And out of her bedchamber."

Anne laughed. "Do they like to go in there?"

"Oh, yes. Especially this one." Barbe gave Babou a firm pat.

"Are we allowed to enter Madame's bedchamber to shoo them out?"

"Of course. And her study, too. If she is in conference, just get Babou out from under her desk, and be on your way."

"He hides under her desk?"

"Under her bed, too."

Anne glanced down at Babou, meeting his amber eyes. "Are you a scamp?" She scratched his muzzle, smiling at the way his eyelashes fluttered.

The dog huffed in agreement.

"Let's see how you do with Madame's birds," Barbe suggested.

"Birds?" Anne echoed, her interest piqued.

"Songbirds. Madame keeps a few in cages in her rooms."

Anne bit her lip. "I hope they'll like me."

"If they do, you might get to join the prince and princesses when they go hawking."

Anne's excitement sparked. "What fun!" Hawking — the royal sport, one she'd always dreamed of mastering.

Barbe grinned. "They mostly use female falcons. They're better hunters."

As Anne trailed behind, she pondered Barbe's words. Everyone said men were better hunters, but her mother had always said that at court, it was the women who hunted down secrets.

*

The next day Lady Elisabeth introduced Anne to her French tutor, a middle-aged man with a stiff posture and a carefully groomed beard.

"*Bonjour*, Monsieur." Anne dipped a graceful curtsey.

"*Bonjour*, Mademoiselle," Monsieur Semmonet replied, his tone clipped and his face unreadable. "You will have your lessons with me at nine every morning, after which you will join the other demoiselles." Without further comment, he turned away.

"Yes, Monsieur," Anne said. It was crucial that she perfected her French as quickly as possible. But the tutor's severe manner didn't seem inviting.

As they stepped into the hallway, Lady Elisabeth offered some words of comfort. "Monsieur Semmonet is strict, but he will perfect your French. You must try to absorb all that he teaches."

Anne hesitated. "I don't think he liked me."

"Nonsense. He is French, that's all. Once you show him your effort, he'll soften."

Anne wondered. She had often heard it said back home that the French were different from the English, sharper around the edges and less patient with fools. The description had appealed to her. But after being introduced to Monsieur Semmonet, she wasn't so sure.

"Madame de Verneuil will take you to meet the archduke and the princesses now," Lady Elisabeth directed as her deputy arrived.

Anne brightened. "Oh, Madame, princesses!" she exclaimed.

"The eldest is Princess Lenore. Then Princess Isabella and the youngest, Princess Mary," Madame de Verneuil told her.

"Thank you, Madame," Anne said. She had never met a princess of her own age. Now she would meet three.

They crossed the street to the Court of Cambrai, its white stone walls glinting in the sunlight. Anne's breath caught at the sight of the palace's spires, proud and pointing heavenward.

"This is the imperial palace," Madame de Verneuil explained as they approached. "It belonged to Margaret of York, Lady Margaret's godmother."

Anne nodded. So, it was true — Margaret of Burgundy had been Margaret of York.

As they entered the courtyard, a short woman with an air of authority stepped forward. Her waist cord held a large set of keys.

"Welcome to the Court of Cambrai," the woman greeted in clipped French.

"This is Madame de Beaumont, Grand Mistress of the imperial household," Madame de Verneuil introduced.

Anne dropped a curtsey, guessing Madame de Beaumont hailed from Spain. Her short, staccato tones sounded like those of the Spanish lady-in-waiting to Queen Katherine back home.

Dazzled to be in imperial surroundings, Anne noted the contrast of the cool, sand-coloured exterior of the palace with the warm red brick of Lady Margaret's residence. Anne followed Madame de Beaumont inside; the palace's stone floors echoed underfoot as they passed down a long corridor. At the end they turned right and stopped before the entrance to a large classroom.

The door opened, and four sets of eyes looked up from their desks.

"Here is Anne Boleyn from England. She is Lady Margaret's newest maid of honour," Madame de Beaumont announced.

Anne curtseyed, bursting with curiosity about the four royals of the House of Habsburg and House of Burgundy combined.

"Hello," the youngest said, staring at her with large brown eyes. She looked to be about seven or eight, a sturdy girl with a prominent jaw.

The other two dipped their heads politely, their eyes remote. One was older than Anne, already a woman, with chestnut hair, a strong jaw and full lips on a face that fell just short of being comely. The other seemed to be about Anne's age, fine-boned and petite like her, but with a timid mien that was nothing like her own manner at all. Returning to their studies, neither looked up again.

Feeling small, Anne's gaze shifted to the archduke. His fair hair framed a face with pale blue eyes, a long nose and pointed jaw that jutted out. To her surprise, his mouth hung slightly open. Glancing at her, Charles of Habsburg dipped his head with the slightest of nods, his expression blank.

Anne's temper flared, but she kept her composure. She didn't enjoy being treated like a nobody, least of all by someone close to her in age — prince or not.

Madame de Beaumont steered her back into the hall. "Once your French improves, you may join them for lessons."

Anne followed the woman down the corridor, careful to hide her disappointment. She had expected the Habsburg prince to be handsome. Instead, he was anything but. God's bones, what would her brother have said if he had seen him? That mouth hanging open would have sent George into fits of mockery. As for the princesses, she had hoped they would be friendly. But their eyes, except for the youngest, had swept over her and slid away.

The message was clear. They were royal and she was not.

*

Back at Lady Margaret's palace, Anne spotted Barbe heading towards her, a shorter girl at her side. Relieved, Anne hurried towards them. After her cold reception across the street, she was ready for more of Barbe's good-natured chatter.

"I was looking for you. Where were you?" Barbe asked.

"I was across the street, meeting the archduke and his sisters."

Barbe's brow arched. "How did it go?"

Anne faltered. "I — I'm not sure."

The older girl gave her a knowing look. "They weren't friendly?"

Anne hung her head. "Not very."

"You'll get used to it." Barbe shrugged, turning to her companion. "This is Jeanne de Rosimbos."

"Hello," Anne greeted.

Jeanne's eyes flicked over Anne. "Hello," she echoed, her tone neutral. With hair the colour of wheat and pale blue eyes, she looked like a faded version of Barbe.

"We're off to check on Madame's birds. Want to come?" Barbe asked.

Anne's spirits lifted. "Oh yes." She trailed behind them as they led her to a section of the palace she hadn't seen before.

Barbe stopped at the threshold of a small room near the chapel gallery. "This is Madame's study," she said with a wink. "The first room of her private quarters in the West Wing."

Anne peeked in, drinking in the art objects placed around the room. A bust of a man with high cheekbones and no collar at all sat on a shelf, his high-arched nose exuding nobility, his expression proud and severe. "Who is that?" she asked.

"An Indian from the New World," Barbe said casually.

Anne's eyes widened. "The New World?"

"Across the ocean, where Columbus sailed," Barbe explained. "The Spanish ambassador gave it to Madame."

Anne nodded, speechless. Hever, with its draughty halls and dowdy decor seemed as far away as the lands from where the noble Indian hailed.

"Wait until you see the other rooms." Barbe led them through the study to another door on its far side.

A symphony of chirps arose as the three girls entered a second, larger room. Sunlight streamed through the tall windows lining the far wall where three birdcages were positioned. Anne paused, charmed by the sight. "Are they finches?"

Jeanne tutted. "They're canaries."

"Do they sing?" Anne asked.

"Not only songs, but arias," Barbe replied.

Anne didn't know what an aria was, but she would make it a point to find out. Putting a finger up to the nearest cage, she prayed she could befriend the bright yellow warblers.

"Don't bother them," Jeanne's voice rang out.

Anne pulled her hand away.

Barbe shot Jeanne a look. "They'll get used to you soon enough," she reassured Anne. "I'll show you where we keep their seed."

Anne's spirits jumped. "I'd love to help feed them!"

Jeanne cut in again. "Only if you're allowed to."

"I hope to be." Anne's stomach tightened at the other girl's coolness. Her mind flicked to the Habsburg royals across the street.

"We keep the birdseed in Madame's cupboard here." Barbe moved to one corner of the room. "The key's in the —"

Jeanne nudged her, whispering something into her ear. "Lady Elisabeth will show you where the key is if she wants you to feed them," Jeanne finished.

Anne nodded, understanding the girl didn't want her to know its hiding place. Trying not to care, she turned back to the birds. Now that Jeanne had told her not to touch their cages and prevented her from accessing the birdseed to feed them, she wanted to sink into the floor. But she also wanted to spend more time with Barbe. Silently, she asked the canaries if they had similar problems when three were in one cage. In answer, the canary nearest her chirped. To comfort or to warn her, Anne couldn't tell.

"Let's go and see Madame's bedchamber," Barbe suggested, heading for the door.

Jeanne blocked her path, frowning. "We should ask Lady Elisabeth first."

"Why? We never have before," Barbe said.

Jeanne gave her another nudge, placing herself between them. A whispered comment ensued, making Anne wish she was elsewhere.

"It's almost time for dinner," Jeanne announced.

"It's only time for the first seating," Barbe objected.

"The first seating?" Anne asked.

"There are two seatings," Barbe explained. "The first is for Lady Margaret and Lady Elisabeth at the head table, with nobles and guests at the rest. We eat at the second seating afterwards, with the stewards, pages, and whoever else is not so important."

Anne nodded, thinking she'd had enough of being reminded of her unimportance for one day. "How many dine here?"

"About one hundred and fifty or so. There are always ambassadors and messengers coming, too."

"And how many demoiselles are there?" Anne asked.

"There are eighteen of us. The older girls are quartered separately, so you won't see much of them."

"We need to take the dogs out," Jeanne cut in, turning to go.

"Have you met Madame's greyhound yet?" Barbe asked Anne as they exited Lady Margaret's private quarters.

"No, only the two little ones."

"Babou likes her," Barbe told Jeanne.

"Good." Jeanne turned to Anne. "You go and find Babou, and we'll find the others." She pointed Anne in one direction then turned to go with Barbe in the other.

"See you at dinner," Barbe sang out as Jeanne hurried her off.

At the midday meal Anne looked for Barbe. Spotting her, she waved then made her way over.

"Did you find Babou?" Barbe asked, attempting to slide along from the end where she sat to make space for Anne.

"In the garden. I took him to his spot; he's all right now." Anne waited to be invited to sit down.

On Barbe's other side Jeanne didn't budge. "There's a place over there." She pointed to a nearby table.

There's a place here if you'd only move over, Anne thought.

"Why can't we make room here?" Barbe asked.

"No table setting here. There's one at the table over there," Jeanne directed.

Barbe looked frustrated. "Just take it from there and bring it over."

"You know we're not supposed to do that," Jeanne snapped.

Anne's stomach churned. She gave Barbe a tight smile. "Please do not worry. See you after dinner."

She walked towards the other table, her thoughts raging. Two girls she didn't know greeted her with polite indifference as she sat down. Returning to their meals, neither spoke to her again. Anne tried to eat, but the lump in her throat made every bite an ordeal, much as her day had been. Barbe was the only friendly person close to her in age she had met thus far. But Jeanne seemed intent on keeping her away.

Taking another bite, Anne's heart hardened. She had played this game before, when cousins visited and three was a crowd. It seemed she would need to refresh her skills, then sharpen them.

THREE

May flew by in a whirl. Foremost among Anne's lessons was French grammar, composition and conversation with Semmonet every day but Sunday. After French, she joined the rest of the demoiselles for lectures in the classics, rhetoric and discourse. For the most part, she listened and didn't speak, something she was unused to doing. Once she improved her French, she planned to catch up to the others, then surpass them.

The midday meal offered lessons in rank and table manners. Admiring the graceful silver ship that sat on the head table, she asked Barbe about it.

"That's to mark the place for Lady Margaret's most important guest."

"It's a wondrous adornment," Anne remarked.

Next to Barbe, Jeanne sniffed. "It's a salt cellar, not just an adornment."

Her hackles rising, Anne quelled the urge to reach out and dump its contents on Jeanne's head. Instead, she trained her thoughts on how much her mother would enjoy impressing guests with a salt cellar so fine.

Afternoons were filled with dancing, music, painting, and sports. Her favourite was archery. Anne relished the snap of the bowstring, a moment when she could forget the strange, careful world around her. But even then, her ears were sharp, absorbing every word the other demoiselles exchanged. When she didn't understand a word or phrase, she asked Semmonet. And if the conversation veered towards less than courtly topics, she asked Barbe when Jeanne wasn't lurking nearby.

On their way to lawn boules one afternoon, Anne and Barbe passed a scullery lad outside the kitchen door. As they walked by, the youth leered at Barbe.

"*Va t'en, cochon*," she hissed as he disappeared into the kitchen.

Impressed, Anne marvelled at Barbe's crisp dispatch. "What did you say?" she whispered.

"*Va t'en, cochon*. Go away, pig." Barbe gave a few grunting snorts and pushed up her nostrils to demonstrate.

Anne laughed, imagining what fun it would be to use the insult on George back home. "I could never say it so firmly," she confided.

"You will need to in the marketplace."

"If we go, wouldn't we be well-attended?"

Barbe smirked. "No matter how well-attended, there's always a way for a youth to sidle up and pass a remark."

Anne frowned. Girlhood was fast fading away. She needed to prepare for what lay ahead. "What else might you say?"

"Depends on whether you like their attention or not."

Anne sucked in her breath. "I've never got that sort of attention."

Barbe looked her up and down. "You'll come in for your share soon enough."

Feeling her face redden, Anne tossed her head. "Teach me another phrase."

Barbe thought for a moment. "You could always say '*laisse-moi tranquille*'."

"Ah, 'leave me in peace' — that's good, more polite," Anne agreed, filing it away.

"And when that doesn't work, as it never does, you can move on to '*fi, manant*' —out of my way, beggar." With a sure hand Barbe swiped outward from under her chin, sending a nearby flock of birds scattering.

"Why shouldn't it work?" Anne asked. She couldn't wait to practise Barbe's gesture. It was the ultimate expression of scorn, impressively delivered.

"Because that's not the way the world works when a youth seeks your attention."

"If I ask politely, why wouldn't he leave me alone?"

Barbe threw back her head, erupting into gales of laughter. "You have much to learn, little one. And if you don't learn the game better than they, you will not be master of them."

"Master of whom?"

"Men. Who else?"

"I shall manage them well," Anne declared. She wasn't sure how yet, but she intended to learn. Already, she had begun by managing George back at Hever.

"Here's another coming up," Barbe warned.

Anne looked. Up ahead a stable boy lounged in the shade of the coach house, eating an apple, his eyes following their approach. "Why do you suppose he'll leer at you?" she asked Barbe.

"I don't suppose. I know."

"What will you say?"

"Nothing. You do the talking."

Anne balked. "I can't remember the pig phrase."

"Just say '*Fi, manant.*' You'll do fine."

Straightening her stance, Barbe slowed as she approached the youth.

Following behind, Anne watched the stable boy run his eyes over Barbe, then her, as if weighing their charms.

"*Fi, manant,*" Anne hissed, summoning Barbe's confidence.

Immediately, the youth slunk back into the shadows.

"Well done, but spit out the 'f' more. You must drive in your sword point," Barbe encouraged.

A rush of triumph swelled in Anne's chest. "It's like training a dog," she crowed, exhilarated at her first attempt to curb a youth.

"You must make them eat from your hand," Barbe advised.

"Like Babou?" Anne asked.

"Like Babou," Barbe agreed. Reaching out, she tweaked Anne's chin.

Anne batted her hand away. "*Fi, manant!*"

"Well done. You will break hearts in no time."

A few weeks later, the demoiselles buzzed with excitement. They'd been told they would accompany Madame to the royal park in Brussels. The Holy Roman Emperor, Lady Margaret's father, had arrived from Austria and had invited her and his grandchildren to join him for an afternoon.

"What do you think he'll be like?" Anne asked Barbe as they passed through Madame's collection room off the garden, its treasures gleaming in the sunlight flooding in through the tall windows. Her father had said he was one of Europe's most powerful rulers, but Anne's imagination floundered, trying to picture such a man.

Barbe's lips twitched. "Not what you expect."

Anne's gaze landed on one of Lady Margaret's odd ractice pieces, its blood-red branches twisting like thorns. Her mistress's surprising art collection was also different from what she might expect. "Will he wear a spiky crown like this?" she asked jestingly.

"Of course not," Jeanne scoffed, coming up behind Barbe.

"Will he wear robes like the Pope?" Anne pressed on. She would not let Jeanne dampen her spirits.

Barbe snorted. "Not likely. From what Madame says, he's no holy man."

"What has she told you?" Anne kept her eyes on Barbe, willing Jeanne to disappear.

Barbe considered. "He likes to hunt. And he's fond of Madame and his grandchildren."

"Does he have a wife?"

"He had one after Madame's mother died, but she died, too," Jeanne filled in.

"What does Madame call him?" Anne asked. Titles danced in her head — Your Holiness, Your Highness, or simply 'Papa'.

Barbe's eyes twinkled. "She calls him Maxi."

Anne blinked in surprise. She recalled the week before, when she had chased Babou from Lady Margaret's study. As she was fishing him out from under her desk, she had heard Madame refer to someone named 'Maxi', complaining about him over money matters to her secretary. Anne knew what that meant. Family members only griped like that when they were close, just as she and George did. And nothing got her mother and father more worked up than a rousing argument over money.

"I wonder if he's a loving grandfather," Anne mused. She didn't have a clear picture of what that might look like. Her own grandfather, the Duke of Norfolk, was as crusty as days-old bread; her other grandfather was long dead.

Barbe smiled. "They say he's like a knight from a chivalric tale."

"What fun it will be to meet him!" Anne cried.

Jeanne sniffed. "You'll not be introduced, as he'll be busy with the archduke and his sisters and not pay any attention to you."

Anne seethed. Not only was she itching to shut Jeanne's sniping mouth, she also didn't like hearing that she wouldn't be noticed. It scratched a wound too raw, one left by her parents, always off on the king's or queen's business. Desperate to steer the conversation elsewhere, she asked, "What happened to their mother?"

Barbe glanced around, as if to ensure they were alone. "She's in Spain."

"Why is she there, with her children here?" Anne pressed.

Barbe's voice dropped. "Because she's mad."

Anne gaped. "Mad?"

"Out of her mind," Barbe confirmed. "She's shut up in some palace over there."

"Who is she?"

"Queen Juana of Castile," Jeanne answered with an air of superiority.

"They call her Juana the Mad," Barbe added.

"She rules Castile?" Anne was surprised. Searching her mind, she remembered her mother saying that the archduke's mother was Queen Katherine of England's sister, both daughters of Queen Isabella of Castile.

"In name only. Her father Ferdinand manages Castile's affairs," Jeanne explained.

Anne's thoughts jumped to the serious-faced prince across the street. "Then the archduke will ascend its throne when he dies?"

Jeanne tilted her chin. "He'll rule all of Spain and the New World, along with the Habsburg lands."

Anne's mind boggled. The youth with the jutting jaw and mouth that hung open would rule most of Europe one day. "How will he manage it all?"

"With helpers like Lady Margaret," Barbe explained, as Jeanne put a hand on her shoulder. She gazed at Barbe adoringly, as if she were Lady Margaret to Barbe's imperial ruler.

Anne wanted to smack off her hand, along with the worshipful look on Jeanne's face. How dare that washed-out shadow act as if she owned her friend? And why was Barbe letting her do it?

Margaret descended from the carriage, aided by the arm of her equerry. Dusting off her black silk gown, she straightened her white pleated collar then raised her head. On the vast lawn to the side of Coudenberg Palace, a burly male figure strode towards her with the gait of a great bear. Her heart swelled as he held out his arms to her.

"Papa!" she cried, forgetting her entourage spilling out of the coaches behind her. She was thirteen again, returning to Flanders from France, meeting her long-lost father at Margaret of York's palace because he didn't have one of his own. She had been hesitant, but he had swept her into his arms, and she had instantly melted.

Maximilian I of Austria had always been an outsider in the Low Countries, accepted there only because of his wife and two children, native-born Burgundian royals. Now two of the three were dead, and only she, Margaret, was left as senior member of the House of Burgundy. But in her father's arms, she was a girl again.

Maximilian caught her to him, his black cape enfolding them both. The scent of Habsburg majesty filled her senses, redolent of horses, leather, and power. Margaret held the key to the Low Countries' prosperity, but Maximilian held the key to something more, as ineffable and glorious as the memory of an epic tale.

"My darling," he exclaimed, lifting her off the ground and making her laugh with joy.

"Maxi, put me down," she protested, feeling the cares of managing seventeen provinces fall away from her like raindrops rolling off a duck's back.

"How is my sweet princess?" he boomed.

"Still your princess, still not sweet," Margaret quipped, as her entourage chuckled and stirred behind her. Already, the air felt festive. Invariably, the court brightened when Maximilian showed up.

"Still as beautiful as always," Maximilian enthused, admiring her with a father's loving gaze.

"I'm glad you think so," Margaret replied, her eyes sweeping him. Older, greyer, but still majestic. She could imagine what he must have been like in 1477 when he rode into Brussels to rescue her mother from her restive Burgundians, ready to throw off ducal authority in the wake of her father's death. God knew they were still restive, but Margaret had found the way to pacify them, providing them with lucrative trade agreements and a peaceable realm in which to make money — then keeping their hard-earned profits out of Maximilian's hands.

"Where are my other princesses?" the emperor asked, looking around for his grandchildren.

Margaret gestured to the princesses to step forward. As Lenore, Isabella, and Mary made their curtseys, their grandfather crouched and crushed all three of them to him, making them giggle and squeal.

Behind them stood the archduke, but Margaret held back from directing him. Charles had given her enough signs recently that he was done with being ordered around. She watched as he stiffly bowed, but his grandfather hugged him before he could finish, pounding his back and making his face redden with what looked to be a combination of embarrassment and affection. All of them loved Maxi. It was impossible not to. His warmth broke through barriers like rays of the sun.

As Margaret watched him melt her mortified nephew's reserve, she thought back to stories she had heard about the Burgundian burghers imprisoning her father after her mother had died. They had locked him in a room with a window that looked out on the square, where they executed two of his most senior Austrian counsellors before his eyes.

But they didn't touch Maximilian. Instead, they let him go, forcing him to concede to their demands to raise his son, heir to the Burgundian ducal throne, in Brussels under a regency council. No one dared to lay a hand on the valiant young Austrian prince who had married their duchess and saved Burgundy from splintering apart.

Margaret could understand why. Her father was a larger-than-life figure, courageous and noble, yet warm and immediate, ready to cut through all class distinctions to connect with the common man. The Low Countries' burghers had recognised his qualities and left him alone. It was something they valued amongst themselves in the new society they were fashioning where merchants and tradesmen sat on the governing councils of their towns and had a say in how they were run.

"Come! The park awaits," Maximilian announced, his voice as deep as his arms were wide, encompassing all of Margaret's entourage in their spread.

Margaret hid a smile as she noted the eagerness on the faces of her demoiselles and pages. Maximilian was well known for his exuberance. When he visited, work stopped and festivities began.

The grand park behind the ducal palace had been prepared with an archery range, a lawn boules court and a stage where something entertaining was sure to happen. Boards for chess, backgammon, and nine men's morris beckoned on gaming tables under the great oaks bordering the lawn. At the side of the pond a large selection of wooden sailboats waited to be launched. As Margaret's party fanned out, gay cries pierced the air and attendants scurried back and forth, offering refreshments.

Margaret sighed with happiness and settled into an armchair next to her father. Today she would enjoy Maxi's mystical, maddening charm. On the morrow they could argue over state affairs and tussle over money and policy. But all that could wait.

Later that day, Anne slowed her steps as she passed the library, her curiosity pulling her towards the doorway. Inside, two voices clashed like swords, Emperor Maximilian and Lady Margaret going at it over someone called Egmond, Duke of Guelders. From what she could gather, he was running wild in the north of Madame's realm, refusing to bow to Habsburg authority.

"You do not understand what I go through with that man!" Lady Margaret's voice sliced through the air, sharp and impatient.

"Of course I do. You must rein him in before summer is out," the emperor responded, his tone unyielding.

"And how am I to do that without money or an army?" Lady Margaret shot back.

"You should have married Henry," the emperor countered, a half-hearted jab. "He could have come to your rescue."

Anne's ears perked up. Henry? The king of England was married to Queen Katherine, her mother's mistress. What was the emperor talking about?

Lady Margaret's laugh sounded bitter. "I don't need a husband to save me. I need money and troops to bring Egmond to heel!"

The emperor pounded an arm on his chair. "You must make him bow to Habsburg authority."

"He insists he has sole authority in his own lands." Lady Margaret's voice matched her father's in volume.

"They are not his own lands. They are Habsburg lands!" the emperor shouted.

"And that is the crux of the matter. He says they are not!" Lady Margaret snapped back.

"You must negotiate," the emperor said.

"I cannot negotiate with someone who refuses to even meet," Lady Margaret replied.

The emperor's lips curled into a wry smile. "No one refuses a sweet enough offer."

"You don't know what drives that man," Lady Margaret said. "It's not money, but honour, and I have no way to sway him!"

"Honour?" The emperor leaned forward. "What honour is there in raiding his neighbours and wreaking havoc on your provinces?"

Lady Margaret's voice dropped, heavy with the weight of her responsibilities. "I rule seventeen provinces. His is just one of them. But to him, it's everything."

"He's wrong, and you must correct him."

"He's wrong, but he believes he's right. And that is far worse."

The emperor sighed deeply. "He is a man of another age, daughter. He's a knight. He will fight to the death for what he thinks is right."

"And my people are not knights," Lady Margaret countered, her tone brusque. "They are merchants, craftsmen. They won't die for some pointless war."

"If only we could marry him to one of our princesses."

Lady Margaret gasped. "He's almost as old as you!"

"It's a better solution than endless fighting."

"I don't want our princesses wasted on a gadfly," she snapped.

"Nor do I," the emperor agreed, lifting his hands in surrender. "But you must find a way to reach an accord."

"I did that last summer, and he has broken it again."

The emperor's voice was quieter now. "Then do it again."

"You are no help, Papa."

"I am here," the emperor said simply.

Anne's heart ached. How she longed to hear her own father say similar words.

The next morning Anne sat with her tutor, her brow furrowed as she recalled the emperor's words. "What did he mean, saying Lady Margaret should have married King Henry?" She hadn't discussed it with Barbe because Jeanne had been stuck to her like a limpet when Anne had gone to find her.

Semmonet cocked his head. "Did the emperor say such a thing?"

"He said Henry would have come to her rescue."

"And you were eavesdropping to hear all this?" her tutor asked.

Anne's cheeks flushed. She glanced down, fiddling with her sleeve. "I — I did not mean to. But I was passing by the library door and … overheard."

Mirth flickered in Semmonet's eyes. "A good opportunity to learn some French, no?"

Anne fidgeted, torn between guilt and honesty.

Semmonet leaned forward. "To answer your question — King Henry Tudor did seek to marry Lady Margaret."

Anne's brows knit together. "But … if she had married him, she wouldn't have been able to rule here."

"Exactly. And she enjoys ruling her realm. She was not about to give it up and move to England to become an old man's wife."

"Maybe she could have stayed here and just visited him sometimes," Anne mused, thinking of her own parents' arrangement. Without fail, they irritated each other after too many days under the same roof.

"There was some talk of her dividing her time between here and England. But Lady Margaret said her people would not be happy having her rule their affairs if she wasn't here to oversee them."

Anne nodded. She could imagine the Burgundian nobles would try to take over if Lady Margaret wasn't at the head of the council table, staring them down in twice-weekly meetings. "I'm glad she didn't marry him," she remarked.

"Why is that, Mademoiselle?"

"Because … she would not have been happy." Anne remembered her parents' complaints about their former king, after he had died. "I heard that Henry Tudor kept a gloomy court."

Her tutor nodded. "I've heard the same."

"Madame would never stand for a dull court," Anne declared.

Semmonet chuckled. "No, indeed."

"And she wouldn't have liked the food," Anne added, thinking how much tastier Burgundian dishes were, so many of them cooked with lardons and red wine.

"The weather wouldn't have pleased her either," Semmonet said.

"Oh, but the English spring is glorious," Anne said, thinking of the lambs in the fields.

"'Tis but a season and the year is long," her tutor pointed out.

"What is winter like here, Monsieur?"

Semmonet pulled a face. "Grey. Very grey."

"Then it's the same as in England."

"With less rain."

"Have you been to England?" Anne asked.

"Never."

"The rain is what makes the grass so green," Anne said dreamily.

"Which makes the sheep produce such good wool."

"It's a good thing for the Low Countries, is it not?"

"It's English wool that enriches us through our cloth industry."

Anne considered. "Lady Margaret must be pleased about that."

"Very. It's why she keeps such close ties with England."

Anne's thoughts drifted to her own place in all this. Had she been sent to the Burgundian court to strengthen those ties? If only her father were there to ask. Thinking of her mistress's joy in the emperor's embrace, she tried hard not to envy her. "Thank you, Monsieur, for such a good discussion," she said, pushing aside her hurt. She felt older, wiser, as though she had stepped into adulthood during their conversation.

"You're welcome, Mademoiselle. Soon, you will be grown, and all you learn here will serve you well."

"May fortune smile on me, then."

"Whatever fortune brings," Semmonet said, his voice turning serious, "hold fast to Lady Margaret's motto — '*Fortune, infortune, fort une.*'"

"What does it mean?" Anne asked.

"Fortune, misfortune — both strengthen one."

Anne considered, noting the feminine object. "It strengthens a woman in particular?"

Semmonet's smile returned, cryptic and amused. "You must ask Madame Margaret. It is her motto and hers alone."

"I shall," Anne vowed.

"Wait for the right moment," Semmonet advised, his eyes twinkling. "And meanwhile, follow the first rule at court — ears open, mouth shut."

Anne pressed her lips together, her thoughts buzzing. Back home her mouth was usually open. But her French was not good enough for her to speak as much as she would back in England. Biting her tongue, she curtseyed to her tutor, feeling like a muzzled racehorse. How she longed for the day when she could fully express herself.

FOUR

Anne stirred as the crisp peal of the church bells of St. Rumbold's filled the air. The day was starting, the sound of noisy songbirds vying with a dog's bark, then two.

Barbe swished by on her way to the garderobe. "Ready for today?"

"We're going to a convent?" Anne asked. She had heard they would go on a charitable outing that day to somewhere that Lady Margaret supported.

"The beguinage," Barbe corrected.

Anne rubbed the sleep from her eyes. "What is it?" she muttered, mostly to herself.

"You'll find out soon enough," Barbe flung over her shoulder and disappeared.

Anne hopped out of bed and sprang to the window. Leaning over the sill, she surveyed the town, its narrow streets winding towards the distant glimmer of the River Dyle. Neatly tiled roofs topped tall, narrow houses of patterned brick and limestone, each with its own design and all exuding wealth and taste. She lingered a moment, then turned to her trunk.

Her smart yellow gown lay on top, its folds gleaming in the early morning light. She reached for it, but Jeanne's voice stopped her, cutting through the silence.

"Don't wear that."

Anne hesitated. "Why not?"

"We'll be helping the older beguines. It might get messy. Wear something you don't mind dirtying."

Anne wondered at her words. Could she trust them? She pulled out a faded rose hand-me-down gown from her sister that her mother had hesitated to pack. Slipping it on, her excitement for the day's outing dimmed at the thought of whatever she might be asked to do.

"That's better," Jeanne approved.

Anne eyed Jeanne, noting with satisfaction that the dull blue-grey gown she wore made her look like one of the Court of Savoy's laundresses.

Outside, the demoiselles grouped into separate gaggles, as excited and noisy as the birds chirping from the trees and vines climbing the walls bordering the Keizerstraat. Trooping through the main marketplace of the Grote Markt and past the soaring tower of St. Rumbold's Cathedral, the lively band of demoiselles turned down a narrow lane. At its end was a small square with neatly tended flowers and a herb garden.

An older woman stepped out from a doorway cut into the stone wall and greeted them. Her grey tunic and white Flemish headdress gave her a modest appearance, but her presence was commanding.

Anne put her mouth to Barbe's ear. "Is she a nun?"

"No, dull-wit, she's a beguine."

"But what *is* that?" Riled, Anne vowed to serve Barbe back in kind once her French improved.

Jeanne rolled her eyes. "It's a type of woman who lives here."

Anne swallowed further questions as the woman addressed Lady Elisabeth.

"I will need four in the gardens, two in the bakery. The rest can help the elderly ones by straightening their houses or offering company."

Anne nudged Barbe as Lady Elisabeth began assigning tasks. "Do they not have families to help them?"

Barbe shook her head. "The beguines are unmarried, without family."

Anne blinked, taken aback. "But they are not nuns?"

"They care for each other in communities like this one. And when they need outside help, they call on great lords and ladies of their town to supply their needs," Jeanne explained.

"But these do not look like almshouses."

Jeanne gave Anne a withering look. "They are far from almshouses. The beguinages are well tended by the women who live in them. But when they get older, they need help at times, so here we are."

"What is all this whispering?" Lady Elisabeth loomed over Barbe, Jeanne, and Anne. Engrossed in conversation, they hadn't noticed her approach.

"Nothing, Madame. Anne was asking if the beguines spoke French and I told her not likely," Barbe improvised.

Lady Elisabeth's expression softened at the anxious look on Anne's face. "That's true, so why don't you two serve one of the beguines together?"

"Oh, Madame, I would be grateful, as I don't know what I should do." Anne breathed out, enjoying Jeanne's glower.

"Do for them what you'd do for your grandmother back home."

"Mostly I talk with her between her naps." An image of her Boleyn grandmother popped up. Irritable and not very fragrant, she nevertheless shared a great deal that Anne's mother didn't have occasion to tell her, as she was away at court most of the time.

Lady Elisabeth smiled. "You will do more than that today. Go with Barbe. The magistra will find someone you may serve."

"The magistra?" Anne asked as she and Barbe moved off, with Jeanne sulking behind.

"That's the *mère des dames*, like Lady Elisabeth," Barbe murmured.

Up ahead a woman in a drab grey tunic waited. "She doesn't seem anything like Lady Elisabeth," Anne remarked.

"She's not nobly born, but you'll see how competent she is. Under her, the beguines bake their own bread, brew beer, sell goods, and earn a living."

Anne marvelled. "I've never seen such a thing before."

Barbe's laugh was short. "You'll see much today."

"What is your choice for service?" the magistra asked.

Barbe pointed to Anne. "We would like to serve together as she has just come from England and speaks some French, but no Dutch."

The magistra tapped a finger against her chin, her sharp eyes peering at Anne. "I'll match you with Mistress Bonnard, who hails from France. She cannot walk well but she'll put you through your paces." Briskly, she handed them off to a woman who had come up next to her.

Alarm bells rang in Anne's head as she exchanged glances with Barbe. Together they followed the woman through the doorway cut into the wall. Proceeding down an even narrower lane, Anne noted small doors lining a long building, each with neat, well-tended exteriors, some half covered with flowering vines and each with a stone bench.

The magistra's assistant stopped before a particularly neat exterior. "Here we are." She rapped on the wooden door, waited, then rapped again.

"What is it?" a voice answered, as irascible as Anne's grandmother's.

"Two demoiselles from Lady Margaret's court to wait on you, Mistress Bonnard," the magistra's assistant called out in French.

The door creaked open to reveal a small, ancient woman with a sharp nose. She scanned her visitors with sceptical eyes. "I do not need any high-minded swans today to do nothing for me."

Barbe stuck an elbow in Anne's side at the beguine's spirited greeting.

"Good mistress, these two are here for you to put them to good use."

"The last two who came did nothing but chatter to each other and drink my elderflower wine," the elderly woman complained.

"These two will do your bidding, if you tell them what you'd like done," the assistant promised.

"I would like them to take me out to sit in the sun. And after they have cleaned my house, they can join me for conversation."

The assistant fixed them with merry eyes. "What do you say, Mesdemoiselles? Can you do it?"

"Yes, Madame. And if the conversation is good, perhaps Madame will offer us some elderflower wine, too, so that it flows even better." Barbe gave a saucy look to the ancient woman.

Mistress Bonnard perked up, either from being addressed as 'madame' or from catching Barbe's lively tone. "Then I'll take these two, and if they only chatter to each other I'll put them to work in separate corners."

Inside, Anne groaned. She didn't care to clean anyone's house, especially on a beautiful spring day. Feeling Barbe's elbow again in her ribs, she smiled at the woman and stiffened herself for the task ahead.

"Come then. You may put my table outside," Mistress Bonnard ordered.

Anne followed Barbe across the threshold, steeling herself for malodorous smells. Could not a page be found to move tables? Then she remembered she was not at court, nor did any men live in the beguinage.

Motioning to a side table with her walking cane, Mistress Bonnard rapped its leg. "Take this outside and set it before the bench. We'll take two stools, too, and after you've cleaned, we'll make good cheer."

Anne peeked at Barbe and suppressed a giggle. What good cheer could one make with an ancient scold who could barely walk? Lifting one end of the table with Barbe at the other, she hauled it outside and set it before the bench. From the doorway the woman held out a cloth for her to wipe down the table.

Anne ran the cloth over the tabletop, but it was already clean. Reaching down to dust its legs, she saw they were as polished and dust-free as any furnishings in Madame's private quarters back at the Court of Savoy.

"Now fetch the stools. After you've swept and tidied inside, I will see to refreshment."

"Madame, it is us who should be bringing refreshment to you," Barbe pointed out.

"Then do so with your conversation. And don't bore me with drivel about gowns and ribbons."

Anne snorted into her sleeve. The day was shaping up well. Returning inside, she picked up a wooden stool and carried it out, noting not a speck of dust on its underside. Grandmother Boleyn would be impressed. The maids back at Hever were forever neglecting to dust the undersides of various pieces of furniture, something she railed over bitterly, to Anne's infinite boredom.

Mistress Bonnard raised a gnarled hand. "Come help me over the doorstep."

Anne and Barbe sprang to assist her, one on either side. With a firm grip on her upper arm, Anne held her breath, expecting the sour smells of age and unwashed clothing. Slowly, they eased her out the door then sat her on the bench. As Anne inhaled, the scent of lavender and peppermint hit her nose. Breathing in again, her senses quickened to the ancient woman's fresh fragrance.

"You may start by sweeping the floor and dusting," the beguine directed.

Anne followed Barbe inside, trying to quell her resentment by thinking of something positive. "She doesn't smell," she whispered.

"Her house doesn't smell either," Barbe whispered back, grabbing hold of a broom.

Anne picked up the cloth she had used on the table outside and swept the top of a sideboard. Examining the underside of the cloth, she held it out to Barbe. "And no dust."

"I can't find anything to sweep here," Barbe said.

Anne looked around. "Try the corners and around the hearth. There must be dirt somewhere."

"Check for cobwebs," Barbe returned.

Anne recoiled. She hated spiders and their webs. And she hated being asked to clean someone's house. Running her cloth down the side of the sideboard to the floor where maids from time immemorial forgot to dust, she found it came up empty. "No spiders. Her house is spotless," Anne announced.

"This is all I've got." Barbe pointed to a miniscule pile of ash from the hearth she had swept.

"What are you doing in there?" an angry voice called from outside.

"Coming, Madame!" Barbe replied.

"What's all that chatter?"

Barbe winked at Anne then addressed the beguine. "We were talking about you, Madame."

"What could you have to say about me, since we've just met?" the Frenchwoman demanded.

"I was saying that you have given us nothing to do, as you have already done it," Barbe explained.

"What do you mean, silly girl?"

"Your house is spotless, Madame. There's not a speck of dust anywhere," Anne put in.

"Of course it is. Why would I wish to live in a dirty house?"

"You are most impressive, Madame," Barbe declared.

The Frenchwoman arched her neck. "You have no idea how impressive I am."

Anne stifled a snort at the elderly woman's confident stance. Her mind ran in myriad directions to conjure up a rich and impressive past for Mistress Bonnard. As for her present, she was becoming increasingly interesting. "Oh, Madame, we should like to know more!"

"Then go and get the pitcher on the sideboard and three goblets from the cupboard. Bring the plate of biscuits there too."

Racing back into the house, they did as she bid them. In a moment they emerged again, with Barbe setting down the full pitcher and plate of biscuits as Anne placed the goblets.

"You will try my elderflower wine?" With a shaky hand, Mistress Bonnard raised the glazed earthenware pitcher.

"With pleasure, Madame," Anne exclaimed. How she loved that phrase in French. '*Avec plaisir*' slipped off her tongue at least once a day, delighting her with its sibilant sound, the final 'r' not pronounced, but implied, leading open-ended into unknown possibilities, much as Mistress Bonnard was doing.

"Allow me, Madame." Barbe took the pitcher and served them all.

"What shall we drink to?" Mistress Bonnard asked, raising her goblet.

"To good conversation!" Barbe cried.

"To your story!" Anne added.

"To lively talk and no dull chatter." Mistress Bonnard clinked her goblet with Barbe's and then Anne's.

Barbe took a deep sip then eyed the surprising woman. "Who was it who visited you last from the Court of Savoy and bored you with their chatter?"

"Two magpies who thought I was deaf, as they didn't bother to address me." The beguine rapped the table with a sharp knuckle. "I wish I *had* been deaf, to not have to hear such blather."

"What were their names?"

"Vanity and Disdain, I would say."

Anne giggled.

"They should have been, but what were they introduced to you as?" Barbe pressed.

Mistress Bonnard's lips curled. "Isabella and Agnes. Two perfectly fine names wasted on perfect ninnies."

"Your wine is delicious, Madame." As Barbe's knee prodded Anne's under the table, she looked pleased to hear sentence passed on two of the haughtiest of their band of demoiselles.

"It tastes almost as good as you smell," Anne quipped.

Mistress Bonnard raised an amused brow. "So, you enjoy my peppermint scent?"

"It's lively, Madame."

"What does it make you want to do?" Mistress Bonnard's voice dropped to a teasing lilt, her eyes glinting.

Anne blinked, her mind racing. No one asked such questions back home. She felt important, as if someone cared what her own thoughts were, without trying to shape them for her. "Toss off my headdress and dance in a field," she blurted, surprising herself.

"Then go and do so right over there. We shall be your audience." The beguine's tone was playful yet commanding. She pointed to the empty lane before them.

Anne froze. "I'll be scolded, Madame, for neglecting my duties."

"Then I shall scold whoever does so and tell them you were doing what I asked you to." A mischievous gleam lit the beguine's face.

Barbe nodded, her mouth working to hold back laughter.

Before Anne knew what was happening, the Frenchwoman reached out. With a flick of her wrist, she sent Anne's headdress tumbling. "Off you go. We'll be your judges."

Her blood rising, Anne took a few steps into the lane. She ran her fingers through her hair and raised her face to the sun. Twirling around, she lifted her skirts and danced a few steps of the basse danse she'd learned just the week before.

Mistress Bonnard's laughter rippled through the air, as carefree as a girl's. "Well done!"

"Pretend you are Princess Lenore!" Barbe called out, her voice a blend of encouragement and jest.

Thrusting her nose in the air, Anne slowed her steps and moved with greater hauteur.

"Be no one but yourself!" Mistress Bonnard overruled.

Anne curtseyed low, humming inside with satisfaction. All day long others tried to mould her into someone else. What joy it was to simply be herself. Leaping into the air, she threw out her arms, at one with the sun on her skin and the spring breeze ruffling her hair.

"More twirls!" the beguine commanded.

Spinning wildly, Anne felt herself grow dizzy. But she didn't wish to stop. Caught up in the cheers of her audience, the sun's warm approval, and spring's intoxicating scents, she forgot everything. It was as if time itself had paused a moment to share her joy. Then an arm grabbed her, and she fell into Mistress Bonnard's embrace.

Righting herself, she gasped as Barbe caught hold of the older woman so that she wouldn't topple over. "Oh, Madame, I didn't mean to bump into you!" Anne cried.

The beguine shook her head. "You didn't. It was I who stopped you from falling."

Anne stared, astonished. "But how did you get over here, Madame?"

"I just walked farther than I have in ages," Mistress Bonnard crowed, looking as vibrant as Anne felt.

"Is that so, Madame?"

"It is, indeed, Mistress Bonnard," a voice called out. "What have these demoiselles done to you?" With her hands on her hips, the magistra stood in the narrow lane, gazing at them.

"It is not what they have done to me. It is what they have done for me," Mistress Bonnard sang out.

The magistra looked undecided. "I hope they have not disturbed you."

"They have brought me back to my youth." Mistress Bonnard's voice rang with merriment.

"Then they must now bring you back to your bench so that you are safe," the magistra said.

"Nonsense. I can do so myself." The elderly beguine moved towards the bench, her cane left propped against the wall.

"Mistress, I have not seen you walk so well for years," the magistra marvelled, shooting a warning glance at Barbe to catch her should she fall.

But Mistress Bonnard didn't fall. Reaching the bench, she waited until Anne and Barbe took an arm each and set her down on it. Then they all looked at each other and broke into laughter.

"Send these two to me again," Mistress Bonnard ordered, her tone leaving no room for argument.

The magistra's lips curved into a smile. "I will see to it."

"They are not dull," the sprightly woman approved.

The magistra's smile widened. "I will let their *mère des filles* know."

Mistress Bonnard thumped the table. "I'm sure she already does."

"I'll leave you to your pleasures. But be careful not to wear out Mistress Bonnard," the magistra counselled the demoiselles.

"We will!" Anne and Barbe chimed together. After watching the magistra disappear through the gate in the wall, they turned back to their host, who was pouring another round of refreshment, this time with steady hands.

Barbe raised her goblet high. "What shall we toast?"

"To pleasing no one before yourself," Mistress Bonnard declared.

Barbe's eyes widened. "Not even our mistress?"

"Or our king or queen if we serve at another court?" Anne added.

"Please yourself, and in such a way, you will most please others," Mistress Bonnard counselled, looking at them each in turn.

Anne sipped her drink, the beguine's surprising words warming her like a fine new cloak. Was it not good advice?

"And you, Madame," Barbe pressed, playful but probing, "did you follow such advice?"

Mistress Bonnard's sharp gaze met hers. "What do you think?"

Barbe's eyes twinkled. "I think you did, Madame."

"And here I am now," the beguine said, looking like the girl she once was.

Glancing around at their tidy, well-kept surroundings, hidden away like a gem in a secret jewel box, Anne thought that to be a beguine was to have a sort of freedom that a courtier never could. "You lead a happy life, don't you, Madame?" she said.

"I do, *ma fille*," the captivating woman agreed. "Especially when the company is good."

Mistress Bonnard winked, and Anne and Barbe winked back.

The following day, Semmonet shut the French textbook with a crack. "Done with grammar, and now for conversation," he announced. "You may tell me about what you have been doing since last we met."

"I visited the beguinage, Monsieur." Anne's insides danced to think about it.

"And I should hope you served with sacrifice there," the tutor responded.

"No, Monsieur. It was no sacrifice at all, but a merry visit."

"You were lucky, then. I have heard the older beguines can be demanding."

"Oh, she was, Monsieur. But in a most enjoyable way."

"I'm not sure I understand."

"I didn't understand, either, at first. And I still don't. She was at once most ancient and yet most young."

Semmonet cocked his head. "What do you mean?"

"She was spirited. And brazen, too." Anne used the word in English, not knowing its equivalent in French.

"Brazen?"

"Playful, Monsieur. At first, she seemed a scold, but then she became like one of us, but with a touch of mystery."

Semmonet's lips curved into a knowing smile. "Was this beguine French, by any chance?" he asked.

Anne's eyes widened. "How did you know, Monsieur?"

"You have just described a Frenchwoman."

"Which Frenchwoman, Monsieur?"

"Most of them."

Anne stared at her tutor. "How so, Monsieur?"

"First she challenges, then if you pass her test, she embraces you but doesn't give all of herself away."

"Yes! That was just how it was! At first, we were frightened, but when Barbe stood up to her, she liked it," Anne told him.

"Frenchwomen like to challenge and to be challenged. There's no other approach for them."

Anne was baffled yet intrigued. "Do they not wish for an agreeable first exchange?"

"Too dull, *ma chère*. Without wit, without challenge, there is only boredom."

Deep inside Anne a string twanged, sharp and bright. "Oh, Monsieur, I feel that way, too!"

Semmonet nodded. "Such is the French way, *ma fille*. And if you don't follow it, you will find no way in with them."

"I would gladly follow such a way! 'Tis much more interesting than just exchanging niceties —"

"— that one does not really mean," Semmonet finished.

"Will you teach me to be French, Monsieur?"

"I will teach you French, and I, myself, am French. It is up to you to learn what you will," her tutor declared.

"I've learned so much from this conversation!" Anne exclaimed. Most of all, she had learned that there was a whole country full of women she wished to be like.

"You will learn more, as time goes on. We have a bit of that French bite here, but the cheese is sharper in France."

"What do you mean?"

"You will discover it once you master the tongue, for you have that same bite yourself."

"I've always known so, Monsieur. But everyone tells me to be quiet and demure and act like a — like a —"

"Like a country cow?"

"Yes!"

Semmonet studied her for a moment. "You are more of a forest ermine."

"What is that, Monsieur?"

"A small animal who stands up to foxes, wolves, and bears."

"How so?" Anne asked, curious.

"She stands on her hind legs and chatters, scolding them fiercely until they back off and slink away."

Anne giggled at the image. "It is what I do back home when my brother or sister cross me."

"And her coat is only to be worn by royals."

"What does it look like?" Anne asked, thinking the ermine image suited her well.

"Black spots on a white field, like Brittany's banner."

"And it is fashioned after the ermine?"

"Indeed, it is, *ma fille*. For Brittany is the ermine and France is the fox. And she has bravely stood up to the fox for centuries, just as Anne of Brittany stands up to her husband, the French king."

"I've heard she's petite like me." Anne recalled the painting of France's queen with her maids of honour that hung in Lady Margaret's bedchamber.

"She is, and brave too, with a fierce tongue."

"Does she get her way in all things?" Anne asked, thinking this other Anne sounded a great deal like her.

"She does, except in the one way she desires most."

"What is that?"

"She has no sons."

"Does the king of France mind?"

"Not as much as she does, *ma fille*. For when he dies, their eldest daughter will marry his chosen successor and bring Brittany into France's realm."

"And if they had a son?"

"He would rule France, and their daughter would inherit Brittany from her mother to rule over herself."

"How sad for the queen to have no sons," Ann mused, thinking of the two her mother had lost at birth, their tiny bodies buried in the family plot back home.

"It's not an uncommon fate," Semmonet noted. "But for queens it is especially harsh, as a king cannot secure his succession without a son."

"My king must be eager for a son himself," Anne mused.

"I'm sure he is. But he is young and there is time."

"My mother says there is always time for men, but not for women."

Semmonet nodded. "The time is shorter for women. And once it runs out, it's gone forever."

"I'll be sure not to let that happen," Anne declared.

Semmonet's eyes held both merriment and sorrow. "No one can be sure of anything. But my wife once said that a woman must keep her years in mind if she wishes for children."

"I didn't know you had a wife!" Anne exclaimed.

The Frenchman's eyes flicked away. "Not only a wife, but a French one."

"Is she here in Malines with you?" Anne asked, hoping she might teach her something more of a Frenchwoman's ways.

"She is with the angels."

"I'm sorry."

Her tutor smiled ruefully. "She used to say that while men play, women plan."

"I shall begin planning now." Anne imagined herself a queen with a nursery full of children and an army of staff to look after them.

Semmonet chuckled. "Leave it to your parents to plan. They'll know where to look for a match for you," he advised.

"But what if my aim is higher than theirs?" Anne asked.

Her tutor regarded her strangely. "Why would you think to aim higher?"

Anne's thoughts flew to Mistress Bonnard. "I should like to please myself before others."

"Even before your parents?" Semmonet asked.

Anne tilted her chin, remembering the French beguine's advice. "In pleasing myself, I will most please others."

Her tutor tutted. "You must be careful in following such a headstrong course."

"Why so?"

"You may find, one day, that those you once pleased by such a policy are no longer charmed."

Anne shrugged. "Then I will go my own way."

"If that is your wish, then do not aim high. For the higher your rank, the less free you will be to go your own way," Semmonet warned, pointing to the door, as their time was up.

Anne thanked him and curtseyed. Escaping to the hallway she smoothed down her mantle, imagining her hands running over an ermine trim. *Of course I will aim high*, she thought. *Why point my arrows anywhere but to the highest target I can reach?*

FIVE

"You will ractice your composition today," Semmonet instructed. The court had moved to Lady Margaret's summer retreat of La Tervuren, just outside Brussels for a few weeks. But, despite the change of location, daily lessons continued as usual.

Anne wrinkled her nose. "Oh, Monsieur, I'm no good at writing in French!"

"I have seen. But you will improve with practice."

"What shall I write, then?"

"An essay, perhaps?"

Anne silently groaned. What a dull prospect to write an essay in French on a beautiful summer day. "I wouldn't know what to say, Monsieur, and no one will ever read it."

"You do not lack for things to say, but who would you most like to say them to?"

She knew instantly. Every day her head filled with thoughts she wished to share with the one person she cared to impress most. "I should like to say them to my father."

Her tutor gave a firm nod. "Then you shall write him a letter."

Anne's pulse quickened. What better way to prove her progress at Lady Margaret's court than by penning her father a letter in French? "But how shall I begin, Monsieur?"

"That's up to you. Write from the heart. Use your own words." Semmonet pointed to the desk in the garden study where quill, inkwell, and several sheets of parchment waited.

Anne moved to the desk, her mind whirling with all she wanted to say. How could she begin to tell him all that she had seen and experienced since leaving England? "But there's so much to say, Monsieur. I'll be here all day and through the night!"

"Nonsense. You'll write one page only and sign off at the bottom of it."

Anne brightened to be given a limit. She wasn't good at keeping to limits herself, just as her thoughts never seemed to end. They kept coming until they spilled out of her mouth. "But how shall I fit all that is new and different here on just one page?"

Semmonet waved a dismissive hand. "Don't bother with all that. Your father spent months at Madame's court. He knows already. Write something that is strictly between yourselves."

Anne gazed into space, her chin propped on her fist. There was so much that she yearned for between her father and herself. Yet in place of warm memories, there was mostly absence and longing. Perhaps she could bridge that gap by letting him know how much she wished to please him.

Picking up the quill and dipping it in the inkwell, she paused.

Her tutor moved to the door. "I'll be back by eleven. Don't be afraid to make mistakes. Just write it all down, and we'll send it off."

Anne nodded, her quill poised above the sheet. What she wished to say to her father was too close to her heart to write with someone else in the room.

Semmonet disappeared, leaving her alone with her thoughts.

Gazing out the window into the garden, Anne collected herself. Beyond all else, she wanted her father to know that she wished to make him proud. She wished for so much more, too — his attention, his time. But it was too overwhelming to express such thoughts in a letter. And it hurt too much to think of them.

Taking a deep breath, Anne put pen to parchment, her words flowing like a river that had been dammed for too long.

Two hours later Semmonet returned, slipping into the room so quietly that Anne barely knew he was there.

"I see you have been busy," he remarked.

Anne bit her lip. "I have made a right mess." But she had done the best she could. All that was left was for her tutor to correct her grammar and atrocious spelling.

Semmonet pointed to the letter. "You must sign it at the bottom, and we shall send it off today."

"But shouldn't we correct it first?" Anne protested.

"This is your work, not mine, *ma fille*. If you wish your father to know what your progress is, you must send him your own letter, not one I have corrected for you."

"Oh, Monsieur, it's such a muddle. I don't know what he'll think," Anne cried, handing the sheet to her tutor.

The older man scanned it, a smile working the corners of his mouth. "He'll think this is truly your work."

"But it's far from perfect!" Anne wailed.

"He's your father. It will be perfect for him." He picked up the quill and handed it to Anne. "Now sign it so you can be off to archery."

Carefully, Anne added her location and the most respectful closing she could think of — *Your very humble and very obedient daughter*, hoping her father wouldn't laugh when he read it. Then she signed the French version of her name.

Behind her, Semmonet squeezed her shoulder. "Does it not feel good to be done?"

"Yes, Monsieur." As she pushed back from the desk, Mistress Bonnard's advice popped into her head — *Please yourself, and in such a way you will most please others.*

She was never sure if she pleased her father. But no matter. She had pleased herself by pouring out her heart to him.

Jumping up, she curtseyed to Semmonet then ran off to archery. There she would fire her quiver of arrows and reap the satisfaction of knowing when she had hit her target.

With her father, she never knew.

"Watch your aim! You will take someone's head off if you shoot that way," the archery master bawled.

"I'm sorry, sir. I didn't know which target to hit," one of the demoiselles answered. She cowered as the master strode towards her.

"Just don't hit a living one," he scolded, as he corrected her position.

"He's on edge because there was an accident a few months ago." Barbe's voice was low.

Anne's eyes widened. "What happened?"

"Someone hit a man, instead of the target."

"How awful!"

"Pinned him to the wall where he was working." Barbe pointed to a nearby building. "That one, right over there."

"Did he live?"

Barbe shook her head. "Dead. Instantly."

"Who did it?"

"The most important person in all of the Netherlands," Barbe murmured.

Anne caught her breath. "Not Lady Margaret!"

"No, you fool. Lady Margaret would never let loose an arrow if she didn't have a good idea of where it might fly."

"Who, then?" Somehow Barbe's insults only grazed her, unlike Jeanne's barbed remarks that hooked under her skin and festered. What pleasure it was to have the day off from Jeanne, with Lady Elisabeth sending her on an errand to the beguinage. If only she might never come back.

"Someone destined for a crown," Barbe hinted.

"The archduke?" Anne whispered.

Barbe nodded.

"I'm sure it was a mistake."

"He was careless, I suppose."

"Poor man," said Anne, thinking of the victim.

"His family is less poor now, since Madame sent them a fat purse for compensation."

"Did the archduke seem upset?"

Barbe shrugged. "I wasn't there. But they say his expression didn't change."

Anne wasn't surprised. From what she had seen of Charles of Habsburg, he didn't show his emotions, whatever they might be. "Perhaps he didn't realise what happened," she speculated.

Barbe snickered. "Of course he did. But his attendants hustled him off and it hasn't been spoken of since."

"Except that you just spoke of it," Anne pointed out.

"Everyone in the kitchen and at the stables spoke of it. But not before the archduke or anyone important."

Anne glanced at the building, pondering the advantages of power. Mistakes made by the important were swept away, while the ordinary were left to grieve in silence.

"Don't mention it to anyone," Barbe added.

Anne nodded. Pulling back her arrow, she released it, just missing the target as certain thoughts flew home. If you weren't important, you were as good as nobody. If you were important, no one could touch you, just like the archduke.

She shot again, hitting the outer ring. She would aim for the bullseye in whatever she did.

*

After practice, Anne and Barbe walked past the building Barbe had pointed out.

"That's the spot, there. Behind those men."

Anne slowed her steps, straining to catch the low rumble of conversation drifting towards them. "Are they talking about it?" she whispered.

Barbe gave a quick nod and pressed a finger to her lips. Together, they eased closer to the corner, just out of sight.

"So, he made a mistake. What of it?" a gruff voice remarked.

"One that cost a man his life," came the reply, lower, steadier.

"A drunk and a roustabout," the first man remarked.

"A man with a mother who mourned him," the second countered.

"Not like the Virgin mourning our Lord."

"Who's to say? Does it not say in the Bible that He comes in disguise, and when He does, we are to feed and clothe Him? Not shoot Him through with an arrow as if He doesn't matter."

The first man let out a short laugh. "How would you know what it says in the Bible?"

"Because a German merchant told me so last week — he said a priest was preaching about it. He said some think the Bible should be in their own tongue so they can read it themselves."

Anne's ears pricked. She would ask Barbe later if she had understood correctly.

"Sounds like they're not sticking to the Mass over there," the first muttered. "Why bother with the Bible when priests read it for us? Going to Mass is enough."

"Some need more, and there are priests now who are saying much more," the second observed.

"About what?"

"About the sale of indulgences, for one," the second said.

Anne started. If they were speaking of what she thought they were, her father had jested about the practice more than once.

"Now there's a nasty business," the first man agreed. "But you want to get to heaven, don't you?"

"There's nothing in the Bible about buying your way into heaven," the second shot back.

Anne glanced at Barbe, who shrugged.

"So, where'd they come up with the idea?" the gruff one asked.

A snort. "The Pope needs money to get St. Peter's rebuilt in Rome."

Barbe raised a finger, confirming Anne's silent guess.

"If the Pope says it's right, then it's right," the first man insisted.

"Any fool can see it's wrong. Didn't Christ toss vendors from the Temple?"

"How would I know?"

"If you could read the Bible yourself, you would know."

The first let out a bitter laugh. "If I could read, I'd know lots of things. But I can't, so I'm not taking any chances. When my time comes, I want to be ready."

The second man's voice dropped. "Pleasing the Pope won't save you. Only asking the Lord Himself will."

"How would I know if He hears me?"

"You don't," the second man said. "You either believe it, or you don't."

"I'll stick with the Pope's orders and leave Bible-reading to the priests," the first said.

"Please yourself," the second answered. The sound of a chisel hitting stone told the girls the men had gone back to work. Barbe tiptoed off as Anne followed behind.

"Well?" Barbe asked.

Anne let out a long breath. "What was that about the Pope and indulgences?"

"He sells them to people who think it guarantees them entrance into Heaven," Barbe explained.

"Do you think there's anything in the Bible about it?"

"It sounds like there's something in the Pope's accounting books about it," Barbe quipped. "Who knows what's in the Bible?"

Anne's voice dropped. "Don't you want to know?"

Barbe shrugged. "Why bother? If the Pope says it's good, that's enough for me."

"You sound like that first man."

"Why should I question it?"

"I thought that's what our lecturers tell us we should do with classical texts."

"Classical texts are one thing. Questioning the Pope is another."

"But we're being taught to go back to the source to seek out answers," Anne countered.

Barbe waved a dismissive hand. "We're being taught the New Learning, that's all. You don't have to apply it."

Why wouldn't I? Anne thought but held her tongue. The last thing she wanted was trouble with Barbe. "Was he saying something about some wanting to read the Bible in their own tongue?"

"If they want to, let them." Barbe's tone was blithe.

"But how can they, if it isn't translated?"

Barbe stared at her. "Why do you care?"

Anne paused, feeling the weight of her next words. "Because it makes sense for people to read what's written there, so they can decide for themselves what they think about it."

"But the Pope does that for us," Barbe argued, her tone impatient.

"Shouldn't we do that for ourselves?" Anne pressed.

Barbe's eyes widened. "You want to take the Pope's place?"

"Of course not! I just don't want someone telling me what to think when I'd like to see what the Bible says about it for myself."

Barbe shook her head, giving Anne an incredulous look. "I'll tell you what I think. You like to stick your neck out, that's what."

Anne shrugged, her resolve firm. What was the point of learning if she wasn't allowed to think for herself?

A few weeks later, the new girl from Bremen shifted beside Anne, her blanket crumpling as she moved. She had been assigned to the same bed, as she spoke some English.

"Are you homesick?" Else whispered.

"Not at all. Why should I be?" Anne asked. To wean herself away from Barbe, with her poison twin Jeanne, she had tried to befriend her new bedmate. But it was hard going.

Else rubbed her eyes as she sat up. "I can't understand half of what's being said."

"I can't either, but that's why we're here." Anne hopped out of bed and moved to the window. Already, she loved the lively tones of French that echoed through the corridors of Lady Margaret's palace, so unlike the schoolbook French she had been taught back in Kent. It was sharper, more musical than English, forcing her to move the muscles of her mouth more. French was like a grown-up gown she would soon fit into, with more accentuated angles than the girlish ones her mother and their attendants had spent the past winter sewing.

"Demoiselles! *Allez-vite*, let's go!" Lady Elisabeth's voice shattered the quiet. "You are expected in the music salon as soon as you've had a bite."

Anne jumped into her pale yellow summer gown, eager to seize the day. She dashed past Else without waiting, a rising impatience gnawing at her. The German girl reminded her of her sister — pretty but dull.

Taking her seat in the music salon, Anne couldn't wait to express with her fingers what she couldn't yet articulate in French. With Jeanne steering Barbe away from her, Anne felt untethered. Thus far her efforts to expand her circle of friends had failed. No one else came close to Barbe, with her lively wit and salty mouth.

Under the watchful eye of the music master Anne strummed her lute, enjoying its mellow tones.

Monsieur Bredemers' voice cut through her thoughts. "You will use your instrument to soothe and to sway, Mesdemoiselles."

The girl next to Anne smirked. "Or to tease and to tempt," she said under her breath, drawing snickers from the girls nearby.

"Come to order, ladies." Monsieur Bredemers rapped his baton smartly. "Each of you will play one passage in turn. Do not rush. And if your fingering is wrong, my baton will let you know."

Anne listened closely as the first of the demoiselles fumbled through her notes. The music master frowned then took a moment to correct her. As he did, Anne silently practised her fingering without plucking the strings. She might be the youngest of the demoiselles, but her slim fingers were more dexterous than the larger hands of the others. When her turn came, she got through the passage with no mistakes.

"Very good, Mademoiselle," the music master commended.

Anne beamed, wondering why the girl she sat closest to glared at her. Was she to be disliked for being the best?

That night Else whispered again, under the covers. "Everything is different here. I don't fit in."

"You will, if you watch and learn," Anne replied, thinking she didn't fit in, either, but she was determined to try.

The German girl sniffled. "I've been watching since I got here, and I've learned that I like home better."

Anne longed to pinch her. "Your father sent you here to become a great lady, did he not?"

"My father lent Madame money to fight the Duke of Guelders, so she took me on as repayment," Else replied.

Anne sharpened her ears. "Is your father lord of Bremen?"

"He is Bremen's largest mercer," Else answered.

A merchant's daughter. The revelation left Anne cold. "Then I'm sure he wishes to raise your station by sending you here."

"We are not of the same rank as the others," Else continued. "They are from the nobility and we —"

Anne cut her off. "Speak for yourself, if you think you don't belong here." How dare a commoner's daughter presume a shared lowly status? Her family had been gentry for generations, rising even farther with her father's marriage to her mother.

"But do you not worry that you don't understand the ways of the others?" Else pressed.

"No. I am fired by it." Anne tapped out her response with a fingernail on her bedmate's back; she fought the urge to scratch it hard. "Do you not wish to gain something new that no one else will have once you return home?"

"I don't want anything new to return home with. I just want to go home."

Anne gritted her teeth. "Do your best to learn French while you're here. The faster you do, the sooner you'll fit in." She needed to find a new bedmate as soon as possible. This one would gain her nothing.

"I'll never understand it," Else moaned.

"You have not been here long enough to know."

"It's not just a difference in tongues. It's a different way to be. I can see it already in the way they carry themselves."

Anne's blood raced. Her bedmate was right. Those at the Burgundian court did carry themselves differently — with confidence born of privilege. She could hardly wait to carry herself in a similar manner. "And don't you wish to do the same?"

"No." The German girl's voice quavered.

"Then go home and be content," Anne advised, struggling to keep a civil tone. Never would she be satisfied to go home and become an English rose like her sister, with all the spirit of a Kentish cow. She had been sent abroad to cultivate her gifts. Being a dutiful, demure Englishwoman was not one of them.

"Do you think my father will be disappointed if I ask to go back?" Else asked.

Anne swallowed her annoyance. "What do you think?"

"He is ambitious. I know he will." Else sounded crestfallen.

"I know of another who is ambitious," Anne couldn't help saying.

"Who is that?"

"My own father."

Else sighed. "I'm like my mother."

"I'm not."

"So, you resemble your father?" Else asked.

Anne paused. In truth, she did resemble him. But since meeting Mistress Bonnard at the beguinage, the idea of pleasing herself over pleasing anyone else had taken root and begun to flower. The more the idea grew, the less it hurt that weeks had passed with no reply from him to her letter. "I resemble myself," she proclaimed.

Else stared. "What does that mean?"

"Nothing. Now go to sleep and dream of home."

Her bedmate sighed. "I will. And God grant that I'll be there soon."

Anne thumped her pillow and turned over. She would dream her own dreams. They would include fending off dull-wits wherever she found them. Especially in her own bed.

The next day Anne spoke to Lady Elisabeth. "Madame, I have thought of a way to learn French faster."

"What is that?"

"I should switch bedmates to one who speaks only French so I may practise during nightly chats." If only she could switch to Barbe. But Jeanne was her bedmate. She could imagine what Barbe's guard dog might do to her if she tried to take her place.

Lady Elisabeth's brow arched. "You are supposed to sleep, not chat."

Anne bit her lip, trying not to appear too eager. "It's just that I want to learn faster."

"Will you not be lonely without your English-speaking friend?"

Anne squelched a snort. "It's she who is lonely, Madame. She longs to go home." Assuming a sorrowful expression, she did her best to show concern for her bedmate's welfare.

Lady Elisabeth regarded her curiously. "Why is that?"

"She says she doesn't fit in here."

"Why should she not fit in? Are you not helping her to do so?"

"I'm trying. But she told me it was not her choice to come."

Lady Elisabeth frowned. "It is an honour to be invited to join Lady Margaret's court."

"So it is, Madame. But she said she is only here to repay a debt Lady Margaret owes her father."

The *mère des filles* looked startled. "What debt is that?"

"She said her father lent Madame money to fight the Duke of Guelders."

Lady Elisabeth's mouth curled down. "How is it she told you all this?"

"Because I'm her bedmate, Madame."

"Not a good idea, I see."

"No, Madame." Anne lowered her eyes as Lady Elisabeth's thoughts drew towards their inevitable conclusion.

"And as for you?" Lady Elisabeth peered at her. "Are you happy to be here?"

"Yes, Madame! I'm so excited to be here that I'm not lonely at all — only eager to learn."

Lady Elisabeth's lips pursed. "Never say 'I am excited to be here.' It is a false friend in French. Say 'I am pleased to be here.' Or 'happy'."

Despite her severe tone, Anne noted a glint in the *mère des filles'* eye. "Why so, Madame? Is it not correct to say I'm excited, when I am?"

"It has a meaning you can't understand at your age. Don't use that expression again."

Anne was astonished. There was so much to learn. Being excited to take it all in was exactly how she felt. "And what is a false friend, Madame?" For sure, she had one in Jeanne. But Barbe seemed true, even with her insults and jabs, much like her brother, George, back home.

"It is an expression for words that resemble similar English words, but which have different meanings in French." Lady Elisabeth paused. "And then there are false friends you will come across at court. You must be on your guard with them. They are everywhere."

"I understand the first, but not the second."

"You will learn from Lady Margaret, who is the master of guarding against false friends. Meanwhile, improve your French and follow my guidelines so you don't embarrass yourself."

Anne dipped her head. "I wouldn't wish to do that."

"No, little one. I see that you would not. Just study and follow for now. Understanding will come."

"I understand."

"You do not yet, but you are clever, so you will learn."

"Yes, Madame."

Before the week was out, Anne had been moved to another dormitory, with Agnes de Middelbourg as her new bedmate. Disdainful and self-contained, from an ancient and noble Burgundian family, the older demoiselle possessed all the hauteur of a grown woman.

Anne studied her every move, the upward tilt of her chin and the slight delay in responding to any question asked by anyone she wished to put at a disadvantage. It didn't take long to discern that less was more where Agnes was concerned. The concept of holding back was ingrained in her, anchored there by generations of breeding. Anne guessed that her own mother would be proud to see her conduct herself in a similar manner.

"Are you picking up any French from her?" Else asked as they crossed paths on their way to the morning lecture. She followed Agnes with her eyes as the older girl swept by, ignoring them both.

"No," Anne replied coolly, mimicking Agnes's posture. "She doesn't speak to me."

Else looked confused. "Do you think she doesn't like you?"

Ignoring her, Anne studied Agnes's back, straight yet relaxed, like a gliding swan. "I don't care if she likes me or not."

The German girl sucked in her breath. "But don't you want to be liked?"

Anne gave her a hard look. Whether she wanted to be liked or not, it made no difference. Barbe liked her; Jeanne did not. There was nothing she could do to sway either of them. "Do you think Agnes wants to be liked?"

Else stared in the graceful girl's direction. "She's different from us. She doesn't need to be liked."

Anne swallowed her disgust. The next time Else presumed an affinity would be the last. Anne was there to become a more polished version of herself, not to be dragged down by some common bore who should never have left home. "That's not the point. It's *us* who are not like *her*. But I intend to be." Anne watched as Agnes picked up an apple, took one bite, lost interest then discarded it, as if her fingers had tired of holding it. Quickly, one of the stable yard dogs pounced on it.

Else sighed. "I'll never be like her, and I don't want to be."

It was the first firm statement Anne had heard the German girl make. At least she knew what she didn't want. Tilting her chin, Anne met Else's eyes. "I do."

"But why would you want to be like that?" Else asked.

There was no point replying. Without a word, Anne moved in Agnes's direction. She would imitate everything her haughty new bedmate did. Then do it better.

SIX

As summer unfolded Anne threw herself into improving her French. One morning, as she passed her former dormitory, Anne noticed the room was empty.

"Else has gone home," Jeanne said, appearing out of nowhere.

"Do you know why?" Anne asked, surprised that Jeanne had addressed her. When Barbe wasn't around, she usually cut her dead.

Jeanne's eyes narrowed. "No. I thought you might."

"Why would I?"

"We thought you might have had something to do with it."

Anne bristled. Who was 'we' and why couldn't Jeanne speak for herself? "Why would you think that?"

"Because you disliked her." Jeanne's smirk was cold. "Even though you had much in common."

"If you mean speaking English, that's not why I'm here."

Jeanne's smile didn't reach her eyes. "That's not what I mean."

"Then what do you mean?"

"I mean you both come from similar backgrounds."

Anne's skin prickled. "Not so. I'm English; she's German."

"And you're both common."

"That's not true!" Anne stopped herself from slapping Jeanne. She mustn't. The more she protested, the more she would not be believed.

Jeanne picked at a fingernail. "That's not what I heard."

"You know nothing of my background." Anne strained to keep her voice low.

"At court everyone knows who's noble and who's just pretending to be…"

Anne's temper shot to the ceiling. "My family is as noble as any."

Jeanne's lips curled into a cruel smile. "If you call being a mercer noble…"

"My great-grandfather was Lord Mayor of London!" Anne snapped.

"I'm sure his success in the cloth trade got him there."

Anne wanted to fly at her. "Who told you such nonsense?"

"Else. Just before she left. Her father's family did business with yours years ago."

Anne's stomach twisted. That part of her family history was never spoken of, at least not by her parents. Grandmother Boleyn had mentioned it in whispers, a secret not meant to be shared.

Jeanne's eyes gleamed. "Think of it as a parting gift to thank you for getting her sent home."

Furious, Anne defended herself. "My mother is from the noble Howards and my father's family is from Ireland's highest ranks."

Jeanne's laugh was short. "Noble chieftains, then? No wonder you are so brash."

"I am not brash. It's you who are brazen to goad me," Anne raged.

"You deserve goading," Jeanne taunted.

"And you deserve a slap," Anne fired back.

Jeanne stood tall. "I dare you to lay a finger on me. I am your superior and it will be to your detriment if you try."

"You are not my superior. You're just older and bigger," Anne spat.

"You are wrong. You are beneath me and always will be. Know your place."

Anne exploded, sending Jeanne flying into the bushes. No self-respecting member of the Boleyn family would allow such talk. Even if it were true.

"Why so feisty? You don't want to get sent home like Else, do you?" Barbe swung one leg over the other as she lounged on the couch in their quarters.

Anne, still simmering, shot back. "Forget Else. Why are you friends with Jeanne? You are better than her."

Barbe chuckled. "Funny, she says the same about you."

Anne's ire flared. "But she just follows you about, copying everything you do."

"Isn't that what you do with Agnes since you got rid of the German girl?"

"I did not get rid of her!"

Barbe raised a brow. "Then why did she leave?"

"She wanted to go home."

"You wanted the same thing."

"I do *not* want to go home!"

"Of course not. You wanted *her* to go. Because she discovered your secret."

Blood rushed to Anne's head. "What secret?"

Barbe snorted. "You know. The one you sent Jeanne into the bushes for."

"She deserved it. She's unkind all the time."

"You're unkind at times, too," Barbe observed. "You weren't so nice to Else."

"I wasn't trying to be. I just had nothing to say to her."

Barbe flicked a hand. "Don't shove Jeanne into the bushes again. You're not going to make friends that way."

"But she insulted me!"

"Everything about everyone gets out at court," Barbe said offhandedly.

"You sound just like Jeanne!"

Barbe reached over and tossed a sugared almond into her mouth. "Don't worry about me. Worry about yourself."

"I have nothing to worry about," Anne huffed.

"If you say so."

Trying to dislike Barbe, Anne found she couldn't. But equally, she could not make herself like Jeanne. Back home, after a scuffle with George, she would be back to being friends within the hour. It wasn't proving so easy at the Court of Savoy.

The next day she was forced to apologise to Jeanne. As Lady Elisabeth watched, Anne swallowed her bile and pretended to be contrite.

"I'm sorry I threw you into the bushes," she lied.

Jeanne held out her arms to show Lady Elisabeth. "I have scratches all over."

Good, Anne thought. "I'm sorry," she repeated, her voice flat.

"What's the problem between you two?" Lady Elisabeth asked, eyeing them both.

"It's nothing," Jeanne said as Anne stood silent.

"It's clearly something. What is it?"

"She won't leave Barbe alone," Anne and Jeanne chorused.

The *mère des filles* looked startled, then broke into laughter. "So that's what this is about," she chuckled.

"It's not right, Madame. Barbe and I were friends first. This one cannot just step in and take up her time," Jeanne argued.

"But we like to spend time together," Anne protested. Following Agnes around and imitating her frozen mannerisms wasn't anywhere near as fun as spending time with Barbe.

"I will speak to Barbe about this." Lady Elisabeth's tone was stern. "Meanwhile, you will stay away from each other, and if one of you is with her, the other is not to approach. Do you understand?"

Anne wanted to object, but kept her mouth shut. With Jeanne stuck to Barbe's side day and night, she would never get a moment alone with her.

"Yes, Madame." Jeanne nodded and curtseyed.

Lady Elisabeth turned to Anne. "And you?"

"Yes, Madame." Anne's heart dropped along with her curtsey.

Lady Margaret joined the demoiselles the following morning as they took their lessons in the library. Despite her stern black taffeta gown and pleated white widow's ruff, her smile was playful. "Now that I have a moment, what questions do you have for me?"

The girls looked at each other, abashed in the presence of their powerful mistress.

Anne raised her hand.

"Yes?" Lady Margaret responded.

"Madame, what is a false friend at court?" she asked, unsure of both Barbe or Jeanne at this point. She was avoiding Jeanne, which meant she couldn't get near Barbe, per Lady Elisabeth's orders.

The archduchess chuckled. "Ah, so you have learned that expression."

"But I don't understand what it means, Madame."

Lady Margaret leaned forward, a knowing look in her eyes. "My child, it means you must guard yourself against those who seek to deceive you."

Another girl, Françoise de Bréderode, spoke up. "In what way, Madame?"

Lady Margaret straightened in her chair, her fingers brushing lightly against her gown. "You are young women now, and soon you will face many who aim to lead you astray. Have you not read my verses on this topic?"

The girls leaned in, intrigued. Françoise broke the silence. "Would you read them to us, Madame?"

Rising with a fluid grace, Lady Margaret moved to a shelf of her library, overflowing with books and manuscripts both classical and contemporary. Pulling out a volume, its binding worn from use, she returned to her chair. The girls rustled in anticipation, their whispers silenced by a single glance from their mistress. Lady Margaret opened the book and began to read, her voice steady and clear: "*Trust in those who offer you service, and in the end, my maidens, you will find yourselves in the ranks of those who have been deceived. They, for their sweet speeches, choose words softer than the softest of virgins. Trust in them? In their hearts they nurture much cunning in order to deceive, and once they have their way thus, everything is forgotten.*"

"But how should we deflect them?" Jeanne asked.

"You must use your sharpest swords," Lady Margaret advised.

"What swords, Madame, as we are women?"

"The sharpest of all weapons, Mesdemoiselles, are your tongues and wits," Madame explained.

The room buzzed with interest. Eyes darted from one girl to another. "But how should we answer them?" Anne asked.

Lady Margaret leaned forward, her tone conspiratorial. "With fine words, of course," she began, her voice once again reading from the text. "*Fine words are the coin to pay back those presumptuous minions who ape the lover by fine looks and such like.*" She snapped shut the book and looked up. "Do you see, *mes filles?*"

"And if they do not heed our words, Madame?" Agnes asked.

Lady Margaret sniffed. "Then they are unworthy of the game of courtly love."

The demoiselles giggled, but the question lingered in the air.

"But what if … if a fine knight turns out to be a low fellow?" Jeanne asked.

Laughter bubbled from Lady Margaret, contagious and sudden. The room joined in, the tension easing. "Ah, my dear. More often than not, such is the case. Never trust a man unless he offers marriage — and even then, let your parents decide if he's worthy."

Eyes darted nervously around the room, the unspoken questions hanging thick. Lady Margaret's gaze softened as she continued, "Many great ladies have written of these things. Their advice fills the shelves of this library."

"Will you tell us which ones, Madame?" Barbe asked.

Anne swallowed her snort. Barbe only bothered with romances and fabliaux. She was just trying to impress their mistress, for which she could hardly blame her.

Lady Margaret rose and went to the bookshelves. Carefully, she pulled out the volume she sought. "This is *Les Enseignements* by Anne of France. I assign it to you all to read. Its contents have guided many daughters."

Lady Margaret replaced the book and retrieved another. She held it up. "Christine de Pizan," she announced, "the most celebrated female writer of her time. She wrote *The Treasure of the City of Ladies*, which you will read once you've completed your first assignment. My ancestors, the dukes of Burgundy, were her patrons." Lady Margaret turned to the front page of the book she held. "Who can read here who it is dedicated to?"

Françoise peered closely. "Is it Margaret of Burgundy?"

Lady Margaret brightened. "It is, indeed. My godmother, after whom I am named."

A chance to display her knowledge welled up inside Anne. "Was she also Margaret of York?" she spilled out.

Lady Margaret nodded. "You are right, *ma fille.*"

Anne's pride puffed. Glancing around to acknowledge the regard of her fellow maids of honour, she was startled to meet hostile looks instead. Quickly, she pinned her eyes back on the regent.

"What are the treasures that fill the city of ladies?" Agnes asked.

"You will soon find out by reading this book. And once you are done, you may read a second work by Madame de Pizan that is somewhat lighter." Lady Margaret went to the shelves again, running her finger along the books in the same shelf she had gone to before. "Here it is," she said, pulling out a slimmer volume and showing the title page to the demoiselles before looking at it.

A hum buzzed through the room.

"So, you are interested in reading *The Book of the City of Ladies,*" Lady Margaret remarked with satisfaction.

"I'm not sure that is the one you are holding," Lady Elisabeth cut in.

Lady Margaret glanced down at the book in her hands. The title page read *One Hundred Ballads of a Lover and a Lady.* With a gasp she returned to the shelf, reshelving it and pulling out the volume next to it. "That was not the book I had in mind. You are to read this one," she corrected, holding up *The Book of the City of Ladies.*

Anne memorised the location of the more interesting book. She would return to the library later to explore what lay between its pages.

"Madame, we would like more instruction on this game of courtly love," Barbe's voice rang out.

Anne's mouth twitched. She missed that bold voice, unafraid to speak up. How could someone as forthright as Barbe be friends with someone as devious as Jeanne?

"I am sure you would, and you will receive it as long as you remain at my court," Lady Margaret replied.

"Could you tell us more, now?" Barbe asked as the room fell silent, the others looking on, rapt.

"The rules of courtly love can only be unfolded bit by bit. You have heard enough for today, so you may think on my words, and consider how you may repay fine words with equal ones to parry false intentions."

"How will we know if they are false?" Françoise asked.

"Assume they are, *ma fille*. For they are in all cases unless accompanied by an offer of marriage. And such an offer is to be weighed by your parents and not by you."

Barbe's brows knit together. "Are we to have any fun at all by following such advice, Madame?"

Lady Margaret chuckled. "Of course you are. You will dance, and sing, and send looks, as well as arrows of wit and wisdom, into the hearts of your admirers to deflect their false speeches. What fun you will have to see the longing in their eyes and know it for what it is."

"But what is it, Madame? Is it something we should fear or enjoy?" Barbe pressed.

"You should enjoy it if you are properly armed. If not, you should flee from such attentions, for they will lead you astray," Lady Margaret admonished.

Wide eyes turned to others, seeking clarification. As the room broke into chatter, Lady Elisabeth glided to the front. "That is enough for today. Madame must return to state matters."

"Thank you for sharing your wisdom with us, Madame," Barbe called out as the others chimed in.

Lady Margaret smiled. "It is my pleasure. And know that when I was your age, it was my godmother Margaret of Burgundy who shared similar wisdom and set me on a good path." Rising, she gave a confident flip of her headdress.

As she left the room, Anne's thoughts swirled. It was her own countrywoman who had taken a role in the regent's education, as well as the formidable Anne of France. Her mistress had been shaped by some of Europe's most powerful women. And now Lady Margaret was shaping her. What did it matter if the others didn't like her? All that mattered was that Lady Margaret did.

SEVEN

The following morning, Lady Elisabeth motioned to the two men standing by the door. "This is Monsieur Contault, Madame's *garde-joyaux* and his assistant, Monsieur Lullier."

Anne curtseyed. She recognised Monsieur Lullier. He was often around Madame's quarters, tending to her needs as her varlet-de-chambre. But why was she being introduced to two important officers of Madame's household?

"They oversee Madame's treasures," Lady Elisabeth went on. "Today, they'll be updating her collections and I've assigned you to assist."

Anne's heart sank. Had Lady Elisabeth arranged this to keep her away from Barbe and Jeanne? "But I'll miss my lessons, Madame."

"You'll learn far more from these gentlemen."

Her heart sank further. "But my French lessons —"

"You'll expand your vocabulary by learning the names of many interesting items in Madame's collections."

Anne silently groaned. Lady Margaret had artwork everywhere; paintings, sculptures, and tapestries adorned every room of the Court of Savoy. Then there were the mysterious natural objects in Madame's collection room off the garden, not to mention the assortment of curios she kept in her private study. Helping Monsieur Contault could take weeks.

"You'll be back at your lessons tomorrow," Lady Elisabeth continued, as if reading her thoughts. "And you can share some of the new words you have learned with Monsieur Semmonet." The *mère des filles* turned and vanished, her footsteps echoing down the hallway.

"Come, Mademoiselle," Monsieur Contault bade. "You will begin in the library with Monsieur Lullier."

Anne brightened. The library was her favourite place. Filled to the ceiling with treasures, it served not only to house Lady Margaret's hundreds of books and manuscripts, but as a reception hall, too. The vast room hinted at a world beyond the court, a place where she could lose herself in pages and ideas.

As Monsieur Contault hurried off, Monsieur Lullier turned to her. "A bit overwhelming, is it not?"

"Oh, Monsieur," Anne breathed, eyes wide. "I have never seen such treasures as Lady Margaret possesses."

"She is Northern Europe's most important art collector, as well as one of its shrewdest rulers."

Anne blinked. "How does she manage all this and everything else besides?"

Monsieur Lullier laughed. "We manage her treasures so that she can manage her realm."

"But why does she have all of this?" Anne blurted out before thinking how silly she sounded.

Monsieur Lullier cocked his head, not looking as if he thought her question silly at all. "Why do you think the archduchess surrounds herself with art?"

Anne paused. *Because she is rich* would be Barbe's response. The thought of it made her chuckle, but it couldn't be all there was to it. "Because it is Madame's passion?"

Monsieur Lullier nodded approvingly. "That is part of it, yes. But what do you think is the deeper reason?"

Anne searched her mind. "I don't know, Monsieur."

"That is well, because Madame does not wish for it to be known."

Anne's curiosity flamed.

Monsieur Lullier studied her with amused eyes. "You wonder if I will tell you, *non*?"

"Yes, Monsieur. If she doesn't wish it to be known, then why am I worthy of being told?"

"She has chosen you as one of her maids of honour. One day, you too may find yourself in a position of importance. When that day comes, you will be well-served to do what Lady Margaret does to strengthen her authority."

Anne sprang to attention. This was far more interesting than being mocked or ignored by the demoiselles back in the classroom. "What does she do, Monsieur?"

"She uses art to assert her power."

"How so?"

The varlet-de-chambre swept an arm over the length of the library. "This room, and every object in it, serves as Lady Margaret's armour. When diplomats and dignitaries come to her court, they see her wealth, her knowledge, and her taste. It speaks to her authority without her saying a word."

Anne studied the suit of armour near the chimney piece, imagining Lady Margaret sitting before it during a negotiation. She could see the way it would lend her weight, silently reinforcing her words. Next, her eyes fell on the lectern beside it. There lay the open prayerbook of the *Très Riches Heures* of the Duke of Berry, the most celebrated book of hours in all of Europe, according to Semmonet. Her gaze moved upward to the tapestries that covered the walls, adorned with heraldic emblems of the Houses of Habsburg and Burgundy, some including Lady Margaret's mottoes. All lent weight to her mistress's authority. "It inspires awe, Monsieur. I can think of no other word," she said.

Monsieur Lullier looked pleased. "And that is Madame's intention."

"If I may ask, Monsieur, whose suit of armour is that?"

"It belonged to Madame's last husband, the Duke of Savoy, and now to her. By placing it in this room, Madame signals to all who enter here that she is fully suited to do battle."

"But, Monsieur, she is a woman."

"And her battlefield is the negotiating table. Or the council chamber. Perhaps this table when an imposing figure comes to call." The varlet-de-chambre slid a hand over the long, polished oak table next to him.

Anne thought of the emperor and Lady Margaret shouting at each other in the library the month before. When she had peeked in, Madame had been seated in front of her suit of armour.

"But Lady Margaret doesn't wish for others to note her methods to wield power," Monsieur Lullier continued. "It would be unseemly for a woman to storm about and command like a man, so she surrounds herself with portraits of powerful rulers, or biblical scenes with her likeness painted in, so that those who view them are reminded of her right to rule."

Anne nodded in understanding. "'Tis clever."

"'Tis more than clever, Mademoiselle. 'Tis what a master ruler does to secure their position and deepen their subjects' fealty."

Anne's mind spun with the implications. Monsieur Lullier had shared a secret truth about the world of power, one that fascinated and terrified her. "Madame is a master, is she not?"

"She is a master at her game. Come, let us see how she plays it in her garden cabinet." With a flourish, Monsieur Lullier gestured for Anne to follow.

They entered Lady Margaret's collection room, its long windows against the far wall opening onto the garden.

Fragrances of lavender and lemon balm wafted in, making Anne's senses dance.

"What do you see, Mademoiselle?" Monsieur Lullier asked.

"I see marvellous objects all about, Monsieur. But I don't know what they are, nor their significance." She had wondered from the first moment she had laid eyes on the small, strange reddish-orange shapes that dotted the room, carefully mounted on wood or plaster bases.

"These are Madame's corals, along with her most prized conches and silver pieces."

Anne surveyed the corals, their spiky tendrils spread out like Medusa heads. "Where are they from?"

"They are from the sea. Some from the Mediterranean and others from across the ocean in the seas surrounding the islands of the New World."

"Are they rocks or plants?"

"No one knows. But they wave like planted dancers under the sea and are thought to have special powers."

"What kind of powers, Monsieur?"

The varlet-de-chambre shrugged. "Some say medicinal. Others say they guard against nightmares or accidents at sea."

"But why does Madame collect them?" Her mistress appeared to be in the best of health. She never spoke of nightmares, to Anne's knowledge, but awoke most mornings with a cheerful countenance and a long list of things to do. Anne knew because she was frequently in Madame's bedchamber when she awoke, shooing out Babou or tending to her caged songbirds, which she had finally been given permission to feed.

Monsieur Lullier moved to a bush-like coral cluster on a table by the window and picked it up. "All say that corals hold powers, but none know what they are." He beckoned Anne closer.

Gingerly approaching, Anne held her breath. Would the coral bush prove friend or foe? Reaching out, she touched one of its spiky red branches, telling herself the coral would not respect her if she showed fear.

"In Ovid's *Metamorphoses*, it is said that the corals are made from drops of blood from the head of Medusa after Perseus cut it off," Monsieur Lullier told her.

Anne shivered.

"And as they are petrified, like those who looked upon the gorgon Medusa, they will protect those who collect them from the evil eye," he continued.

"'Tis a good story, Monsieur."

"And do you believe it?"

"If Lady Margaret does, then so do I."

Monsieur Lullier shrugged. "Lady Margaret knows that those who pass through this room will sense they are in the presence of mysterious powers."

"I see."

"And she intends for the feeling that comes over them to extend to the feeling they hold for her."

Anne cocked her head. At the very least, she understood that her mistress knew how to create an effect that magnified her position. And that effect was aided by the carefully chosen treasures with which she surrounded herself. "Then, it doesn't matter whether Madame believes the corals have powers or not?"

Monsieur Lullier nodded. "It doesn't matter at all."

"So, there you are," a voice sounded from the doorway.

"Are we ready to begin?" Monsieur Lullier asked.

Monsieur Contault shook his head. "We are called in to meet with Lady Margaret."

"What about the inventory?"

"It's off. Lady Margaret has just sent word that she needs us for something else today."

Monsieur Lullier turned to Anne and made a short bow. "If you will excuse me."

"But, Monsieur, I have done nothing yet to help you."

"Lady Margaret calls. We shall leave it for another day."

"Oh, Monsieur, I have learned a great deal from you!"

"Because you have the ability to understand the significance of what I have told you."

Anne beamed. "Thank you, Monsieur." She curtseyed deeply; when she rose, the two men were gone.

Left in the collection room alone, Anne approached the coral cluster once more. Reaching out, she stroked its spiky branches, no longer afraid. Whether Lady Margaret's treasures held powers or not didn't matter. What mattered was that Madame enhanced her own powers by making others believe they did.

Anne smiled to herself. One day, she would do the same.

Later that day, Anne stepped into the music room, a heavenly combination of singing voices filling her ears. The intricate melodies interwove like musical threads in a rainbow-hued tapestry of sound.

"It's beautiful," she said to Barbe. Finally, Anne had found her without Jeanne around. She wanted to tell her so much, but she didn't yet have the words to say it all in French.

"It's a work by Master Josquin. Lady Margaret says he's a genius."

"Who is he?"

"The greatest composer in Flanders — some say in all of Europe." Barbe pointed to an old man, his Flemish hood askew as he conducted the singers with hands gnarled with age.

Anne edged closer, ears pricked to understand why the music seemed so different from anything she'd heard before.

"Do you like to sing?" Barbe asked.

"Yes!" Anne stopped herself from saying she loved to sing. Semmonet had taught her that one did not say in French that one loved to do this or that. It was another false friend. Anne recalled her Howard grandfather complaining it was no wonder the English had pulled out of France at the end of the Hundred Years War, as they were fed up with trying to speak French. She was determined not to make the same mistake.

"You could ask to join them in practice for the midsummer festival," Barbe suggested.

"I'd like that."

"Don't be so sure. Monsieur Josquin is short-tempered and doesn't suffer fools who can't learn their lines quickly."

"Good," Anne said. She couldn't suffer fools either.

Barbe gave her a curious look. "Why is that good?"

Anne reined herself in. "I mean, I can pick up my lines quickly, so he may not scold me."

"Silence!" a voice roared from the far end of the room.

Anne jumped, suddenly aware that the rehearsal had stopped. The conductor glared at them.

"Excuse us, Monsieur," Barbe stammered. "I was only saying—"

"Out, you magpies! Go chatter elsewhere," the old man barked. He moved towards them with a determined gait.

Barbe darted for the door, with Anne close behind. Rounding a corner, they stumbled into a storage room, collapsing into laughter.

"Mother Mary, save us!" Barbe choked out, her eyes dancing.

Anne shook with mirth, tinged by remorse. "Do you think he'll recognise us if he sees us again?" She so wanted to be one of those singers.

"He's almost blind, but he hears everything. He won't know it was you if you don't open your mouth, unless it's to sing."

Anne started to reply, but Barbe stopped her mouth with a well-placed hand. "Silence, you magpie! Do not interrupt the unfolding of my genius."

The door swung open to reveal Madame de Verneuil's stern figure. "What is going on in here?" she demanded.

"I'm showing Anne her duties," Barbe said.

"And what duties might those be?"

Barbe hesitated. "To keep quiet in Monsieur Josquin's presence unless she is opening her mouth to sing."

Madame de Verneuil's gaze narrowed. "So it was you two who disrupted the rehearsal."

"We were praising his work," Barbe defended, but Madame de Verneuil remained unimpressed.

"You were disturbing him," Madame de Verneuil corrected.

Barbe made a face. "We didn't mean to."

"You will answer for it."

"No, Madame! Not really?"

Madame de Verneuil gave a wry smile. "He told me that if either of you can sing, you will report to his rehearsal tomorrow morning."

Barbe groaned. "But I sing like a frog!"

Madame de Verneuil turned to Anne. "And you?"

Anne's heart leapt. "With pleasure, Madame!"

"Good. But don't test his patience. He has no time for slow learners."

"So I have heard," Anne said, her senses alight. What a chance lay before her — to learn from a genius and add her voice to a heavenly chorus instead of labouring over a French textbook that contained nothing anyone ever said in conversation.

With a side glance at Barbe, she slipped on her headdress and stumbled out of the storeroom after her. There was no one else she had such fun with. It was a pity Barbe couldn't sing.

Over the next few weeks Anne joined Monsieur Josquin's rehearsals daily. Quickly memorising her part, she gained confidence as she sang. What a pleasure it was to hear her voice soar over the others.

Until one day it wasn't.

"Stop!" the maestro screamed. "You! *Anglaise*! What do you think you're doing?"

Anne froze. She had thought she was doing her utmost. What more could the exacting master want? "I — I don't know, Monsieur. Singing the best that I can," she stammered.

"That is not the point. You are to blend in, not drown out the others and show off your skills over all the rest," Monsieur Josquin scolded.

Anne reddened. Why shouldn't she show off her skills over all the rest? It was when she felt most herself. "I'm sorry, Monsieur. I'll try harder."

"You are already trying too hard. The point of polyphony is to imitate and blend. Do you understand?"

Anne shrank inwardly, nodding. "I think so."

"Let us begin again." The maestro raised his hands to direct the group.

Chastened, Anne sang the motet again — less beautifully, less outstandingly, and more to the maestro's satisfaction.

The rehearsal came to an end and Monsieur Josquin grasped her arm on her way out. "That is what I want you to do, Mademoiselle. See that you continue in such a way."

"Yes, Monsieur," Anne replied, assuming a courtier's smile. It was not what she wished to do. She had wanted to stand out, to soar above the others and be complimented on her skills.

But this was not the moment. Anne swallowed her frustration. When would that moment come?

That evening Anne flung herself onto her bed, face down.

"What were you thinking?" Barbe asked. Agnes de Middelbourg had been invited to join Lady Margaret's card game, so Barbe lay stretched across her side of the bed, rumpling it to perfection in her absence.

"I was thinking I want to be the best," Anne blurted out.

Barbe tutted. "We are not here to be the best. We are here to make our mistress look the best. That is the job of a maid of honour."

"I know," Anne moaned. "But I don't want to blend in!" At home she had been the best at everything. Was that not why she had been chosen to go abroad?

Barbe gave a snort. "At least you're honest. But you won't get far at court unless you do."

"But I'm no good at it," Anne griped.

"'Tis true," Barbe agreed cheerfully. "You're always itching to stand out. But you'll make enemies that way."

Anne stared at her. "What enemies?"

"Those who envy you."

"What do I care if others envy me?" Anne asked, brightening at the thought. A vision filled her head of returning home and sprinkling Continental flair over others like fairy dust. Cow-like English maidens would topple at her touch.

Barbe waved an airy hand. "All I know is that my mother says pride goes before a fall."

Anne's thoughts flashed to her proud mother and even prouder grandfather, the Duke of Norfolk. Neither seemed in danger of falling.

The next day at lute lessons, Anne fared better. Her slim fingers were nimble, deft at creating sounds like a faded wall hanging, adding ambience, but not shouting to be admired.

"You are coming along with that piece," the music master approved. "Tonight, you will play at Lady Margaret's card game."

"Oh, Monsieur, I'm not ready!"

"Nonsense. If you falter, play softly until you find your way," Monsieur Bredemers advised. "Your playing is better than your French, so we will use you to lull Lady Margaret's guests into unsuspecting relaxation."

Anne's ears pricked. "To do what?"

The music master winked. "To bathe them in pleasure, so they bet more at the gaming table."

"I see." Anne strummed a bright arpeggio in agreement.

"You will not see until you have sat across from Lady Margaret at a card game, lulled into tranquillity until the evening ends and you realise you have lost every coin you came with."

Anne giggled. Her father had played cards with Lady Margaret. He had joked that he rarely won. "But I only know a few tunes, Monsieur."

"Mademoiselle Veronique will join you. Take turns and learn from each other." With a firm pat on the back, the music master motioned for her to go.

*

That evening, Anne perched on a low stool in the corner of Lady Margaret's grand salon, half-hidden from where the guests would sit. Beside her was Veronique de Hallewijn, one of the older demoiselles.

"When do we begin?" Anne whispered.

"Just before Lady Margaret comes in from supper."

"Will someone give us a sign?"

Veronique assumed a droll expression. "You will hear her laugh and know she is on her way."

Within minutes, Anne's heart sped up as the great doors creaked open. A murmur of voices swelled, growing louder as they approached. Then, it came — a joyous musical laugh, soaring over the others. Only Lady Margaret possessed such a laugh, at once confident and confidential, embracing all who heard it.

On cue, Veronique bent over her lute, a glossy lock of chestnut hair cascading down one shoulder. She strummed the beginning lines of a slow, wet, woodsy tune, each note like a droplet falling from a leaf in a forest. The room quietened, lulled by the soothing sound.

Anne's gaze followed the approaching figures. Lady Margaret glided in, a stately presence on the arm of an older ambassador, his coat made from a shimmering brocade that hinted at distant lands — perhaps Venice. Her father had said that of all the ambassadors, the Venetians possessed eyes and ears above anyone else, attuned to the smallest gesture or expression, and to every detail of those they were sent to report on.

Anne straightened, using her mistress's erect bearing as her guide. Like a proud caravel sailing into port, the Netherlands' ruler glided to her seat at the centre gaming table. Behind her a bevy of Burgundian nobles flowed into the room. Among them were the archduke and his close advisor, William de

Croy, Lord of Chièvres, an elderly man with a distinguished manner.

Anne noted that her mistress made room for her nephew but not his advisor. She had heard from Semmonet that Madame was not fond of the Lord of Chièvres, finding him too aligned with French interests for her Habsburg tastes. As Anne took in the power positioning in the room, a nudge to her foot brought her back to her duties. Veronique was approaching the end of her piece, signalling for Anne to take her turn. She flexed her fingers and began to strum. It was her moment to aid Madame in enveloping her guests in Burgundian pleasures.

As her fingers found the opening chords, the French word for 'pleasure' lingered in her mind. How frequently the term 'plaisir' was used, on the tip of everyone's tongue all day long, unlike in England. Back home one did not go on about pleasure to others, although one sought it as much as the next person. Yet in French-speaking Burgundy, pleasure was considered a worthy pursuit, to be sought without a trace of guilt. No wonder the English clung so tightly to their one remaining French foothold in Calais. Her father had told her mother that young King Henry was eager to expand England's presence in France once more.

Leaning over her instrument, Anne matched her tempo to the pace of the players as they took up their cards and studied the first round of their hands. The minutes slipped by, and before she knew it the card game had ended. The players stood, mingling with those at other tables as attendants circled with trays of hippocras.

Anne ended her wandering tune and looked up to see Veronique's eyes on her.

"You change when you play the lute," Veronique observed.

"I do?" Anne blinked, unsure.

"You are in a world of your own, not trying to be seen."

"Is it a good or bad thing?" She didn't wish to be scolded later for her usual crime of calling attention to herself.

"It's good." Approval swam in Veronique's eyes. "By not seeking notice, you'll be noticed all the more."

"I'm trying not to *want* to be noticed," Anne said, wrestling with her usual struggles. Could a cat be a dog? Could a swan be a duck?

"But you do, and it shows."

"Does it show too much?" Anne's discomfort deepened. Apparently, Barbe wasn't the only one who had noticed her hunger for attention.

"At times." Veronique's lips twitched. "But you'll learn."

"How so?" Anne pressed, desperate to understand. She wanted so much, but it seemed wanting was the very thing she must conceal.

"Keep playing," Veronique advised. "And forget the others. Soon, they'll be somewhere else — wherever your music takes them."

There was so much Anne needed to know. Daily, she fought an endless struggle against herself to never seem too much of anything — too eager, too sparkling, too clever. How and where would she ever be appreciated for being who she was?

"Let Lady Margaret be your guide and don't show your hand." Veronique picked up her lute and strummed as the guests regained their seats at the gaming tables.

Anne glanced at her mistress, her face serene, her eyes giving nothing away as she looked at her cards. The ambassador studied her for a moment, then emptied his coin pouch onto the table. With a gracious smile, Lady Margaret laid down her hand and swept the pile of coins into her already sizable winnings. The room stirred in admiration and disbelief as the ambassador dabbed at his brow with a silk cloth, watching his silver pieces disappear.

Anne marvelled. If Lady Margaret could bluff so effortlessly at cards, what wonders must she work at the diplomatic table? Exchanging a smirk with Veronique, she stifled a giggle. They had played their part well in adding to their mistress's allure.

EIGHT

"The lesson for today is on the art of the entrance," Madame Filiberti announced, her Italian accent curling over her words like gusts from a warm breeze.

The maids of honour turned to each other, curious.

"What is it, Madame?" Françoise de Bréderode asked.

"It is your moment to make an impression," Madame Filiberti explained. While her husband, a friend of the ambassador from Milan, was in Antwerp acquiring paintings to round out their collection, Madame Filiberti had been invited by Lady Margaret to add some additional polish to the demoiselles of the Court of Savoy. "I will choose a few of you to demonstrate."

"But how can we demonstrate something we don't yet know?" Barbe asked.

Madame Filiberti rapped her fan on her lectern. "You will know it when you see it."

A hum throbbed through the salon as Madame began to stroll amongst them, her gaze unhurried but deliberate, as though selecting her subjects was itself an art. In accompaniment, a lute and a tambourine player tucked into a corner of the room began a slow, meandering tune, feeding a growing excitement.

After a moment the Italian woman stopped in front of Isabelle de Longueval, her porcelain beauty admired by all. "Go to the door then enter the salon as if you are entering a roomful of strangers."

"What kind of strangers, Madame?" Isabelle asked, her voice tight.

"Ones you must impress."

"Ahh." A general stir sounded as the tambourine player shook his instrument in agreement.

Anne's stomach tightened. This was a game she was keen to play, one her parents had been playing for years.

Isabelle hesitated, her cheeks flushing at the challenge. Going to the door, she disappeared through it. In a moment she re-entered the salon. With hands clasped in front of her, she cast her eyes to the floor. Without looking up, she melted into a corner of the room.

Madame Filiberti gave a noncommittal shrug, then turned to Françoise. "You next."

Françoise sprang up, her steps lighter than Isabelle's. Exiting the room, she re-entered with a smile. Her gaze roved over the group, gaining smiles in return from most of the girls. But Madame Filiberti remained impassive. Her eyes moved once again, this time settling on Agnes de Middelbourg. "Now you."

Agnes strolled to the door, her gown swishing as she left. When she re-entered the room, she took her time. With her chin held high and her eyes averted, she glided into the salon, her gaze fixed on some invisible horizon, distant and unattainable. Picking her way around the room, she came to a stop before Anne. Then, much to Anne's astonishment, Agnes offered a radiant smile to her alone. Enraptured, Anne smiled back. But the older girl's smile had vanished, as if it had never been there. As she turned away, Anne longed to feel it on her again.

Madame Filiberti beckoned to all three maidens. Tapping a finger on Isabelle's shoulder, she said, "You entered the room perfectly but made no impression." She moved to Françoise. "You called attention to yourself and made a momentary impression. Nothing more." She turned to Agnes, who stood like a statue beneath her gaze. "You captured the room. Just right," she approved.

A stir rippled through the group, quiet murmurs of speculation on what Agnes had done that the others had not.

"Who can tell me what made the third entrance the right one?" Madame Filiberti asked, her challenge dangling like a key ready to unlock a door.

"Agnes was the most graceful," Veronique ventured.

"It has nothing to do with grace," Madame Filiberti said dismissively. "All three were graceful, as we saw."

Claude de Saillant frowned in thought. "She smiled, but so did Françoise."

"Françoise smiled at everyone in the room," Madame Filiberti observed.

"Is that not a way to make a favourable impression?" Claude asked.

Madame Filiberti sniffed. "Some might find it pleasing. Others might think the one who smiles at a roomful of strangers has no discernment."

Claude looked puzzled. "Then what did Agnes do that was different?"

Madame Filiberti narrowed her eyes. "She took control of the room."

A collective hush fell as the girls weighed her words.

"Tell me, one of you. How so?" Madame Filiberti scanned the girls' faces, searching for a glimmer of understanding in any of them.

Anne gathered her words and raised her hand.

"Yes, little one," Madame Filiberti called out.

"She smiled at only one person. And then she withdrew her smile," Anne answered in halting French.

Madame Filiberti's face lit with approval. "And why is that powerful?"

"Because it made people wonder," Anne continued. "Why did she smile at just one person? And why did she immediately withdraw it?"

A satisfied smile curved Madame Filiberti's lips. "Exactly. It provokes interest. It gives and then withholds, leaving others curious, wanting more. With everyone watching what took place, she seized control of the room."

Dumbfounded, Anne realised that Agnes did that sort of thing all the time. It was why she couldn't help noticing her.

"Is there a simpler way to remember such a trick?" Claude asked.

"It is not a trick. It's a skill. An important one. And yes, there is a term for it," Madame Filiberti replied.

"What is it, Madame?" a chorus of voices resounded.

"You may put this lesson in your quivers," Madame Filiberti said, leaning forward. "Entice, then deny," she enunciated, each word clear and ringing.

The room erupted in expressions of wonder as the girls took in the dictum.

Anne tucked the three short words into her heart and mind. More useful than the ramblings of their male lecturers, this was something that could change the power balance between her and others.

"Madame, you must come back soon and instruct us more!" Claude exclaimed.

"Only if you give me a topic you'd like me to teach on."

"Oh yes, Madame! There are so many you might advise us on!"

Madame Filiberti tossed her head and laughed, her tones tinkling like chimes in a summer breeze. Reaching out to the girls on either side of her, she gave each a hug.

Anne crowded in for one, too. As she did, she met the eyes of Agnes. In them was the same hint of approval that Anne's mother offered at rare moments. But when she looked again, it was gone.

The following week, Madame Filiberti glided into the room, her presence commanding. The girls straightened in their seats as she began, "Today, we shall learn how to walk."

"My mother has already taught me that, Madame," Jeanne spoke up.

"Fine. Then walk to the door and back, and we shall see what you know," Madame Filiberti replied.

Jeanne's face reddened. "I only meant to say so, not to demonstrate."

"Show us or don't bother telling us." Madame Filiberti's words sliced through the air like a sharpened sword. "We would all rather see what you have learned."

It was true, Anne thought. Far stronger to show what you knew than crow about it to others.

Rising with a wobble, Jeanne cleared her throat. Then, looking at a spot above the door, she proceeded towards it with a slow, stately gait.

"Not bad, but raise your skirts a bit so that we may see your feet. Then walk back to your spot."

Jeanne blushed but raised her gown so that her black embroidered slippers showed. Walking carefully, her eyes flicked nervously towards Madame Filiberti.

"Now, place one foot in front of the other and walk back to the door."

Jeanne did so, slowly.

"What is the difference, my ladies?"

"She seems more grown up," Françoise remarked.

"How so?"

"I don't know, Madame."

"Anyone else, who can defend their thoughts?"

"She swayed more from side to side," Anne observed.

"Correct. And why is that important?"

"Because women have … hips." Anne still didn't have any, but she hoped she would soon.

"Precisely."

The girls tittered amongst themselves.

"Begging your pardon, but men have hips, too, Madame," Barbe pointed out.

Madame Filiberti looked smug. "Ones meant for riding or fighting. Nothing as important as the purpose for which our hips are made."

"What do you mean, Madame?" Claude asked.

"I mean that our hips serve a purpose for which all mankind admires our sex," Madame Filiberti answered.

"I know what it is, Madame!"

"What is it, then?"

"It is because men are bewitched by seeing our hips sway," Claude replied, to much laughter from the others.

"You have a point, *ma chère*, but there is a reason beyond that," Madame Filiberti said.

"Is it because we bear children?" Veronique asked.

"Exactly so. Without our wide hips, our babes would not pass through, and mankind would cease to exist."

"But not all of us have wide hips, Madame," Françoise put in querulously.

Anne silently thanked her for speaking up. She had not wished to mention it herself.

"And that is the point of walking with one foot in front of the other," Madame Filiberti explained.

"Do you mean our hips will look wider?"

"Our hips will make their presence known. And all men take note of such a sight, as it reminds them of who made them," Madame Filiberti intoned, as if reciting a line from Scripture.

"I thought men don't like to be reminded of their mothers when admiring demoiselles," Claude remarked.

"They don't wish to be reminded of their mothers at certain moments, but deep inside they look for them in younger and different versions."

"My mother says men like variety, which is why they're always mooning after women everywhere," Barbe noted.

Madame Filiberti's smile was coy. "They can't help themselves, dear. Their minds are as enslaved to our bodies as our bodies are enslaved to bearing children."

"But not all of us bear children. Lady Margaret has no children and neither do the nuns," Barbe challenged.

"But we are all enslaved to the monthly rules that makes it possible for us to bring forth children," Madame Filiberti pointed out.

Anne avoided looking at the others. She was not yet enslaved, but she desperately wished to be. Lady Elisabeth had assured her *les règles* — the rules — would soon come. She couldn't wait to find out what these monthly rules meant, although every older demoiselle she knew complained about them.

"Madame, why is it that nuns have courses?" Barbe asked. "I would guess they have no use for them, so why should they suffer like the rest of us?"

"No woman escapes these rules, be she a nun or a *beguine*."

"It seems unfair, Madame."

"All women think it unfair. Just as men think it unfair that they must go to war and be killed for petty squabbles between kings," Madame Filiberti remarked.

"Do you think it is men who are more unfairly burdened? Or women?" Barbe asked.

"Ah, *mes chères*, 'tis a big question. I leave it to those who like to debate to answer. But where women have power, they are wise to exercise it. And there is great power in their walk, if they know how to do it well."

"What about running, Madame?" Claude asked.

Madame Filiberti pursed her lips. "A lady does not run. A lady appears calm and unrushed at all times to show she is in command of herself."

"But in the event that we must hurry somewhere, how should we do it?"

"Or when one is playing at games?" Jeanne added.

"It is simple. One does not appear to run, but to glide or to float."

The girls looked at each other, impressed.

Anne eyed Agnes, who toyed with a strand of golden hair that had escaped her headdress. She always appeared to float when she walked — never rushed, never clumsy.

"Like a youth or a man, Madame?" Barbe asked.

Madame Filiberti frowned. "Never like a man. Like the work of art that you are."

"A work of art?" Françoise asked, her eyes wide.

"Each of you is a work of God's hands. And each of you reflects His glory," Madame Filiberti declared, surprising Anne with a spiritual departure from her usual tone.

"How do we do that while running, Madame?" Claude asked.

"You bunch a fold of your gown in each hand, then take small light steps. Keep your head up, eyes straight ahead, and move your shoulders as you run."

"It is too complicated, Madame. Show us!"

"Like this, then." Madame Filiberti raised her skirts to reveal red beribboned slippers. Lifting her head, she skimmed across the room with small sure steps. As she ran, her shoulders danced backwards and forwards in a motion that highlighted her throat and neckline.

"You seem to float, instead of run," Jeanne remarked.

"That is because I took small steps and kept my head up," Madame Filiberti explained.

"I shall try it later," Jeanne exclaimed.

"You will know if you have succeeded by the reaction of whomever you pass," Madame advised.

"What will they do, then?"

"They will note you, then turn away, if your gait is clumsy," Madame Filiberti warned.

"And what if it is not?"

Madame Filiberti smiled slyly. "You will rivet their attention."

A collective sigh rose as each demoiselle contemplated such power and its uses. But Anne was contemplating something else. Next time she saw her father, she would dazzle all present with her graceful walk or run. And if her father didn't notice, at least he would note that those he was trying to impress were noticing her.

Françoise broke into Anne's reverie. "Madame, why is such a simple thing so powerful?"

Madame Filiberti's face took on sibylline mystery. "It is always the simplest things that are most powerful."

"What else then?" Françoise looked mesmerised.

"The tone of voice in which one speaks," Madame Filiberti divulged.

Another hush descended over her audience.

"And what else, Madame?" Claude asked.

"The way one uses one's eyes," Madame went on.

"Ah, yes," Claude said, as Anne considered her own eyes. Her childhood nurse back home had called them dark and dancing.

"And the neck," Madame Filiberti added.

"The neck, Madame?"

"The way to use one's neck is important, *mes chères*. Yet another arrow in our quivers."

Anne gazed at her colleagues' baffled expressions. Once, she had overheard her grandmother comparing her to her sister, saying that Mary was a beauty but "the little one has grace, with that lovely long neck." It had meant nothing to her at the time.

"What could be important about a neck?" Barbe scoffed.

"It is not to be underestimated, especially as attached to a young demoiselle," Madame Filiberti proclaimed with unfathomable wisdom.

"Tell us, Madame!" Claude persisted.

"I am done for today. But you must all practise your gait before I see you next. And whoever has improved the most will choose our next topic from the ones I've given you."

Anne quivered. She might not be blonde or rosy, or a woman yet, but she had a long neck, dancing eyes, and a lithe gait. Madame Filiberti would show her how to use such attributes to get herself noticed by those she wished to impress. As for those she didn't? Glancing at Agnes de Middelbourg, she assumed the older girl's indifferent expression. Why should she care?

*

The demoiselles spent the rest of the week vying to outdo each other with graceful gaits. Anne worked hard at hers, placing one foot in front of the other and swaying daintily as she walked. The hips she longed for were sure to come. She would be ready, when they appeared. But what she enjoyed most was to ractice her run. Lithe and light, she swung her shoulders, feeling her breaths deepen as she shortened her stride. What joy it was to forget her cares and leave every worry behind. But best of all, she knew that the others were watching, admiring her grace.

"You are a sight to behold," the head cook remarked as Anne breezed past, her skirts brushing the bushes along the path like butterfly wings.

"If you run so fast, you'll trip," Barbe chided, swiping at Anne's gown as she flew by.

"Next time, slow down, or you'll be taken for a child," Madame de Verneuil advised as she came to a stop at the end of her first pass around the garden.

"But I feel so free!" Anne twirled as the spring breeze lifted her headdress.

"Madame Filiberti is teaching you to be a lady. Slow down and act like one when you move."

"I'm not just moving, Madame. I'm flying!" Anne sang out.

Madame de Verneuil caught Anne's arm as she passed, her grip firm but gentle. "Too fast. A lady never rushes."

Anne laughed with joy, her cheeks flushed with exhilaration. "But it feels so good when I do!"

"Run more slowly so that we may admire the lady you're becoming," Madame de Verneuil corrected.

At the thought of being admired, Anne slowed her steps. What rush was there, anyway? It was the job of men to rush about, battling with each other at contests, or at war. Madame

Filiberti had said each of the demoiselles was a work of art. She would ensure that any who saw her thought so, too.

Taking her next turn around the garden at a more sedate pace, Anne had time to note the faces of those she passed. The old gardener straightened. The assessment in his gaze made her heart flutter. By the time she made it back to where Madame de Verneuil and Barbe sat, she understood what Madame Filiberti meant. She felt as if she were floating, rather than flying.

"My turn, now," Barbe announced, rising and setting off.

Anne dropped onto a stone bench and turned her face to the sun.

"You are a flower, *ma fille*, about to unfurl your petals," Madame de Verneuil remarked.

"When will they unfurl, Madame?" Anne's voice was wistful.

"When you forget all about wondering when," the lady-in-waiting admonished.

"It's hard to forget when the others are women already and I'm not."

Madame de Verneuil chuckled softly. "Patience, child. You won't miss it."

Trying to take her mind off her worries, she watched Barbe's lumbering return, her steps lopsided and awkward. Faced with such a ludicrous sight, Anne burst out laughing. "You're like a lame horse on a loose rein!"

Barbe's face darkened. "And you're a nasty child with a loose mouth." Kicking a cluster of pebbles in Anne's direction, she took off again.

Anne's smile faltered, her laughter dying in her throat.

Madame de Verneuil tutted. "You don't think before you speak at times."

Anne crossed her arms. "Barbe says whatever she wants to me. Why should I not do the same to her?"

"Because you were unkind," Madame de Verneuil scolded.

"She is bigger and stronger than me, and can take any dart I send her way," Anne argued.

"You'll find that it is the biggest and strongest who are sometimes least equipped to deflect a dart," the lady-in-waiting advised. "And if they're powerful, you will have made a dangerous enemy with a thoughtless remark."

Anne bit her lip, wanting to argue more. But a cold knot in her stomach stilled her.

"When she comes around again, compliment her," Madame de Verneuil urged.

When Barbe returned, Anne called out, "You're better now — your steps are shorter."

Barbe stopped and dusted off her gown, not meeting Anne's eyes. "And you're better now that you've curbed your tongue," she retorted, her voice icy.

"I didn't mean what I said before," Anne said.

"Then why say it?" Barbe spat, each word a dagger thrust.

Anne hung her head. "Because I didn't think before I spoke."

"Then you did mean it. And so did I," Barbe shot back.

A lump rose in Anne's throat. "Let's forget it and go find the others."

Barbe glowered. "I'll find them on my own." She turned and ran towards the palace without a backward glance.

NINE

The following week, Madame Filiberti returned, to the delight of the demoiselles. "Who among you have racticed your gaits?" she asked.

"I have, Madame!" Jeanne said.

"May I show you, Madame?" Claude asked.

"You may all line up along the far wall and walk across the room. Then I will choose one of you to decide on our topic today," Madame Filiberti directed, her tone leaving no room for hesitation.

Anne fell into line next to Françoise. Barbe had deserted her since their falling out, always in the company of Jeanne when they passed in the halls and at mealtimes. Swallowing her hurt, Anne focused on her steps, crossing the room swiftly, her lightness outpacing the others, undoubtedly more graceful. Surely, Madame would notice.

"You have all improved, but I see one swan in particular," Madame Filiberti announced, a smile lifting the corner of her mouth.

Anne's pride swelled. Determined not to preen when Madame called out her name, she waited. Madame Filiberti strolled among them, finger raised thoughtfully, then stopped. She tapped Barbe on the shoulder. "You will decide our topic today."

"But I'm far from the best, Madame!" Barbe burst out.

"I didn't say I would choose the best," Madame Filiberti corrected. "Who recalls what I said?"

Anne's mind raced. Hadn't Madame said she would pick the best? Why choose bumbling Barbe? Her confusion bubbled into frustration.

Claude raised her hand. "Did you say you would choose the one who had improved the most?"

"Exactly. Mademoiselle Lallemand has shown the greatest improvement." She gazed at Barbe with approval. "Now, what shall our topic be today?"

Barbe beamed. "I'd like to learn about the neck."

"Ah, the neck. An excellent choice," Madame Filiberti agreed.

"What is so special about the neck?" Jeanne asked.

Madame Filiberti's eyes sparkled. "It is not the neck itself, but how one uses it."

Eager eyes scanned the room as various necks were noted.

"I will need some models," she continued.

Hands shot up, a sea of hope. Anne's hand was among them, but Madame Filiberti chose Barbe, Claude, and Isabelle.

Disappointment flooded Anne. Was she being punished for her cruel words to Barbe? She already felt punished enough by the older girl's cold manner.

"You will all pretend you have just entered a room," Madame Filiberti began. She pointed to the row of windows lining one wall of the garden salon, punctuated by tables on which Lady Margaret's mysterious coral collection was displayed. "Now face the windows and pretend that someone of interest is to your right," she continued. "How will you turn to look at them?"

"It depends on if it's a man or a woman, Madame," Isabelle said.

"Let us say it is a man whom your parents wish for you to meet," Madame Filiberti instructed.

A buzz resounded through the room. Everyone knew such a moment would come.

"You wish to make an impression," she continued.

"But what if I don't?" Barbe asked.

Madame Filiberti's mouth twitched. "Then you let him know you are far above him, without saying a word."

"Ah," a collective chorus sounded, much impressed.

Anne was impressed, too. What good advice to take charge of the moment, whatever one wished its outcome to be.

"Before you turn your head, you roll back your shoulders and push them down," Madame Filiberti instructed.

The three models complied.

Anne marvelled to see their throats and chests puffed out like proud doves. Instantly, their collarbones appeared more defined, the line from neck to shoulder more attractively curved.

"Now raise your chin slightly then tip it down just enough to create a curve."

Barbe frowned. "How do I raise it then tip it down at the same time?"

"Watch." Madame Filiberti demonstrated. The move was subtle but powerful, a graceful tilt that made her neck appear both elegant and strong. The girls tried to mimic her, some succeeding, others faltering.

"Now turn to the right and meet his eyes."

Barbe smiled, her turn too eager. Claude turned and looked frightened. Isabelle turned and managed a perfectly cool glance, chin tilted just so.

"Very nice, Isabelle. Where did you learn to do that?"

"I watched Lady Margaret," Isabelle divulged. "When envoys come, she looks over their heads to remind them of her higher station."

"Well done," Madame Filiberti praised.

Anne considered carefully. What did Isabelle and Agnes possess that she didn't? Pondering Isabelle's chin tilt and Agnes's hauteur, Else's words drifted back to her. It wasn't beauty or rank that made them different. It was how they carried themselves.

Rolling back her shoulders, Anne lifted her head and pointed her chin out then down. The goal was within reach.

"Today we work on the eyes," Madame de Filiberti announced the following day.

A swell of excitement rippled through her audience.

"Now, how do we use them?" Madame Filiberti asked, peering out towards her decided admirers.

"To see, Madame!" Françoise called out.

"Evidently. But how we move them will determine how others see us," Madame Filiberti elucidated.

Anne glanced at Barbe, who narrowed her eyes and turned away. Stung, Anne did the same. How well she knew what Madame meant.

"I need two of you to demonstrate."

Hands flew up.

"You, and you," Madame Filiberti said, pointing to Jeanne and Françoise.

Anne's spirits sank. Would she ever again be chosen for anything?

"First, we will demonstrate social rank," Madame Filiberti began. "Jeanne, you are the mistress of your household. Françoise, you are her serving maid. I want you, Jeanne, to instruct Françoise to prepare three bedchambers for guests." She turned to Françoise. "You will ask Madame if you should use the same coverlets or put on new ones. Then Jeanne will tell you to ask the head housekeeper."

The girls giggled as they assumed their roles.

"I need three bedchambers prepared for our guests," Jeanne began, eyes fixed on Françoise then glancing down.

"Should I use the same coverlets, Madame, or new ones?" Françoise responded, looking straight at Jeanne.

"You will ask the head housekeeper. She will know." Jeanne's eyes skimmed Françoise then shifted down again.

"Good. Now, I will play the part of the mistress," Madame Filiberti said. "And, Françoise, when you ask your question, you will immediately lower your eyes, as you are addressing your superior."

Françoise dipped her head. "Yes, Madame."

"I need three bedchambers prepared for our guests," Madame Filiberti said, glancing at Françoise then past her at a point slightly above her head.

"Should I use the same coverlets, Madame, or put on new ones?" Françoise asked, this time glancing away and downwards.

"You will ask the head housekeeper." With an upward swish of her hand, Madame Filiberti dismissed her.

Anne watched closely as Françoise stepped back and curtseyed. She had seen Lady Margaret use a similar hand gesture countless times, both graceful and commanding.

Madame Filiberti turned to the room. "Now, what did I do differently from Jeanne?"

"You swept your hand upwards, dismissing her," Claude replied.

"Correct. And after I told her to ask the head housekeeper, I did not say, 'she will know.' It is the mistress's job to know everything. Never say someone else will know, when it is you who must always know."

"But, Madame, what if you truly *don't* know?" Barbe asked.

"Never let on that you don't know something about your own household. Simply direct your servant to the person who can best answer their question. You will look weak if you say you do not know," Madame Filiberti explained. "And your staff will feel uneasy to serve a mistress who is not in command of her domain."

Anne thought of Lady Margaret. She never said she didn't know to any question asked. No wonder her countrymen took heart from her leadership.

"Now what else did I do that was different from Jeanne?"

Anne flashed through the scenario, delighting in Madame Filiberti's sharp questions. They probed for the 'why' behind the way things were done, just as Semmonet did. Raising her hand, she wasn't sure what her answer would be, but she wanted to draw Madame's attention.

"Yes?" Madame Filiberti called on her.

"Was it that you looked beyond Françoise after addressing her?"

"Correct. When I looked away, my eyes moved beyond Françoise to a point slightly above her head."

"Who would notice all of this, Madame?" Barbe asked.

"No one must notice, but all who command must be aware of such details, as must all who serve," Madame Filiberti instructed.

"But what if you are of equal rank?"

"That depends on whether you are dealing with a man or a woman."

"Tell us about a man!" Claude said eagerly.

"First, I will show you how to exchange glances with a woman, as it is simpler."

"But my father says women are less simple than men," Françoise remarked.

Madame Filiberti's mouth twitched. "And he is right. But between women, it is far less dangerous to give the wrong cues than it is with men."

Anne's ears perked at Madame's admonition. Whatever dangers lurked from men, she would match with her own manoeuvres. Did Lady Margaret not do the same with her council members?

"With a woman of equal rank, you glance at her briefly, then look to one side at eye level," Madame Filiberti continued.

"What if she looks above you?" Barbe asked.

"She is trying to assume power."

"What should we do, in that case?"

Madame Filiberti grinned slyly. "Mirror her. You will beat her at her own game."

"Mirror her, Madame?" Claude asked.

"Exactly. If she is examining a point above your head, examine a point above hers."

"Oh, Madame, what fun!"

"It is rather fun, especially when the other party becomes aware of what you are doing."

"How far should we go?"

"Don't play the monkey. But match her subtly. Imitate her gestures, move your eyes, head, neck, and hands in the same way."

Anne looked forward to practising such a manoeuvre. But with whom?

Glancing at Barbe, she received a cold gaze that passed over her head in return. Flitting her eyes away, they fell on one of

Lady Margaret's prized corals. If, indeed, they possessed healing powers, Anne needed them desperately. She begged the spiky reddish orange cluster to help her repair her rift with Barbe.

"Now tell us about the case of a man, Madame!" Claude persisted.

"Oh yes, the men. I had forgotten about them," Madame Filiberti remarked.

"One of equal rank, Madame," Françoise reminded her. "What do we do, in such a case?"

"In such a case, it all depends on if you wish to draw his interest or to discourage it. Now I will play the young demoiselle, and Françoise will play a man of equal rank who has come to court me." She turned to Françoise. "Give me an interested glance. I will do something with my eyes and one of you will tell me if I return his interest or not."

Squeals of excitement broke out as Françoise gave Madame Filiberti an admiring look.

Madame Filiberti pursed her mouth as she glanced back at Françoise then looked away at the same level.

"You are interested!" Barbe said.

Madame Filiberti frowned. "No, I am not."

"But you looked away at the same level!"

"I have let him know I am his social equal and that is all."

"And if that is not all?" Jeanne asked.

"Françoise, give me that look once more."

Françoise repeated her admiring glance.

This time, Madame Filiberti cast her eyes to the side, slightly downwards, and smiled.

"You are interested!" Claude said.

"Yes, I am." The demure smile on Madame Filiberti's face demonstrated her point.

"Now what will you do?" Isabelle asked.

Madame Filiberti buttoned up her smile. "That is beyond the scope of this lesson."

"Oh no, Madame! Do tell," a flurry of voices urged.

"Then I would play the modest maiden to ensure my suitor's flame leaps higher," she advised.

The demoiselles stirred, elbowing each other.

"But if I'm interested, why shouldn't I let him know?" Barbe asked, her honest approach tugging at Anne's heart. She would never use a similar strategy, but she admired Barbe for suggesting it. For the first time she understood how being different might be precisely why two people could be friends — except they no longer were. Anne's spirits sank.

Madame Filiberti tutted, shaking her head. "You must give a man room to pursue you. If you throw yourself at him, you will be like a blanket snuffing out a fire."

Anne gazed at her instructor with worshipful eyes. Madame Filiberti seemed to know all the most important secrets. If only she could master a few to win back Barbe.

"Madame Filiberti is giving today's lecture!" Françoise de Bréderode announced the following morning, her fingers moving quickly as she pinned a pearl comb into her dark-blonde hair.

"What will it be on?" Anne asked.

"Some Italian word I can't remember." Françoise waved her hand airily.

Anne admired the way Madame Filiberti kept them all on their toes. Her sharp, peppery delivery made everything she said seem like something worth knowing. Whatever the topic, the demoiselles paid attention when she addressed them.

At the sound of heels tapping against the stone floor, Anne straightened. Madame Filiberti swept into the room, her headdress crowned with a white ostrich plume that bobbed as she moved. On anyone else's head it would look laughable. But the Italian woman wore it with the sort of self-assurance Anne longed to possess.

"*Mes filles*, have you practised all I have taught you since last we met?" Her sharp eyes flicked over the group like a hawk surveying its territory.

"Oh yes, Madame, we have worked on it." A hint of mischief laced Barbe's tone.

Madame Filiberti's eyebrow lifted slightly. "So, we need not review?"

"No, Madame. Let us move on," Barbe urged.

"Very well. Today I will present on a concept we Italians admire." She swept out a hand to one side, as if introducing an important guest. "*Sprezzatura.*"

The word hung in the air, mysterious, almost magical.

"What is it, Madame?" Isabelle asked.

Madame Filiberti looked down her nose. "Something you should know," she replied, her ostrich plume waving in agreement.

The room buzzed with whispers, curiosity igniting the group as Anne leaned forward, eager for more.

"*Sprezzatura*," Madame continued, her tone serious, "is the art of seeming effortless while performing with excellence."

"What do you mean, Madame?" Claude asked.

"You practise a skill until you can do it without appearing to try. It is not virtuosity, though it requires mastery. It is subtlety — perfection that looks like ease."

Barbe raised her hand. "But why should we act like we're not trying when we are?"

Madame Filiberti's lips curved into a knowing smile. "Because, *ma fille*, the exercise of *sprezzatura* will place you above the rest."

Anne's stomach thrummed. Her father had sent her here for exactly that — to rise above the rest.

Françoise broke the spell. "Give us an example, Madame. How do we practise such an art?"

Madame Filiberti stepped forward, her gown brushing against the floor like a whisper. "One day, many of you will manage great households. You will oversee grand gatherings."

A murmur arose. It was the hope of all in the room to do so.

"When your guests arrive, you will appear calm, as if the event unfolded perfectly under your direction," Madame Filiberti continued, her tone commanding. "Not a hair out of place, not a worry in sight."

Françoise grinned. "My mother does that before the guests. Then she shouts at the kitchen staff and my father on the other side of the house."

Anne giggled as cascades of laughter broke out. Her mother would do the same.

"As do many," Madame Filiberti nodded, acknowledging the truth behind the humour. "But to exhibit *sprezzatura*, you must appear as though it costs you nothing."

Anne leaned forward, soaking up every word. This was no ordinary lesson. It was a key to something greater — a way to navigate the world with grace, to control without showing strain.

"And if we have no household yet?" Barbe asked.

Madame Filiberti's gaze sharpened. "You have yourselves to manage. You must act as if you are not doing your utmost, even when you are."

Anne spotted Agnes de Middelbourg shift slightly, the subtle nod of her head revealing she knew what was meant. Anne wanted to know, too. Then master it over Agnes.

"Is such a way not deceptive, Madame?" Barbe asked.

"Not deceptive, but artful." Madame Filiberti's voice cut through the room. "Court life itself is an artful presentation. To serve your sovereign, you must be more than competent. You must be artful."

"Give us an example, Madame," Jeanne urged.

"You are with the king..."

"We have no king," Barbe pointed out.

Ignoring her, Madame Filiberti continued. "You are with Lady Margaret. She is at an archery contest, and you are on her team. You have practised your skills for months. You hit the target and win the competition. Then, what do you do?"

"Jump up and down and shout, 'Hooray, I've won!'" Barbe waved her arms in the air, forcing those closest to her to back away.

Madame Filiberti's lips pursed. "No, you do not. You do the opposite. You shrug and say luck was with you that day. Then you present your prize to Lady Margaret and ask her to give it to someone who needs it more than you do."

"But I would like to keep it for myself!" Barbe protested.

"That may be, but that is not the way of *sprezzatura*. You act as if you are surprised that you hit the target at all. Then you hand over your win to someone in need, in an act of nobility."

"So, this *sprezzatura* has something to do with nobility?" Jeanne asked.

"*Sprezzatura* has everything to do with nobility," Madame Filiberti affirmed. "And as you are being trained to take your place amongst the nobility, you must possess it."

Anne eyed Jeanne. She would master enough *sprezzatura* to stuff Jeanne's mouth with it next time she opened it to question her background.

"Let us take a walk," Madame Filiberti continued. With a shake of her ostrich-plumed head, she smoothed down her gown and made for the door, motioning for the girls to follow.

"Where are we going, Madame?" Françoise asked.

"We will search for *sprezzatura* in Lady Margaret's quarters."

Anne had glimpsed the paintings on the walls of Lady Margaret's bedchamber. With their mistress away in the north, putting down the latest disturbance by the Duke of Guelders, now was the perfect moment to view her treasures under a trained eye.

Leading them straight into the archduchess's large, luxurious bedchamber, Madame Filiberti stopped before a painting of the Virgin's Assumption. "This work is by Michel Sittow, who was at the court of Queen Isabella of Castile when Madame Margaret was there," she announced.

Anne sucked in her breath. So Lady Margaret had lived in Spain.

"Do we see any *sprezzatura* here?" Madame Filiberti asked.

The girls murmured, studying the painting. Françoise broke the silence. "There's nothing artless about it."

"Correct. This is all art and no *sprezzatura*, so let us move on."

"It's just another dull Virgin portrait," Françoise whispered as Anne passed by.

Glancing more closely, Anne's blood coursed through her veins. The painting moved her, with or without *sprezzatura*. She imagined that a ruler like Queen Isabella would have treasured it, with its careful composition drawing the eye to the Virgin's contemplative pose. Her mother had told her that Queen

Katherine's court was more formal than King Henry's due to her strict Spanish upbringing. Perhaps they didn't go in for *sprezzatura* in Spain.

The group then moved past Lady Margaret's three bird cages to another corner of her bedchamber. Anne visited the red-and green-draped room almost every morning to collect Madame's lapdog when he had escaped to find his mistress. But this time, she looked around with sharper eyes.

"Now here is a painting by one of Madame's favourite artists. Who can tell me what they see?" Madame Filiberti asked.

"There are two small boys playing. It seems that one is teasing the other," Agnes observed.

"And who are these two small boys?" Madame Filiberti asked.

"Two Italian princes?" Isabelle asked.

"They are the Christ child and Saint John. But why do you guess Italian?"

Claude spoke up. "The painting looks Italian."

"And why is that?" Madame Filiberti asked.

"I don't know. It just does."

Madame Filiberti frowned. "That is not enough. You are here to learn the art of conversation. To hold up your end well, you must defend your opinions and not offer vague comments with nothing to back them up."

Anne agreed. There was nothing more frustrating than when she asked her sister what something or someone was like, and Mary replied that she couldn't quite say. Anne always wanted to pinch her at such moments but held back to avoid her mother's wrath, although she knew her mother felt the same about Mary's lack of mental rigour.

"I-I suppose it looks Italian because the children are naked," Claude stammered out.

"That is not all, but is a point, as Italian artists have begun to depict the human body in its full glory in their works."

"Did not the ancient Greeks and Romans do so as well?" Claude asked, summoning some backbone.

"Yes, *ma fille*. The new emerging art takes its inspiration from classical times. But what else about these children makes you think this painting is by an Italian artist?"

Anne spoke up. "It's in their playfulness. They aren't stiff and frozen."

"That is so. And what else?"

"They are exhibiting *strezzapura!*" Barbe called out.

Madame Filiberti chuckled as the demoiselles laughed scornfully. Anne didn't join in but moved to Barbe's side.

"You are on the right path, Mademoiselle, but try saying it correctly," Madame Filiberti encouraged.

"*Spezzatura!*" Barbe amended.

"So close, *ma fille*. Try again." Madame Filiberti held out a warning hand to quell the mocking laughter.

Barbe glanced around, a humiliated expression on her face. As she turned her head, Anne leaned in and whispered in her ear.

"*Sprezzatura!*" Barbe sang out, in a final valiant effort.

"Well done, Mademoiselle." Madame Filiberti squeezed her shoulder.

"It was nothing," Barbe rejoined.

Madame Filiberti stopped her. "Do not explain; do not complain. It is the first rule of the wellborn."

Barbe looked confused. "What do you mean, Madame?"

Madame Filiberti sniffed. "It is self-evident."

Disappointed cries ensued. "Oh, Madame, explain more, for we should like to know!" Jeanne exclaimed.

"Some of you already do. As for the rest — reflect and absorb." Madame Filiberti looked over their heads at the *mère des filles*, who had appeared in the doorway.

Anne pondered Madame Filiberti's words as they left the room. Her mother had said the same to her once — never complain, never explain. When she had tried to justify something she had done, her mother had cut her off and told her not to explain her actions, as it would only weaken her position.

In a flash, Anne saw that all of Madame Filiberti's lessons were of a piece. *Sprezzatura* wasn't just about appearances — it was about moving through life with grace, about holding power without seeming to.

The others chattered around her, but Anne held her breath as the lesson settled into her bones. She could see it now — Lady Margaret, her cards held loosely, her face serene, winning every hand without a flicker of effort. This was *sprezzatura*.

Anne blew out her breath. She would master it.

TEN

"Today we will cover the art of conversation," Madame Filiberti announced.

The girls exchanged puzzled looks. Wasn't conversation something they engaged in all the time? What more did one need to learn?

"You will pair off. Each of you will find a bench with your partner while I walk amongst you."

Anne darted a hopeful glance at Barbe. But she was nudging Jeanne, her face hidden. The nudge — a familiar gesture that Anne had once relished — now seemed worlds away.

To her relief, Madame Filiberti paired them off, sparing her the indignity of not being chosen. "Anne, you will work with Isabelle." She pointed to a bench. "Seat yourselves there."

Anne noted Isabelle's hesitation before picking up her skirts and moving to the bench. Among the most beautiful of the demoiselles, with her honeyed curls and slanting blue eyes, Barbe had dubbed her 'a doll almost come to life'. God's bones, how Anne missed her irreverent companion.

As Isabelle sat, she flounced out her skirts, making even less room for Anne.

What had Mistress Bonnard nicknamed her? In a moment it came to Anne. The beguine had dubbed Isabelle and Agnes Vanity and Disdain. Watching Isabelle fidget with her skirts, Anne guessed she was Vanity. Then the demoiselle fixed her eyes on a point straight beyond her, and Anne settled upon Disdain.

Madame Filiberti clapped her hands twice — a sharp, commanding sound. "We will simulate dinner party conversation," she began. "You are seated next to an important guest, and you must make conversation."

Barbe's hand shot up. "If they're so important, they may not wish to speak to us."

Madame Filiberti smiled knowingly. "Politesse demands acknowledgment. Eventually, they will turn to you. When they do, you must be ready."

Anne thought of the archduke. He didn't bother to converse with anyone if he didn't care to. And when he made mistakes, they were covered up. All at court, other than Lady Margaret, regarded him as untouchably important.

Anne's imagination flamed. She might not be royal now, but women like her had the power to ascend through marriage. The story of a common widow who had become Queen of England floated through her head. Anne's mother and grandmother never tired of discussing how Elizabeth Woodville had stood on the side of the road with her two small sons and waved down the King of England, who had been instantly smitten.

Elizabeth Woodville had not agreed to a tumble in the hay. Refusing to become the king's mistress, she had driven him mad with desire until she got the result she was after — a ring on her finger, a crown on her head. Edward IV had married her, upending the age-old rule of royals marrying only royals.

Yanking Anne from her reverie, Françoise spoke up. "What shall we say, Madame? Especially to an important person?"

"You may begin by asking if they are enjoying themselves."

"And if they are not?" Barbe put in.

"They will not say so, but if they show a glum face, your job is to brighten their mood," Madame Filiberti explained.

"What if we have nothing in common?" Jeanne asked.

"Sooner or later, all of us find something in common to share."

"Perhaps the weather?"

"You may begin with the weather. But if you end up there, too, you will soon be abandoned by your conversation partner."

"A remark on the gardens?"

"As a starting point, yes. But you must seek to draw out your dinner companion."

"How so, Madame?" Barbe asked.

"Probe gently to learn something about him. Then steer the conversation in that direction," Madame Filiberti specified.

"And if we are seated next to a woman?"

"The same. But at a formal dinner it is customary to seat a woman between two men."

"Why is that, Madame?"

"To ensure élan and to prevent the men from engaging in dull or combative talk." Madame Filiberti rolled her eyes.

"How do we ensure élan, Madame?" Claude asked.

"You show wit and confidence." Madame Filiberti tossed her head. "Above all, you sparkle." She extended an arm in languid invitation.

Exhilarated, Anne's blood coursed. Their instructor had described the woman she intended to become.

"But what if we are not witty or sparkling?" Barbe asked.

Anne stifled a chuckle. Barbe had wit, but her delivery tended towards blunt over sparkling.

"Should you fail to captivate, there is a stronger strategy that always works," Madame Filiberti advised.

The demoiselles leaned closer.

"Every important person likes to be noticed," she proclaimed.

Anne's insides skipped. Unimportant people liked to be noticed, too.

"You must seize on something he says about himself and draw it out further," Madame Filiberti filled in.

"But what if he doesn't wish to be drawn out?" Barbe asked.

Madame Filiberti sniffed. "If he is important, he will enjoy talking about himself."

"If he is already important, why should he care?" Barbe challenged.

"It is an infallible truth that everyone likes others to note one's importance." Madame Filiberti lowered her voice. "Especially men."

Especially me, Anne thought.

"What a good trick!" Barbe enthused.

Madame Filiberti's smile held secrets. "It is not a trick, *ma fille*. It is the job of a courtier, and it is my job to teach you to do yours well." She thrust up her chin and clapped her hands twice. "Now, take your roles and let us begin."

Anne glanced at Isabelle. The older demoiselle sat like a statue carved from ice. "I'll start," Anne broke the silence. "Shall I be the important person, or will you?"

Isabelle passed a frosty eye over Anne's head. "What do you think?"

A spark of mischief lit within Anne. "Then it's settled. I'll be the important one, and you can address me."

Isabelle's face darkened. Before she could respond, Madame Filiberti appeared. "Have you begun?"

Anne faced her. "We were just deciding who is who."

Their instructor looked vexed. "Pick a role. You'll switch in a moment, so you will play both parts." She moved to the next bench where the girls were busily engaged.

As Isabelle fluffed her sleeves, Anne shook out some imaginary dust from the hem of her gown. Two could play this game. Several moments ensued as both girls outwaited each other.

Madame Filiberti again clapped twice. "Now you will switch roles."

Groans went up, alerting Anne that there were others who thought themselves too superior to play the lesser role.

"May we change partners, Madame?" Agnes asked.

"You may not," Madame Filiberti snapped. "This is an exercise, and you are all to remain with your partner but reverse roles."

"But why should we practise being of lower rank than we are?"

"All rank is relative. If you are lucky, you will one day sit at a table next to someone more highly ranked. Now is the time to learn how to manage that moment."

More groans ensued, but conversations began as Madame Filiberti strolled among them.

Anne turned to Isabelle. Isabelle crossed her arms, staring into the distance.

"I trust you are enjoying your visit?" Anne asked, adopting her best imitation of a polite dinner companion.

Isabelle wrinkled her nose. "What visit? I'm not visiting."

"I'm pretending you are a visiting dignitary."

"Well, I'm not," Isabelle retorted.

Anne tried again. "Did you enjoy yourself this morning?"

Isabelle's gaze remained fixed on a point over Anne's head. "I did. Until this lesson."

"What did you do before?"

Isabelle's smile was smug. "I tried on hair ornaments sent by a suitor."

"Only a king or emperor could be worthy of you, I'm sure."

Isabelle's smile faltered, her eyes dimming. "That's what my mother says."

"And your father?" Anne pressed, curious despite herself.

Isabelle's smile vanished entirely. "He doesn't say anything."

Anne's heart dropped, along with her urge to prick. How familiar it sounded. "Neither does mine," she blurted.

For the first time, Isabelle's eyes met hers. "Why is that?"

"He's always busy. Or away," Anne spilled out.

"Mine, too."

"And now *you* are away at Madame's court," Anne noted.

"So I am. What of it?"

"One day you won't care if he tells you anything or not."

"Why so?" Isabelle asked.

Anne leaned closer. "Because what is most important is what you tell yourself," she said, sharing advice she gave herself at times.

Isabelle looked at her curiously. "And?"

Anne noted the lump in Isabelle's throat. "And that's all that matters."

Isabelle nodded, the lump disappearing. Anne's ill will melted like snow in a February thaw. Isabelle had problems similar to her own.

Madame Filiberti loomed over them. "How did you fare?"

Anne glanced at her partner, their moment of connection hanging between them like a fragile thread.

"She understood what's important," Isabelle said.

"And that is what counts," Madame Filiberti said before moving off.

Anne and Isabelle exchanged a look, a secret understanding passing between them. A connection had been made where none existed before. Madame Filiberti's advice had reaped powerful rewards.

Later that day, Anne was to hunt with falcons. It was a sport much enjoyed by the nobility. She had gone hawking back home with neighbouring gentry-folk. But this would be her first time in royal company.

Lady Margaret had instructed Lady Elisabeth to send Anne with a few other demoiselles to accompany the archduke and two of his sisters on their outing.

"Why did she choose you?" Barbe asked, looking miffed.

Anne shrugged. Barbe had finally begun speaking to her again, but it was not the same as before. "Perhaps because I asked to borrow Dame Berners' book from the library."

Barbe looked suspicious. "What's that, and who's Dame Berners?"

"It's a book on hunting and hawking by an English nun."

Barbe lifted incredulous brows. "A nun wrote a book on hunting?"

"It's the most prized work on the subject in all of England." Anne's grandmother had mentioned it when Anne asked if she knew of any books written by women.

"What's it called?"

"*The Boke of St. Albans*," Anne said.

"And it's in Madame's library?"

"It was on the shelf where she keeps her books in English." She had only skimmed it, but Barbe didn't need to know that.

"I wonder if Henry Tudor sent it to her."

"I don't know, but I'd like to," Anne said. So Barbe had heard about that chapter in Madame's life before they joined her court.

"Are you afraid?" Barbe asked.

"Of the falcons?"

Barbe cast a knowing glance. "Among other things."

"Of course not," Anne replied, although she was, a little. But the honour of being included in this highest of aristocratic pursuits offset her fears.

"Remember, most of the falcons here are female. They may not like you," Barbe tossed off as she walked away.

Anne watched as she joined Jeanne under the loggia. Their heads together, they broke into giggles as they glanced towards her. Moving to her horse being readied in the stable yard, she stepped onto the stable boy's intertwined hands and mounted it. As she arranged her skirts, she saw him look in Barbe and Jeanne's direction, paying her no mind at all. When would the day come when all that would change?

She clucked to her mount and moved off, joining the princesses up ahead. Shaking off her worries, she smiled brightly at Lenore and Isabella of Habsburg.

Their lips curved slightly in return, their eyes remaining cool. The message was clear — 'I am being civil, but do not get too close.'

Averting her gaze, Anne tried not to care. But their polite froideur cut deeper than any of Jeanne's digs about her family.

A scurry of hooves sounded behind. Anne turned to see the posse of falconers draw up. Their noble hunters were clamped onto their arms, the birds' leather hoods covering their heads and eyes, topped by multi-coloured plumes, far more splendid than the hoods on the hawks back home. Instantly, Anne forgot her troubles, intent on the wild creatures next to her, readying for duty.

Catching up to the archduke, the head falconer reined in. "If you please, Your Grace and Graces, Mesdemoiselles, you will form a circle around our group so that we may begin."

Anne and the other demoiselles flanked the princesses and their attendants' horses.

On the far side of the circle, the archduke rode up, flanked by his entourage. Charles of Habsburg wore his usual glum expression, as if it were beneath his dignity to associate with the party across from him. Nevertheless, his eyes flicked to the hooded birds, as did Anne's.

"To begin, you will remember that these noble hunters are not our friends, nor will they ever become such," the falcon master opened.

Anne wondered at the man's words. Did not dogs and horses become friends with their masters? Even the caged canaries in Lady Margaret's quarters flew onto her shoulders when she let them out. Why not falcons?

"Then what are they, Monsieur?" Agnes asked.

"Killers," the falconer said, stroking the back feathers of the creature that perched on his leather gauntlet. "Nothing more."

Anne shifted uneasily on her mount.

"But they become attached to their masters, who feed and care for them, do they not?" Agnes persisted.

"No, they do not. And it is a mistake to think otherwise. A wild creature is ruled by instinct alone. It is not a creature such as a household or stable yard one."

"It is attached to its home in the mews, is it not?"

"It is chained to its perch in the mews, that is all. If it were not chained, it would fly off and leave its handlers far behind, to seek its natural pursuits."

"But the one on your arm seems to like you."

The master falconer shook his head. "She likes to be petted at this moment and that is all. When she is done with me, she will let me know."

Anne stifled a giggle. It did so sound like the ladies featured in stories of courtly love that she had come across in Madame's library.

"I will show you how to throw her off and then you will all do it together."

Anne caught the eye of Princess Isabella next to her. The Habsburg royal returned a blank gaze. Observing that gaze, Anne understood why falconry was reserved for the highest circles. Trained to do their duty, but friends to no one, the falcons kept by princely houses showed royals their role.

"Once you are all fitted with gauntlets, we will perch one of our beauties on each of you," the falcon master instructed.

"What if my falcon hops off?" Claude asked.

"It will behave, if you are at ease," the falcon master answered.

Claude looked nervous. "But what if I'm not?"

"You will school yourself," the master instructed. "Whatever worries you have, set them aside and think only of guiding your bird to its task."

What if my falcon doesn't mind me? Anne thought. Then she realised it was up to her. She would be cool, self-possessed, like the two princesses beside her. The falcon would do its job, as she would do hers.

An equerry approached and fitted a thick gauntlet on her right hand. Anne's blood rose to breathe in the smell of rich leather, ripened with the scent of countless fierce hunters whose talons had gripped its surface.

Once all in the party had been fitted, the falcon master called them to attention. "You will see my lady has bells attached to her ankles. With the sound they make we will track her, once she has made her kill."

Anne shivered. In a moment, a well-dressed killer would perch on her arm. She must master it or be mastered by it.

"I will remove her hood then raise my arm to send her on her way," the falcon master continued.

The group watched in silence as the master grasped the plumes atop the falcon's hood with a gentle hand, lifting it off to reveal the cold, fierce eye of his lady.

With a slow, graceful move that reminded Anne of the beginning steps of a basse danse, the man raised his arm. Jerking it forward in a lightning thrust, he catapulted the bird into the sky.

Anne exhaled as the bird soared off, as noble a sight as any she had seen.

"When you throw her off, you must do so quickly, with no hesitation," he instructed.

A second equerry rode up beside Anne, a small merlin falcon atop his arm, its plume waving the Burgundian colours of yellow and blue. Grasping it, the man pulled off the bird's hood.

"Hold out your arm, Mademoiselle. I will perch Lady Merlin on you. Then you will hold steady until the master gives the command."

As Anne extended her gloved arm, the merlin hopped onto it. She studied its talons, three in front and one at the back. They reminded her of curved scimitars used by Saracens in chivalric tales she had read. Sucking in her breath, she imagined its talons grasping its prey in a final death flight. Would the joyful jingle of the bells attached to the falcon's ankles be the last sound its doomed victim heard?

Nervous giggles formed in the back of Anne's throat. She stifled them, remembering her grandmother's rebukes when she dissolved into laughter at serious moments.

"Once you all have a bird on your arm, the dogs will be released to flush out the prey. Then you will follow my two commands — 'arms up' and 'thrust.' Any questions?"

"May I pet my bird?" Agnes asked.

"You may stroke its feathers lightly."

Anne reached out slowly and paused before touching her bird. Sensing no alarm, she stroked the merlin's breast feathers. How she would love to make friends. But the falcon master's words rang in her ears. He had not suggested making friends was unlikely; he had said it was impossible. Glancing at the princesses next to her, she understood only too well.

At last, all the birds were settled. The master signalled to release the dogs to flush out game in the field ahead.

A din of barking ensued as the hounds bounded off, tightening the nerves of all present.

"Is everyone ready?" the falcon master asked.

"Yes," a chorus of voices answered, Anne's among them, her tone low, her giggles at bay.

"Prepare to raise your arm," the falcon master commanded.

All rose in their saddles as they straightened their arms.

"Arms up!" the master barked.

Anne lifted her arm to the sky, surprised at the weight of the merlin upon it.

"Thrust!" the master cried.

Anne jerked her arm forward and the merlin flew off, in a movement so quick that it was gone before she knew what had happened. Shielding her eyes from the sun, she tracked it for a moment but soon lost sight of the bird at the dizzying speed with which it flew.

"Well done," the falcon master grunted.

Anne glanced at the others. All faced heavenward, wonder straightening their carriage. Even the archduke looked rapt, his long jaw pointing up, his torso ramrod-straight as he tracked his bird. His had been larger than the others. Anne guessed it was to do with rank, as was most everything at the Burgundian court.

"Will they return to us?" Claude asked.

The falcon master shook his head. "No. We will track them or track the dogs to them and see what they have brought down. Then their keepers will reward them with a bone or feather from their kill."

Anne spurred her mount, the world falling away as she followed the others. Her spirits flew with her falcon, soaring above all thoughts of cutting princesses and envious peers. She was one with her well-dressed killer, on its way to dispatch its enemies.

"How did it go?" Semmonet asked the following morning.

Anne's eyes lit up, her voice spilling over with excitement. "I loved it!"

Her tutor frowned, waiting.

"It pleased me greatly," Anne corrected. What a gulf lay between expressing herself in English and French, far wider than the English Channel.

"Why so?" His tone sharpened, curious.

"I understood something new."

Semmonet tilted his head. "And that is?"

"That the royals are like trained falcons."

Her tutor eyed her with interest. "In what way?"

"They do their job, but do not become too attached to those around them."

Semmonet's eyes flickered with understanding. "Why do you think that is?"

"Because, for them, duty trumps all."

A slow nod came from her tutor, lost in thought. "So, it does, Mademoiselle. Although I know of one royal who became so attached to her falcons that she kept them in her bedchamber."

Anne clapped a hand to her mouth. "Really, Monsieur? Who was it?"

"It was Lady Margaret's mother, Mary of Burgundy."

Anne leaned forward, eager to hear more about her mistress. "I only know that she died young."

Semmonet's gaze drifted to the window, as though seeing something long past. "The duchess was fond of hunting and hawking. She loved animals — her dogs, horses, monkeys, and parrots. She even had a giraffe."

"Oh, Monsieur, I do so hate monkeys." Anne wrinkled her nose. "But I would have liked to see her giraffe!"

"There is a tale told of her when she wed Maximilian," Semmonet mused, warming to his subject.

"Do tell, Monsieur!" Tales were so much more interesting than texts.

"She informed him that her falcons and greyhound would share their bedchamber."

Anne erupted into giggles. "Did he mind?"

"She was the richest bride in Europe and had paid for him to travel from Austria to wed her and rule over Burgundy together. What do you think?"

"I would guess he agreed." Anne struggled to visualise the grizzled, bear-like emperor as a young, handsome prince.

"He did. And he fell in love with her, too."

"How did he put up with all the animals in their bedchamber?" Anne asked, giggles welling up again.

"They all obeyed their mistress and made no fuss at all. And Maximilian shared her passion for hunting, so he indulged her."

Anne grew wistful. "How is it she died so young?"

Semmonet's eyes dimmed. "Riding accident. She was out hawking, and her horse threw her."

Anne could picture it now — the thrill of the hunt, the danger of a fall. "Did she die instantly?"

"She lingered for some weeks, but her back was broken."

"Poor woman," Anne murmured.

"She left a rich legacy by uniting Burgundy with the House of Habsburg."

Anne's thoughts took flight. "And she gave us Lady Margaret, too."

"As well as Madame's older brother, Philip."

She had heard Lady Margaret had a brother. But her father hadn't had time to tell her the full story. "What happened to him?"

"He died young, much like his mother."

Anne blinked. "Was he the father of the archduke?"

"Yes."

"Is the archduke like him?"

Semmonet's eyes rolled. "Nothing like him at all, God be praised."

"Why do you say so, Monsieur?"

"Philip was led by his counsellors. They called him Philip-follow-counsel behind his back."

"Is not the archduke led by his counsellors?" Charles of Habsburg's sullen face flashed before her. Perhaps not.

Semmonet shook his head. "He shows signs of being his own man."

"Is that a good thing?"

"In his case, it is a very good thing. He reserves judgment and doesn't speak until he has considered carefully."

Anne pursed her lips. "I thought he was just sulky."

Semmonet shot her a sharp look. "Mind what you say about the archduke. He is a boy turning into a man. They all go through such phases."

Anne thought of George back home. When next she saw him, her mischievous brother would be on his way to manhood. How she missed their romps and spats. Would he turn sulky, too, becoming even more impossible than he already was? She sighed. "How sad for the archduke and his sisters that they have lost their parents."

Her tutor shrugged. "Their duty is to sow Burgundian and Habsburg seed across Europe, and they have their aunt and grandfather to show them how to do it."

"Will they have any say in their marriages?" Anne asked.

"The princesses will have none," Semmonet replied, "and the archduke is promised to the English king's sister."

"Princess Mary?"

"Yes."

"But will it come to pass?"

Her tutor's mouth twitched. "That remains to be seen."

"Lady Margaret would welcome it, I should think." An image of the paintings of Henry Tudor, Henry VIII, and Katherine of Aragon that hung in Madame's portrait gallery came to her, amongst other royals from Europe's great dynastic houses. For the first time, it occurred to Anne that not a single French king's portrait hung there.

"She's set on it," he agreed. "But remember what I said. The archduke shows signs of being his own man."

*

That afternoon Anne encountered Charles of Habsburg on his way to the stables, trailed by attendants, as usual. This time she viewed him with new eyes. Perhaps he wasn't sulky so much as fed up with his minders telling him what to do and how to behave. What must it be like to be surrounded everywhere one went, never given a moment alone to jest with a companion or pull a prank?

Strolling past the archduke, she suppressed an urge to snatch the plumed Burgundian cap from his head. How satisfying it had been at home when she had knocked off her brother's cap at unexpected moments. God's bones, what fun they had shared tormenting each other.

Instead, she poured her high spirits into an impish smile. Perhaps they might exchange a remark about their outing of the day before. "Good day to you, Your Grace," she called out.

Charles turned, his expression a mixture of surprise and annoyance. "Good day, Mademoiselle," he muttered.

Anne's heart raced. "Did you enjoy the hawking yesterday?" she asked.

The archduke shrugged, as if to shake her off. "It was as usual."

Anne pressed on, undeterred. "I felt as if I were a falcon, myself."

Charles raised an eyebrow, his gaze drifting past her. "So you did," he mumbled, turning away.

Heat rushed to her cheeks. His entourage exchanged amused glances as Anne's sense of humiliation flared. How could he be so dismissive?

"My, that was awkward," a voice behind her said.

Whirling around, Anne came face to face with Barbe and Jeanne. They were the last two people she wished to have seen what had just taken place.

"Have you had any better luck?" she responded, her embarrassment flaming into anger.

"What were you thinking?" Barbe challenged.

Anne's blood boiled. "That he might have noticed I was in his hunting party."

"Do you think he cares?" Jeanne sneered.

"Apparently not," Anne tossed off. Why should she care if he did or didn't? Except that she did.

"Do you not know that you are not to address the archduke unless he addresses you first?" Jeanne asked.

"He looked as if he could use some cheer," Anne argued.

"Obviously not," Barbe shot back. "Otherwise, he wouldn't have dismissed you."

Waves of humiliation engulfed Anne. Indeed, he had. Most cuttingly. "Perhaps he's shy," she parried.

"Reserved, not shy," Jeanne corrected. "And he doesn't take kindly to nobodies addressing him."

Anne's control collapsed like a wall of ice in a spring thaw. "I am not a nobody!" she spat.

"So you think," Jeanne scoffed.

"And who are you to say?"

Jeanne stepped closer, eyes narrowed. "I know who I am and what my place is. Which is more than you do."

Anne clenched her fists, incensed at her adversary's sting. Should she not be allowed to hold a conversation with a youth of her own age with all the charm of a rock? "Why must we be chained to our places when we are all human beings?" she cried.

"So sanctimonious," Barbe prodded. "Would you say the same if the stable hand there strolled over and started a conversation?" She motioned with her thumb to a youth lounging at the other end of the stable yard.

"Of course, not. What are you thinking?" Anne protested.

"That's what I asked you," Barbe threw back.

"I told you. The archduke and I went hawking together, so I asked him how he enjoyed it."

"And he let you know he was not amused to have you address him without permission."

"God's bones, why do we all have to stay in our place and never venture out of it?" Anne railed.

"You did venture out, and you got slapped down," Jeanne observed.

Anne's rage rose. "That was not a slap down. He was just not in the mood to talk."

"Of course he wasn't," Jeanne agreed. "He's not in the habit of responding to bold English girls who force conversation." Her upper lip curled into an ugly sneer.

Anne stamped her foot. "I didn't force anything."

Jeanne chortled. "You tried and got nothing in return."

"Unlike you, who will get this in return," Anne erupted, shoving Jeanne to the ground.

Immediately, Barbe pounced on Anne, knocking her down. Reaching up, Anne grabbed Barbe's ankle and brought her down on top of her.

"*Arriviste!*" Barbe screeched, yanking off Anne's headdress and pulling her hair.

Several moments of combat ensued with Anne absorbing a number of French phrases Semmonet had not covered in class. Then, the stable boy and several equerries were upon them, pulling them apart and to their feet.

"Enough, Mesdemoiselles," the senior of the men counselled. "Go and find Lady Elisabeth," he ordered the stable boy.

The youth stood rooted to the spot, his mouth gaping wide as he took in the sight.

"I beg you, Monsieur, don't send for Lady Elisabeth," Barbe pleaded.

"If you say it's over, then I won't," the man grunted, laying a hand on the stable boy's arm. The lad seemed stunned to have seen Lady Margaret's fine young ladies go at it like stable yard cats.

"But you should have alerted us first so we could draw bets," a second man jested.

Jeanne dusted off her gown as she glared at Anne. "We didn't expect to be attacked by this one here."

"So, the *anglaise* threw the first jab, did she?" the first man joked, assessing Anne with admiring eyes.

"I was goaded," Anne huffed, then drew herself up. Why should she address a stable hand?

In a flash, the severity of her blunder with the archduke rained down upon her. Should the youth who would one day rule most of Europe address a demoiselle serving in his aunt's household any more than she should answer to a horse handler?

As the men mocked them, Anne clapped her hands to either side of her head to hide her shame. God's blood, what would Lady Margaret say if she heard about this?

ELEVEN

"You will accompany Lady Margaret to Lille next week," Lady Elisabeth said, smoothing the folds of her gown.

Anne's eyes lit up. "I will?"

"Lady Margaret has need of you to help her entertain some English guests."

"Will the other girls go too?" Anne asked, awash with relief that her recent scuffle had escaped the ears of the *mère des filles*.

"Agnes and Veronique, yes. And one of the older girls."

"Who, Madame?"

"Étiennette de la Baume."

Anne only knew Étiennette by name. The daughter of a great Burgundian lord, she was quartered in the older girls' dormitory, a world apart from Anne's.

"And the guests?" Anne's heart leaped at the thought that her father might be among them. Lille, near Flanders' border with France, wasn't far from where Lady Margaret's father and King Henry had just triumphed over the French, capturing the town of Thérouanne.

"Important ones." Lady Elisabeth reached out and heightened the shoulder poufs of Anne's gown.

"Will the emperor and King Henry be there?" Anne asked, beside herself with excitement.

"It's not your concern who will be there. Your job is to help translate from English to French for Lady Margaret. And —"

"And what else?"

A smile lit Lady Elisabeth's face. "To add lustre."

Anne caught her breath. "And how shall I do that?"

"You will play your lute and speak only when spoken to. But there will be evening occasions…"

"With dancing?"

"Of course."

"Oh, Madame, I cannot wait!"

The full splendour of the Burgundian court was on display at Lady Margaret's Rihour Palace in Lille. Tapestries transported the week before from Malines adorned the walls of its high-ceilinged entrance hall.

Portraits of Lady Margaret's parents, Maximilian, Holy Roman Emperor, and Mary of Burgundy, hung in the gallery above the curved main staircase. Most prominent was a portrait of Burgundy's most illustrious duke, Philip the Good. On the way to Lille, Lady Elisabeth had told Anne he had built the tall, narrow palace to use as an urban residence from which to collect taxes.

Anne guessed her sovereign would be impressed. She hadn't yet met the twenty-two-year-old king, but she knew that if she succeeded at Lady Margaret's court, she might one day be asked to serve Queen Katherine back home.

"Be available but invisible," Madame de Verneuil instructed, showing her to a spot just inside the library door that opened onto the entrance hall.

Anne smoothed down her skirts as she peered out. Lady Margaret stood at the top of the stairs, the black velvet of her gown catching the light, its slashed sleeves with cream-colored satin peeking through in perfect symmetry. Thinking she had never seen her mistress look so magnificent, Anne jumped as a burst of trumpets announced their visitors' arrival. She flew to the window and peered out onto the courtyard.

Horses snorted and dust flew up as the red, blue, and gold banners of the English crown flapped overhead. Equerries rushed to help the party dismount, and within minutes two tall, broad figures bounded up the steps.

"The King of England, Henry VIII, and his captain, Viscount Lisle," a voice blared as Lady Margaret made her way down the broad, winding staircase.

Through a crack in the library door Anne watched as her mistress approached the men, a figure of stately grace. The serene look on her face bespoke immutable confidence.

"The Lady Margaret, Archduchess of Austria, Dowager Duchess of Savoy, and Governor of the Netherlands," Lady Margaret's steward announced, bowing to his mistress as she approached.

"Madame Margaret, I am honoured to meet you," King Henry said in passable French. Bending over her hand, he kissed it heartily.

"As I am to meet you, Monsieur," Lady Margaret replied, maintaining a neutral expression.

"May I present my captain of the vanguard, Charles Brandon, Viscount Lisle?"

Lady Margaret flicked a cool eye over King Henry's companion, then returned her gaze to him.

Anne sucked in her breath as the king's companion reached for her mistress's hand, not noting that she hadn't offered it. With a flourish, he bent over and kissed it.

Lady Margaret retracted her hand and turned to the king. "I trust your journey from Tournai was not too tiring?"

"If it was, I have forgotten already, now that I have met Europe's most sought-after woman," King Henry replied.

Lady Margaret broke into a radiant smile, her laugh tinkling like windchimes. "Your Grace is too kind."

King Henry stepped back and put a hand to his heart. "I am not too kind, Madame. I am dazzled."

Lady Margaret tilted her chin higher, a sign that she was pleased with his compliment.

Anne watched the eyes of both men travel over the reception hall, taking in the exquisite Flemish and Brabantine tapestries and fine *objets d'art* on marble tabletops. She had not yet been to the English court, but her father had jested that it was a backwater compared to the Burgundian one.

Anne pressed her back against the library wall, noting the enormous tapestry that Lady Margaret had brought with her, featuring Burgundy's coat of arms. On it was written, '*Groigne qui groigne, vive Bourgogne.*' She stifled a giggle. Her French was not yet flawless, but the meaning was clear: 'Grumble those who may, long live Burgundy.' How apt the motto was for the powerful woman on the other side of the door.

Anne peered out again. King Henry cut a fine figure. Tall and broad-shouldered, he exuded vitality. A reddish gold beard adorned his broad, youthful face, punctuated by two small, birdlike blue eyes.

The other one sized up well, too. Equally tall and strongly built, Charles Brandon looked to be older by a few years. With a full head of thick dark hair and deep brown eyes, he matched his sovereign in size. Both exuded high spirits and confidence.

"The emperor sends his regrets that he will not be able to join us this evening," Lady Margaret was saying.

"What regrets, Madame? He joined me in battle and spurred his troops as a god come down from Heaven," King Henry jested.

"He does have a way about him, does he not?" Lady Margaret said.

"It was as if Roland had joined us on the battlefield. His men almost genuflected when they realised who he was."

Lady Margaret looked amused. "So, he showed up unannounced?"

"He did, Madame. But when his men spotted the black eagle on his banner, they were overjoyed."

"As were we," Charles Brandon cut in.

"But he is not one for dining and dancing," Lady Margaret informed them. "He has returned to Malines, where he is most likely recounting the battle to my nephew."

King Henry beamed, looking unconcerned if the emperor came or not. "Madame, it was not a battle, but a rout. Already they are calling it the Battle of the Spurs, as the French turned tail and spurred their horses to run away."

All three laughed heartily, Lady Margaret's tones skimming over the men's. Anne had never seen her in such sparkling form, her laughter as beguiling as any of her demoiselles. "In any event, you have joined my father in victory, and I am here to help celebrate your win," she declared.

"I look forward to it, my lady." King Henry's tones oozed gallantry.

"You must rest and recover, for a celebration awaits this evening that will challenge your dancing spurs."

"You will find our spurs more to your liking than the ones the French used to run from us," the king quipped.

The roar of laughter that ensued made Anne's skin tingle. The evening ahead promised to be a glittering affair. If only her father might be there to see her shine.

"We are at your service, Madame. Your word is our command." King Henry dipped his head, as did his companion.

Precisely what my mistress wishes for, Anne thought.

As the men were led to their chambers by Lady Margaret's steward, Anne sank into a chair, her mind racing. Lady Margaret had used all the weaponry of femininity to melt the king of England into her willing servant. How clever her mistress was to charm and dazzle her quarry into dancing to her tune.

"May I have the pleasure?" a towering man asked at the dance that evening. He was not addressing Anne, but Agnes de Middelbourg next to her.

He wore a mask, but there was no mistaking the tallest, broadest, most exuberant man in the room. Perhaps the other one came in a close second, but one could see the tufts of reddish-blond hair sticking out from each corner of the Venetian mask this one wore, leaving no doubt as to his identity.

Anne watched closely as her comely colleague curtseyed then hesitated a moment before taking the English king's outstretched hand. Noting how the king's interest flamed at Agnes's calculated delay, she tucked away the ploy for future use.

As the king whirled Agnes through a spirited galliard, Anne thought how much quicker and livelier she would be at it than her glacial bedmate. But she was too young to be asked to dance.

Or so she thought. A slim English officer, also masked, bowed before her. Her heart racing, Anne smiled gracefully then took his hand and glided onto the dance floor. Soon the entire room was whirling and jumping, the men making lively leaps until one took centre stage.

As the thinly disguised English king displayed a well-muscled leg in leap after leap, Anne heard Lady Margaret's laughter float above the general hum. The young king wasn't the only one showing off his skills tonight. At age thirty-three, Lady Margaret was in the prime of life. She had succeeded in all she had put her hand to and now it looked to be the case that she would succeed in charming King Henry to serve her aims for the Low Countries.

Noting her mistress's high spirits, Anne saw it was the king's companion she danced with, recognisable by his height and dark brown mane of hair. He appeared to be handling her masterfully — turning, twisting, and drawing her towards him in a way Anne had never witnessed any man do with Lady Margaret before.

Anne snuck further peeks as her capable but mute masked officer managed his steps. Two performances were beginning to stand out from the others — the king's, and Lady Margaret's with Charles Brandon.

Agnes de Middelbourg had faded into the circle surrounding the king and was doing what she had been trained to do — support the wishes of Lady Margaret to add lustre to the occasion but not call attention to herself. With a jolt of envy, Anne noted how well she did it.

The galliard ended with exuberant applause for the king's performance. Anne curtseyed to her partner and hurried off to see if her mistress needed anything. Lady Margaret's tinkling laugh led Anne to her. This evening it was more vibrant, dancing and skimming above the sounds of the crowd.

Rounding the corner to a quiet nook off the great room, Anne stopped short. Charles Brandon, Viscount Lisle, was deep in conversation with Lady Margaret, his head bent towards hers, his muscular thigh brushing her gown.

Anne noted that Lady Margaret had exchanged her previous black gown for one of shimmering cloth of gold. On her head she wore a Burgundian headdress, bedecked with emeralds, rubies, and pearls.

For the first time, Anne noticed the regent's hair. Dark blonde and wavy, it was caught up in a cloth of gold caul that glittered in the candlelight. Peering closer, Anne saw what appeared to be tiny diamonds sewn into it. Lady Margaret looked enchanting.

Apparently, the king's close friend thought so, too. Anne's breath hitched as she saw Brandon take Lady Margaret's hand and stroke her knuckles with his fingertips. Anne wasn't sure if that was a liberty or not, but she had never seen any other man attempt anything with Lady Margaret other than a courtly kiss on the cheek. This was something more.

Averting her eyes, she told herself she should retreat. Whatever was transpiring between them, Lady Margaret didn't appear to need her help, nor her lustre. She was exhibiting more than enough of her own.

Anne tiptoed away in search of refreshments.

"Where have you been?" Veronique de Halewijn asked, sidling up to the long trestle table laid out with delicacies, sweetcakes, and huge silver bowls of punch.

"Just checking if Madame needed anything." Anne waved vaguely towards the alcove.

"Does she?"

Anne hid her smile. "No. She's quite fine."

"She is more than fine this evening," Veronique remarked. "I have never seen her look so beautiful."

"Nor I," Anne agreed. "She looks like one of us, only better."

"Better in what sense?"

"Queenlier," Anne decided.

Veronique nodded. "She is a queen in all but name."

"But without a king."

"Better off without one," Veronique said with a shrug. "She is master of her country and her household. Unlike queens who serve at their husbands' pleasure."

"She had a few husbands, did she not?" Anne asked. Her father had promised to fill her in on Lady Margaret's background before she left England, but the king had called him away before he'd had the chance.

"She had two. Three, if you count the first one."

Anne raised an eyebrow. "What do you mean?"

"She was sent to the French court as a young girl to be married to the French king."

"Which one?"

"Charles, the one before Louis. But he married Anne of Brittany instead."

"He jilted her?"

Veronique smirked. "It gets better. Anne of Brittany jilted Lady Margaret's father to marry the French king."

Anne stared. "The emperor must have been furious!"

"Why do you think both Lady Margaret and the emperor hate the French?" Veronique asked.

"Is that why she's so keen on an English alliance?" Anne asked, her mind spinning.

Veronique nodded knowingly. "Why do you think we're here?"

"Because she wishes to impress my king."

"Who is young and ambitious. And eager to impress her, as she's the link to an imperial connection."

"A perfect match…" Anne mused, the pieces falling into place.

"And our mistress will do everything in her power to ensure your king doesn't move in France's direction."

"My father says whenever England moves towards France, it ends badly," Anne remarked.

Veronique's gaze sharpened. "Your father has taught you well."

Anne's heart caught. *I wonder if he's here.*

As Veronique turned to assess the crowd, an uneasy swirl of pride and yearning rose in Anne's chest. Had he received her letter? She longed to know. But she hadn't seen him. Even back home she rarely saw him. Was that not also the case with Lady Margaret and her father? Yet Lady Margaret didn't seem to suffer from their distance. Instead, it appeared to have helped her stand on her own.

Remembering that what was most important was what she told herself, Anne straightened. She would do the same.

The next day Lady Margaret walked with the king and his party in her gardens, her burgundy gown shimmering in the late summer light, the rich fabric matching the rubies in her headdress.

Anne joined them, along with the handful of other demoiselles invited to Lille. Enjoying the light breeze that sent butterflies dancing across their path, she tried to carry out her duties to her mistress. But Lady Margaret seemed entirely wrapped up in the attentions of the tall Englishman next to her. Charles Brandon had once again attached himself to her side, the murmur of his deep voice mingling with Lady Margaret's melodious one.

"Don't worry about Madame, *ma fille*. Just listen and watch," Lady Elisabeth advised Anne. "And if a word or two is not understood, fill it in, and offer the translation."

"The king's French is good, Madame. It's his friend who doesn't seem to speak any," Anne observed.

"He is managing well enough without words." Lady Elisabeth peered over Anne's head at Lady Margaret and Charles Brandon up ahead. Tightening her lips, she steered Anne towards the gaggle of demoiselles surrounding the king.

Gay cries rang out as Étiennette de la Baume offered a posy to King Henry. In return, the king jumped to capture a blossom from an overhanging branch and presented it to her.

"Thank you, Your Grace. I will treasure it forever," Étiennette gushed.

"Jewels last longer," the king's jester quipped, making the group break into laughter.

"I will treasure it as if it's a jewel," Étiennette added.

"You will not need to, as I have something better for you," King Henry returned. With a sweep of his hat, he plucked a jewelled pin from its crown and presented it to her.

"No need, Your Grace! You have already presented me with a gift," Étiennette protested.

"Do you refuse my offer, then?" King Henry looked amused.

"Of course not, Your Grace." Étiennette blushed as he leaned over and pinned it to her bodice, his eyes fixed on the abundant charms swelling from its top.

Anne blushed too, as she considered that in his own realm the king was all-powerful. Whatever else the king might choose to give to a favourite, one must accept or face his displeasure.

With a shiver, Anne wondered how Queen Katherine managed him. Did she look the other way when he flirted and cavorted, or did she bridle him with her own blend of enticements?

Veronique nudged her. "Looks like the king has found a favourite."

"She must be careful not to lead him on."

"Why do you say so?"

"Does not Lady Margaret advise us to guard against false friends?" Anne reminded her.

Veronique shrugged. "Étiennette is already spoken for. Her future is set, so why shouldn't she have some fun?"

Anne stared, shocked. "Would her intended be pleased to hear she is flirting with a king?"

"The lord of Marnay is so ancient that he's probably deaf," Veronique told her. "And from what I know, Étiennette is in no rush to warm his bed."

"How old is he?"

"Over sixty, with two wives dead already."

Anne shuddered to think of a wrinkled old man touching a bride just a few years older than herself. "Is she happy to have made such a match?"

Veronique snorted. "It's her father who made it, and she is happy to put it off for as long as possible."

"Why do you laugh?" Anne asked.

"I heard that she begged Madame to keep her on for another year in hopes that he might die."

"'Tis sad," Anne remarked.

"She's not sad now, so be happy for her," Veronique advised, her eyes travelling to where King Henry walked arm in arm with Étiennette, his green and white slashed sleeve brushing her bodice.

"I'm glad it's not me the king is flirting with." Anne's voice was low.

"Glad? Or jealous?" Veronique returned.

Anne lifted her chin. "I wouldn't wish to be in thrall to a king's beckoning finger."

"You wouldn't know until you have."

"I know what I'd do if I was."

"And what is that, little one?"

"I would refuse, if I chose to."

"So easy to say. So hard to do," Veronique teased.

"I should like to belong to myself," Anne replied stubbornly. "Not to a man, nor to the Church."

"You would end up like Lady Margaret then."

"I would be perfectly happy to."

"It is a pity you don't have a country to rule."

Anne shrugged. "I would rule my own heart."

Veronique scoffed. "You would rule nothing. We are all of us chosen to join Lady Margaret's court so that we make good marriages one day. What would your parents say if you refused?"

"What's all this babble, ladies?" a booming voice cut in. The tall, broad figure of the English king loomed over them.

"We were just musing, Your Grace." Honey dripped from Veronique's tones.

"Come muse with me, then," King Henry commanded. "I enjoy the chatter of beauteous maidens."

Veronique flung Anne a triumphant look and moved off with the king.

Anne waited for her sovereign to beckon her, too, but he had turned his back. She watched as he tucked Veronique's arm under his own, oblivious to her. Plucking a flower from the nearest bush, Anne pulled off its head. She would show the world what sort of marriage she would make. While biddable beauties dulled the interest of their suitors, she would sharpen the right man's desire by refusing it. After that, she wasn't sure. But experience had taught her that if she submitted to one who liked to be challenged, she would end up like her sister Mary when she and George teased her — humiliated and at a disadvantage.

Tossing the flower stalk to the ground, she sniffed. She would play a better game.

That evening Lady Margaret outdid herself. Wearing an emerald-green gown with a cream-colored front panel in tribute to Tudor colours, she sparkled with élan, resplendent in the candlelight.

Peering down at her own demure gown and paltry chest, Anne couldn't wait to be a year or two older. Poised on the brink of womanhood, she was not yet a full player in the courtly games taking place on the dance floor and in the far corners of the great hall.

"Go on, Anne. Dance with the others," Lady Elisabeth urged at the opening strains of a pavane.

"They're all taken." Anne's tone was mournful as she eyed several of the other demoiselles being led to the dance floor.

"Stand up straight, believe you will be chosen, and soon you will." Lady Elisabeth moved off amidst the excited hum of the crowd.

Anne did as she was told, giving herself over to the music. She imagined herself as a fairy sprite, lithe and mysterious, different from the other demoiselles, so uniform in their bovine charms.

Her pulse quickened as a young officer approached. She held her breath, half-expecting him to pass her by, but he stopped before her.

"Would Mademoiselle care to dance?" he asked in halting French.

Anne curtseyed. "Thank you, sir. But you may speak English, as I am English myself."

Relief flooded his face. "Thank you, my lady. It's my first time out of England and that was all the French I know."

"You did well," she encouraged. "But you're off duty now."

"I'm never off duty under His Grace's eye, but I'm glad not to mangle any more French."

"I don't think the king is paying close attention, so you needn't impress him, at least for this dance." Anne noted King Henry partnering Étiennette, his eyes glued to the low neckline of her gown.

"Then I'll try to impress you," the officer said, leading her to the dance floor.

Anne's heart sped up at the thought of being taken for a full-grown woman. "Thank you." She fluttered her eyelashes the way Veronique had at the king's approach in the garden.

"What brings a lovely English maid here to grace us?" the officer asked.

"I am one of Lady Margaret's maids of honour at her court in Mechelen," she answered, using the English name for Malines.

"You are highly placed to be amongst that great lady's court," he remarked.

"It has been beyond all expectation."

The officer looked interested. "In what ways?"

"Madame seeks to educate us in the same way she, herself, was educated."

"Since your mistress rules the Netherlands, I suppose you are not just learning needlework and dancing," he jested. "Although you dance quite well," he added with a grin.

"Her library is enormous, as is her art collection. And when important visitors come, they sometimes address us."

"Filling your head with new ideas?" the officer asked.

Anne nodded. "My head is ready to burst with all the New Learning I've gained since joining her court."

"Name some of these visitors that I may test my ignorance," the officer requested.

"Sire Erasmus of Rotterdam has spoken to us several times on topics to do with the Church."

"That's beyond my ken. Who else?"

"Emperor Maximilian visited a few weeks back and set us all afire."

The officer's eyes lit up. "He set his German troops afire, too. When they saw him, it was like a spark catching dry timber — as if he ignited them to fight."

"He's like a hero from an old romance," Anne enthused, thinking of how larger-than-life the emperor was. It wasn't his size; it was the way he drew people to him from all ranks and made them feel as if they were players in an epic tale.

"There's something about the man. Although —" The officer stopped.

Anne's ears sharpened. "Although what?"

"Nothing, Miss. Just my own lack of understanding."

"Do tell, sir. Perhaps I can help, as I've been on the Continent for some months."

The officer looked around. Seeing no one nearby, he bent his head and lowered his voice. "I don't understand why the Holy Roman Emperor would show up like a conscript in our king's army."

"He's a great man but likes to be a friend to the common people." There was more, but she wouldn't say, as it wouldn't add lustre to her mistress's mission. Lady Margaret had argued with her father the month before, when he had visited on his way to join King Henry's forces. The emperor had shouted that he needed money, and Henry had agreed to pay him one hundred pounds a day to serve alongside his troops. Lady Margaret had been mortified.

"'Tis similar to our King Henry the Fifth of bygone years," the officer remarked. "You probably don't know of him, but his troops loved him dearly."

"Agincourt," dropped from Anne's mouth. On the frequent occasions when her mother lorded her superior family background over her father, he would fling back at her that his ancestor, Baron Hoo, had fought at Agincourt under Henry V.

"That's the one, my lady. You're well-educated, indeed. Fathoms beyond me." The officer's mouth curved into a puckish grin.

Anne giggled. "Don't say so, sir. You are here on the Continent seeing new sights and learning new ways, just as I am."

"I'm learning something new this moment, in talking to you."

"And what is that?"

"That a young lady of your age can be as polished as a steel sword," the officer replied.

Blushing, Anne felt her mother's poke, urging her to handle the compliment well. "I'm honoured to have an officer of the English army say so."

"Many will say so in years to come, my lady. Mark my words."

Anne's pride flared. "Sir, I —"

"You have occupied this young lady's attention for far too long, Thomas. Why not let someone else have a chance?" a confident voice cut in.

Astonished, Anne looked up to see a second officer wresting Thomas away so that he could take his place. She felt a twinge as she thought of her father. If only she might hear a compliment from him like the one this Thomas had served.

"May I, Mademoiselle?" the second officer asked.

"I'm flattered," she responded, then remembered that her mother told her never to say she was flattered, as it diminished both parties to the exchange.

"I heard you speaking English and I can't take any more French for the moment. Will you humour me?"

"Of course." She brushed away the thought that the attention she was receiving might be due to being one of the few English-speaking ladies present.

Her new partner was no-nonsense, less conversational than the previous one, with eyes that skimmed the crowd. Soon her pride had shrunk back down to size.

"How is it that your English is so good?" the officer asked.

"I *am* English, sir."

"Do I detect a Kentish accent?"

"You do, sir. I'm from Hever, near Edenbridge."

"One of the king's close men at court is from Hever."

Anne's insides tightened. "That would be my father, sir."

"You are Thomas Boleyn's daughter?"

"I am."

"He must miss you while you serve on the Continent," the officer remarked.

Again, she felt a twinge. "He seeks to better me by time spent at Lady Margaret's court."

"Already, you are far ahead of the young ladies back home."

"Thank you, sir," she replied, noting Lady Margaret swirling by, partnered by Charles Brandon.

The officer's eyes followed them. "A handsome couple."

"They dance well together, do they not?"

"Like a glove to a hand," he remarked.

"Who is the glove and who is the hand, sir?"

The officer scrutinised her more closely. "I can see why your father chose to send you abroad."

"What do you mean, sir?"

"You're a quick one for such young years."

"I'm not sure that age moves in step with quickness." Anne's thoughts flew to her older sister.

"And I'm sure that you will sharpen up further with age."

"May I not be too sharp for my own good," Anne quipped.

"You're wise to say so," the officer commented. "I know some who are, and one day they meet the axe's edge."

A shiver ran down Anne's spine. "I'll take care not to let that happen."

The officer laughed. "Of course you will, young lady. I wish you the best during your time on the Continent." The pavane ended, and with a courtly bow he turned and melted into the crowd.

Behind him, Anne wondered at his words. Had he complimented her or warned her? And who did he refer to who was too sharp for their own good?

Certainly not her mistress, whose grace and charm melted any who stood in her way. But what about the king's companion? Trailing after them, she noted Charles Brandon's hand on the small of Lady Margaret's back. They looked as if they were dissolving into the mists of an unguarded state the regent had warned her demoiselles against countless times.

Yet the summer evening was full of wonder, and her mistress was queen of it. Sharp swords had been laid down after a successful battle, to be replaced by something soft and yielding, something Anne could not yet fathom.

TWELVE

Returning to Malines, Anne noted her mistress seemed younger, more vibrant and girlish than she had before. It was as if the vivacity of the English king and his entourage had rubbed off on her, returning her to girlhood days and brightening the court.

Making headway after his win at Thérouanne, King Henry and the English army next besieged Tournai, an enclave on the Franco-Flemish border that Lady Margaret wished to see set free from French control. On the twenty-fifth of September, 1513, after an eight-day siege led by Charles Brandon, the city's gates had opened, and the English had marched in. Lady Margaret learned that the king had honoured his close companion with the keys to the city.

Sending her compliments, Lady Margaret received back an invitation to join them in Tournai for a victory celebration. King Henry requested her to bring her nephew Charles.

"Anne, you'll be needed again to translate any words Madame may be unfamiliar with," Lady Elisabeth informed her.

"I'll gladly go," Anne exclaimed, bursting with eagerness. "Though I was hardly needed last time," she added.

"You performed a great service to Madame by making the English officers feel at home," Lady Elisabeth observed. "This time, the archduke will join us, and he doesn't speak a word of English."

Anne didn't look forward to more time spent with Charles of Habsburg, especially after their last encounter. She wondered if he would be accompanied by his tutor. "Will Monsieur de Croy join us?"

Lady Elisabeth gave her an impatient look. "What do you think?"

"I think not," Anne said, feeling foolish for asking. Lady Margaret made no secret of her dislike for her nephew's tutor, with his pro-French leanings.

"Correct. This will be the archduke's first time meeting your king. You must help him shine, as you did for Madame at Lille."

"Madame shone at Lille without help from any of us," Anne noted. How sparkling her mistress had been. Now another round of festivities awaited. Inside her slippers, she wiggled her toes at the imagined sounds of the lively galliards ahead.

"That is true, but the archduke is only thirteen. He'll need your help."

"But he never speaks to me," Anne protested, thinking no matter what polish was applied, the archduke was unlikely to shine anywhere.

"All demoiselles are more grown up than male youths of the same age. Don't concern yourself with whether he speaks to you or not. Just fill in the words he needs should a blank moment arise."

"Yes, Madame. Will the same demoiselles go who went to Lille?"

"Barbe will come, too. You must be helpful and remain invisible unless you are needed."

Anne's heart leapt. With Jeanne not among them, she had a chance to make up with Barbe. "I already feel invisible next to the others," she confessed.

"You are not invisible; you're just younger than the others. Soon, you will blossom and then you will take your place as Lady Margaret's most sparkling brunette."

"Really, Madame?" Anne liked the sound of Lady Elisabeth's prediction.

"You're coming along, *ma fille*. Your gifts will be different from the others. But they are still gifts."

"What are they, Madame?" Hungry for praise, Anne longed to hear more. But instead, she clasped her hands and pretended to be as demure and modest as she was not. And never would be.

"Get along with you," Lady Elisabeth replied, shooing her away. "A demoiselle as clever as you already knows what they are. I will not puff your head further."

Forced to content herself with the *mère des filles'* heady morsels, Anne went to join the others. As she sailed down the corridor, she savoured thoughts of becoming Lady Margaret's most sparkling brunette. It would make her father proud. *May he be there*, she prayed.

That evening Anne found a place by the hearth next to Veronique, the excitement of the upcoming journey filling her thoughts.

"Madame is taking you to Tournai?" Veronique asked, arms flung out in a languid stretch.

"Yes. And you?"

The corners of Veronique's mouth turned up. "Of course."

"She needs me to translate," Anne said. After Lille, she and Veronique had grown closer. Not as close as she felt to Barbe, but no one could take Barbe's place.

Veronique rolled over and addressed the ceiling. "How I should like to misbehave with one of those handsome officers the English king has around him."

Anne sucked in her breath. "That's exactly what Lady Margaret warned us against."

Veronique shrugged. "Are you sure about that?"

"Has she not said many times that a man's suit is not to be trusted?"

"She seemed to be enjoying the one Brandon was making in Lille," Veronique remarked.

Anne's thoughts shifted uneasily. "Perhaps she liked the attention."

"Madame is always the centre of attention," Veronique said. "That was different."

"Perhaps there's a girlish side to her."

Veronique propped herself up on one elbow, shooting Anne a knowing look. "I wouldn't call it girlish. Madame is a woman, and not an old one."

Anne's mind whirled. "But the king's captain is an army officer, and Madame is the daughter of an emperor."

Veronique waved a dismissive hand. "She's wealthy and powerful and can do as she pleases."

Anne gaped. "Do you not think she cares to guard her reputation?" Her mother had warned her countless times that a woman must do so. She had not fully understood what she meant, but she knew it was important.

"I think she cares to enjoy herself. And why shouldn't we do the same, before we're tied to dull husbands?"

"You'd be sent home if you disported with a man!" Anne cried.

Veronique rolled her eyes. "You're still a girl, *mignonne*. Wait until your blood runs hot and you weaken at the knees when a man dances with you."

Anne recoiled. Were they not at court to master the art of self-possession? "I'll never do any such thing!"

Veronique's laughter poured over Anne like a rushing waterfall. "You'll see. All the advice that is in the books and on the lips of our chaperones is there for a reason."

"What reason is that?"

"That so few follow it." Veronique rose from the couch and strolled from the room, her laughter echoing behind.

The journey to Tournai was long, but finally Anne saw the royal banners fluttering in the distance. King Henry himself was there, his standard gleaming under the autumn sun — bright reds, blues, and the golden lions of England, paired with the fleur-de-lis of France.

She leaned out of the carriage window, her voice rising in excitement. "'Tis the king himself come out to greet us!"

Barbe, beside her, furrowed her brow. "Why does the king of England fly the French fleur-de-lis?"

"He has just captured Tournai from the French and wants the people to know they are now held by the English," Lady Elisabeth explained.

Barbe frowned. "Will Madame be pleased to see those fleurs-de-lis?"

A good question, Anne thought.

"She'll be delighted to see the fleur-de-lis on the English king's banner as opposed to the French king's one," Lady Elisabeth replied.

The demoiselles nodded as lessons outside of the classroom sunk in. Europe's chessboard had just reconfigured with another English and imperial win against the French.

Anne watched closely as King Henry and his captain of the vanguard flanked Lady Margaret's coach, trotting gaily alongside as they entered the city gates. She wasn't sure if the archduke was with Lady Margaret, but she guessed a thirteen-year-old youth would not wish to bump along in a coach full of women if he had a choice.

Tumbling out of her carriage, Anne moved ahead to Lady Margaret's. She arrived just in time to see her mistress stepping daintily from the inside with one hand extended to grasp the hand of Charles Brandon.

Charles of Habsburg was nowhere in sight. Anne guessed he had chosen to ride a mount in princely fashion.

Trumpets sounded and the crowd murmured and parted ways as England's monarch strode to meet the Netherlands' ruler. Wearing a cap adorned with an enormous tear-drop pearl hatpin, King Henry bowed low over Lady Margaret's hand and kissed it.

Lady Margaret did not curtsey; not being his subject, she had no need to. Instead, she pressed his hand with both of hers. "I am delighted to be here," she greeted, then turned. "My nephew, Your Grace."

As if out of nowhere, the young Habsburg prince appeared, his posture straight, his face composed.

"Prince Charles of Habsburg, Prince of Castile, Archduke of Austria, Lord of the Netherlands and Duke of Burgundy," an equerry bawled.

The youth met King Henry's eyes, his expression solemn. Anne noticed him stiffen as the English king, nine years older, a head taller, and half an arm's length broader, clasped him on each arm with a hearty welcome.

"Our prince held his own, did he not?" Barbe whispered.

Surprised, Anne studied the young archduke. She had not expected him to handle himself so well. His calm demeanour made the English king look as if he were trying too hard. The pale, reserved prince had grown more formidable, his titles reminding everyone of the numerous territories he would rule over one day.

"Come, let us take refreshment before we show you the city," King Henry said.

"With pleasure," Lady Margaret assented. Anne noted her eyes moving to Charles Brandon, who stood just behind the king.

Lady Margaret's entourage blended with King Henry's attendants as the merry group moved towards the palace he had secured for their lodgings. Once inside, the demoiselles were directed to a suite next to Lady Elisabeth and Madame de Verneuil.

Wondering where Lady Margaret was lodged, Anne did not ask. She had grown up quickly since Lille. There, she had learned that her mistress might have a side to her she had not previously seen. If Veronique's predictions were to be believed, she might have such a side to herself one day.

That evening a great banquet was hosted by King Henry to honour his Low Countries guests. The table groaned with delicacies as servers brought out course after course of venison, pheasant, duck, goose, lamprey, and even a swan.

Finally, the meal was over, and the tables cleared for dancing.

The sounds of the orchestra tuning up coalesced into the opening chords of a stately pavane. King Henry, in towering splendour, extended his hand to Lady Margaret, leading her to the centre of the polished floor. His officers fanned out, ready to engage with the fair ladies of the Burgundian entourage.

As usual, Agnes was chosen first, followed by Veronique.

Anne hovered at the edge of the dance floor, her heart pulsing to the beat of the music. To avoid looking desperate, she watched the archduke out of the corner of her eye. His attendant leaned in, whispering something, prompting a frown from the Habsburg prince. She could guess he was being encouraged to ask a demoiselle to dance.

She looked around to see that there was no one left but her. Had not Lady Elisabeth told her she was there to assist the archduke?

Moving to where he stood, she shook off Barbe and Jeanne's taunts over not knowing her place. They had decided their place was set, but she had other ideas for herself. "Are you enjoying yourself, Your Grace?"

Charles glanced at her, his face carved from granite. "Not really."

A spark lit her eyes. "May I help, my lord?"

Her address did nothing to brighten his demeanour. "I don't like to dance."

"I've noticed, Your Grace. Yet your aunt wishes you to make an impression," Anne encouraged.

Charles didn't budge. "I have no need to make an impression."

"'Tis true, my lord. Your titles make all the impression necessary for any of us," she observed.

He shot her a stony glare. "Then that should be enough."

Anne couldn't resist pushing further, the rhythm of the music daring her on. "It's enough for everyone, except for Madame."

Charles rolled his eyes. "Soon, it must be enough for Madame, too," he stated flatly.

Anne considered. Up ahead, Lady Margaret would face relinquishing rulership when her nephew came of age. Wishing to steer away from such a sensitive topic, she changed course. "Soon you will wish to make an impression on someone you admire."

The archduke frowned. "I don't know what you mean."

"I don't really, either, but that's what lies ahead for both of us," Anne riposted.

Charles looked down his nose. "Do not presume to speak for me."

"Forgive me, Your Grace," Anne said, swallowing her annoyance. "I thought of you at dancing lessons and hoped that you might show off tonight how well you had learned them."

Charles's upper lip curled. "I am not a show-off like your king."

About to protest, Anne glanced at the dance floor. There, King Henry was lifting an elegant leg, exhibiting exactly what his Continental counterpart alluded to. "You're right, my lord. You have no need to strut like a peacock to prove to others what all of us know."

"What is that?"

"That you will one day rule vast realms."

"'Twill be a large job." Charles's mouth turned down, his jaw jutting even farther than usual.

"It will, my lord. Which is why you should enjoy playful moments when they come."

"I am not feeling playful at the moment," he said.

"What are you feeling, if I may ask?"

The archduke's gaze slid past her, scanning the wall behind. "I am wondering what possesses you to speak to me so freely."

Anne's temper sparked. If he were her brother, she would have boxed his ears. "We are at the same court, my lord. I learn what you learn, and I can guess what you face ahead."

"It's a heavy load," he groused.

"Would you take a moment to forget about it?"

"If they play something lively, I will."

Anne flipped her veil behind her. "I'm sure a better tune will come along soon." Unwilling to be further insulted, she glided to the other side of the dance floor. There she waited for the pavane to end while nursing her latest defeat. A pity the future leader of most of Europe was such a bore.

Tossing her head, she noted two officers halt midsentence to take in the sight. Ignoring them, she looked out at the dancers, her spirits rising at the sight of King Henry performing a final leap. At least her own king knew how to make good cheer.

The next day was filled with festivities from morn till night. Two representatives of Tournai's finest tapestry-makers presented six silk tapestries to Lady Margaret, depicting scenes from Christine de Pizan's *City of Ladies*. It was a worthy gift to assure her of their imperial allegiance.

Anne looked to be of service, but Lady Margaret floated on a cloud under Charles Brandon's attention and Charles of Habsburg had gone off with King Henry to tour Tournai's ramparts.

"Do you think Lady Margaret fancies Viscount Lisle?" Anne asked Barbe as they strolled behind the two on a walk through the town.

Barbe rolled her eyes. "Do you think the sun will rise tomorrow?"

Anne giggled. "I wonder that our mistress would let an army officer turn her head."

"It would seem that your king is encouraging their interest on both sides."

"Why do you say so?" Anne asked.

"He is throwing his friend in her path so that she might marry him and strengthen their alliance."

Anne stiffened. "Lady Margaret would never marry a man so basely born."

"Didn't your mother marry a man so basely born?" Barbe asked casually.

Like a torch set to dry tinder, Anne flamed. She pinched Barbe's arm, hard. "Did Jeanne say that?"

"I am just saying what people know. Your father was clever to land so wellborn a wife."

Anne flushed. Once again, her family's secrets were being aired. "My father is highly favoured by both Lady Margaret and my king."

"So he is. But your mother is from one of your realm's noblest families and your father is not," Barbe pointed out.

She suppressed the urge to pinch Barbe again. Not here. Not now. "Who told you that?"

"A little bird. Do you not know that everyone at court gets talked about?"

Anne seethed beneath the steady gaze of her fellow demoiselle. She knew from countless screaming matches between her parents that Barbe's words rang true. But she didn't wish others to know it. Her father was talented and ambitious. But it had been his marriage to her mother that had raised him high enough to catch Henry Tudor's notice. Her mother would not let him forget it. And now, others would not let Anne forget it, either.

*

The days passed in a merry whirl, filled with promenades, picnics, archery contests, card games, banquets, and dancing. On the eighteenth of October, a tourney was held, with the king and Charles Brandon challenging all comers.

A perfect autumn day, neither too hot nor too cold, the red and gold leaves on the trees seemed dressed to honour the English king.

It was Anne's first time attending a tourney. She was mad with excitement. Wearing the green and white striped gown that had been made for the invited demoiselles, she felt very grown-up.

"Look!" Barbe nodded in Charles's direction. "Our sullen prince has perked up."

Anne glanced to where the archduke stood with his attendants, at some distance from Lady Margaret. He was leaning on the railing in front of his seat, engrossed in the action on the field below. "I'm happy for him. And he isn't sullen. He's just a thirteen-year-old boy," she argued, surprising herself.

"Ah, and you are an expert on such a matter, I see."

"When we are of foul temper, we must hide our feelings with false smiles and good manners," Anne countered. "But he doesn't need to answer to anyone."

"He answers to Lady Margaret," Barbe corrected.

Anne glanced back at Charles. "He won't answer to her forever. He told me so himself."

Barbe looked curious. "So, you attempted another tête-à-tête with him?"

Anne pursed her lips but resolved not to rise to the bait. "I was trying to make good cheer, but he wasn't having it."

"You're a slow learner, for one so clever," Barbe goaded.

Anne did not respond to the taunt. "He'll have the weight of the world on his shoulders one day."

"But not today," Barbe observed.

"Soon enough. When he comes of age."

"Less than two years from now. He comes into his majority on his fifteenth birthday."

"I wonder how Lady Margaret will manage him once he becomes a man," Anne said, congratulating herself. Her strategy had worked. By not responding to Barbe's jabs, she had allowed the storm to pass. Barbe had lost interest in poking her further.

"I can guess what will happen before she works it out," Barbe answered.

"What's that?"

"I'd wager he'll take her position for himself."

Anne sucked in her breath. She knew her mistress. She would not like to lose her position. "But she's good at it."

"He's Lord of the Netherlands, is he not? He'll want to try that on for size and see if it fits."

"If he's clever he'll ask his aunt to continue to rule. He'll have enough to do with his other realms," Anne guessed.

"Especially after his grandfather dies."

"Which one?"

"The Spanish one," Barbe explained. "King Ferdinand. Can you imagine becoming king of a realm you've never been to and whose language you don't speak?"

Anne shook her head. "No, but once he's run the Netherlands for a time, I'll bet he'll hand them back to our mistress when he goes to Spain."

"Do you think he'll marry someone his aunt picks out for him?" Barbe asked.

"I wonder." Anne glanced in the archduke's direction. But her thoughts scattered as the crowd went mad, cheering for Charles Brandon, who had shattered a spear, unseating his opponent. The archduke cheered too, his hands thrown in the air and his hat askew, looking almost handsome. Her gaze shifted to Lady Margaret, standing proudly and clapping with delight at the viscount's triumph.

Barbe nudged her. "It's a good thing Madame left her widow's coif at home."

Anne took a closer look at her mistress. "I've never seen her so rosy and flushed."

Barbe's elbow dug into her side. "I can tell you why."

"Why, then?"

Barbe narrowed her eyes. "You're too young to know."

"I am not! And I know very well."

Barbe looked down her nose at her. "What do you know?"

"That she enjoys Viscount Lisle's attentions," Anne said.

"What attentions?"

"You know. His sweet words and close attendance," Anne replied.

Barbe chortled. "Hah! That's not all."

"What else, then?"

Her chortle grew louder. "So much more, little one. More than your tender ears can manage."

Anne reddened. "What do you know of what Madame enjoys?"

"Do you know what makes a woman's face glow?"

Anne thought for a moment, then stared. "Surely you don't think Madame is with child?"

"Of course not, you ninny." Barbe lowered her voice. "There are far more blissful delights than being with child that a woman might enjoy."

"I'm sure she's not enjoying them with Viscount Lisle," Anne countered, not certain at all of what they were.

"How sure are you?"

Anne tried to look knowledgeable. "She would not disport with one out of wedlock."

"Do you really know that? And do you think it takes wedlock to disport?"

"I don't — I don't know what it takes, but it's not done among respectable people," Anne hissed, doubly enraged.

Barbe threw her head back and laughed. "Oh, little one, you have much to learn."

"My mother says a woman's reputation is precious beyond jewels." Anne's tone was hot. Was it possible her mother had harped on that point because her own reputation had been in question? Her face loomed in Anne's head — haughty, snobbish, above reproach. Was there something behind her mother's proud demeanour that she didn't yet know?

"Of course, it is. Which is why Madame will disport and go no farther."

"What do you mean by 'farther'?"

"I mean she'll never marry him."

"Then I'm sure she'll allow him no liberties."

Barbe patted her head as if she were a small child. "Do you not know that women enjoy the sport of love as much as men do?"

Infuriated, Anne threw off her hand. "I would not call speaking honeyed words and exchanging glances 'sport'."

"Nor would I, little one." Barbe erupted into gales of laughter, unnoticed by the others who were cheering on the latest broken spear of the English king against a comer.

"You have no idea what she is doing with Viscount Lisle," Anne snapped.

"No, I don't. Nor do you. Do you know why not?" Barbe looked mysterious.

"Because we are not in her room at night to know."

"Precisely. And have you noticed that none of us know where her room is?"

Anne paused. "What do you mean? Is it not next to Madame Elisabeth's?"

"Not that I have noticed."

"Then where does she sleep?"

Barbe lowered her voice. "Perhaps she doesn't sleep at all."

"But her ladies must know where she is. Do they not attend her?"

"If she wants them to. But I don't think she does at the moment." Barbe looked at her slyly.

Thoughts swirled in Anne's mind. Her mistress was ruler of the Netherlands and head of her household. Just as her nephew would do one day, Lady Margaret answered to no one. She could do what she liked, within reason.

Thinking back to Mistress Bonnard's advice, Anne considered. What was wrong with occasionally being able to do what one liked?

That evening the banquet King Henry hosted was beyond compare. Anne felt stuffed to the gills. Then the music started up and she joined the other demoiselles in a graceful ladies' dance, the flicker of candlelight catching the folds of their silken gowns as they twirled and swayed.

While they danced, the king and several of his men disappeared. Wondering where they had gone, she guessed something special was in store.

"Look there!" Barbe cried.

Anne followed her gaze to the far corner of the great hall. A ripple passed through the guests as masked men, their hats glittering with cloth of gold, streamed in. Spreading out among the guests, they surrounded the dancing ladies and began to close in on them.

Her blood racing, Anne saw that one of the tallest ones presented himself to Lady Margaret. She watched as they twirled and glided, the masked man attending as she reeled away, then reeling her in until he pulled her tightly against his chest.

Anne's thoughts spun along with them, the scene unfolding like a story she had heard before. Had her own father once danced like this with her mother at Henry Tudor's court? She had heard whispers of how they met, though her mother was always tight-lipped about details. Elizabeth Howard, proud and relentless about rank, had married a man beneath her. How and why had that happened?

The sounds of her parents' arguments flooded her — raised voices, bitter words exchanged behind closed doors while Anne and George pressed their ears to the other side. Their father had ambition to match their mother's pride. Who could blame him for reaching beyond his station to grasp what he had the ability to hold? She and George would both do the same.

Looking around, Anne marvelled that one masked man might be an army officer — another, the King of England. The king's closest friend was his former master of the horse. Perhaps social positions were loosening back home. Were they also loosening on the Continent?

Glancing at the archduke, she doubted it. He might not marry the woman his aunt chose for him, but he would marry as well as he could, just as Thomas Boleyn had done. If there was anything she had learned about the Habsburgs since arriving at Lady Margaret's court, it was that all four of the Burgundian-Habsburg children knew they were duty-bound to make royal marriages. There would be no exceptions and no dissent.

Charles of Habsburg barely condescended to talk to her. He thought of her as a servant or attendant. She was that, of course. But one day she planned to be much more. Why should she not, when her father had pulled himself up to become one of the most highly ranked men at King Henry's court?

Turning her gaze to Charles Brandon, Anne saw his game in a flash. He was pulling himself up, too. And King Henry was extending a helping hand. The young English king was opening doors. If her father and Brandon could step through them, so could she.

As a masked man approached, Anne smiled, imagining what opportunities might await once she returned home. Accepting the officer's invitation to dance, she threw off her hurt feelings at the archduke's disdain. The future ruler of most of Europe might think her beneath his dignity, but she would show him differently one day.

THIRTEEN

"Why no, Monsieur! I have no plans to marry again, as I don't need to." Lady Margaret's laughter burbled like a spring stream.

"Madame, you must look to your future happiness," Charles Brandon counselled.

Anne drew in her breath as Brandon's hand grasped her mistress's. One moment it lay serene on her lap; the next it was enveloped in the large, sure hand of the king's close friend.

"I am happy as I am. No future beckons that I would choose over this moment," Lady Margaret said.

"I would choose nothing over this moment, my lady." Brandon's eyes sought Lady Margaret's. "But once this moment is past, I will not be able to forget you."

Lady Margaret looked confused. "You will forget something?"

Anne cleared her throat, drawing her mistress's attention. With a curtsey, she asked, "Madame, shall I translate?"

Lady Margaret withdrew her hand from Brandon's enormous one. "Yes, do."

Anne translated his words to French as Lady Margaret's cheeks flushed, a faint pink creeping up to the hint of fair hair peeking out from under her headdress.

"Tell her I have thought of nothing but her since Lille," Brandon told Anne, his eyes fixed on his royal target.

Translating, Anne recalled Lady Margaret's admonitions to guard against the dupery of honeyed words from dishonest chevaliers. Was she in the company of one, now?

Margaret of Austria looked anything but on her guard. She fluttered her eyelashes at her suitor and toyed with her veil, a picture of everything she had warned her maids of honour against.

"You may tell Monsieur that I am pleased he remembered me," Lady Margaret responded.

Anne translated, then waited.

"You are the queen bee, Madame. And now that I am stung, I shall not recover," Brandon declared.

Anne relayed his words, struggling to keep a serious face. Such lines were straight out of the textbook of what not to believe when pursued by light suitors. Had Lady Margaret not penned verses to guard against such sweet speeches? What about the books from her library by Christine de Pizan and Anne of France?

Lady Margaret's tinkling laugh floated towards the Englishman like water moving downstream. In an instant Anne saw that all the admonitions of the sages were as grains of sand against such a strong current.

"What say you, Madame?" Anne asked, as her mistress made no reply, her gaze fixed on the velvety brown eyes of Charles Brandon.

Lady Margaret waved a dismissal. "I will manage from here."

Anne backed away, wondering how Lady Margaret would fare without her. She turned and peeked back. Brandon's hand had once again captured Lady Margaret's. What more would he capture before the night was over?

No longer needed, Anne rounded the corner of the alcove. The crowd was dense as she picked her way through it, looking for a familiar face.

Suddenly, she froze, her breath catching in her throat. There stood her father, talking to an English officer.

Papa! She wanted to cry. But she held her tongue. Now was her chance to display the skills she had learned at Lady Margaret's court. Straightening, she raised her chin and glided towards him.

The officer spotted her first, followed by her father, who turned slowly, his eyes sweeping over her like a stranger assessing a new face.

"My daughter, Anne," he introduced, as if they had parted only days, not months, ago.

"How do you do, Monsieur?" Anne asked. Turning to her father, she resisted the urge to fling herself into his arms. "How nice to see you, Father."

He offered a tight smile. "You have grown, daughter."

"Have I?" she asked, tingling to hear more. Grown in what way? Statelier? More beautiful? More self-possessed?

"Have you met Officer Scroggs?"

"'Tis a pleasure, Monsieur." Anne wished he would disappear, and her father would sweep her into his arms the way Lady Margaret's father had done the month before.

"A pleasure, Mademoiselle." The officer bowed as if searching for something.

What was he looking for? In a flash, Anne had it. Putting out her hand, she allowed him to brush it with his moustache. Would her father notice she was being taken for a woman, no longer a girl?

"I have so much to tell you, Father!" Anne burst out, unable to contain herself any longer.

Her father's smile widened, although still tight. "I have heard all about it from Lady Margaret."

"Did you get my letter?" Anne asked, doubting Lady Margaret had taken a moment to tell him anything. She was very much otherwise engaged.

Thomas Boleyn's face went blank. "Your letter?"

"The one I sent you from Tervuren."

Her father waved an airy hand. "I'm sure I did. So much comes in every day."

"But you must remember if you got it, do you not?" Disappointment crept over her. How could he not know if he had read it or not?

The officer cleared his throat. "I'm off to find refreshment," he announced, looking as if he wished to give them a moment.

Anne's father put a hand to his shoulder. "Don't go, Scroggs. We need to finish our matter."

"Rightly so." The officer's eyes flicked to Anne.

Her father's eyes followed. "Will you go and find refreshment for us, Anne?"

Her heart sank. "Of course, Father."

"Take your time."

Anne moved off, stunned. Was she a serving girl to be sent off to fetch ale? Her father had dismissed her only moments after a six-month separation. Why was something else always more important than spending time with her?

"Who was that you were talking to?" Veronique asked at the refreshments table.

"My father. And an officer."

"Your father is here? You must be so happy!" Veronique exclaimed.

"Yes," Anne replied, trying not to sound as numb as she felt. She busied herself getting the requested drinks.

Her elation upon spotting him had vanished. Perhaps once her father finished with the officer it would return. But the first moments of their reunion had fallen flat.

She made her way back with the ale, mindful that he had told her to take her time. Slowing her steps, she weaved in and out between the clusters of chatting and laughing guests. Soon she, too, would join in with the merriment. In a moment, her father's eyes would be on her, noticing and admiring her as if she were the most important person in the world.

At the spot where she had left them, Anne glanced around. Her father and the officer were nowhere in sight.

"Did you see where Sir Boleyn and Officer Scroggs went?" she asked a nearby English officer.

"Who?" The officer peered at her. "Ah, yes. They went off with a messenger. Something important, no doubt."

Something more important than me, she thought. "But — but I brought their drinks for them," she spluttered, trying not to let her face fall.

The Englishman eyed the mug in her raised hand. "I'll find a home for that ale, if you're offering."

"Here, sir. May you drink it with pleasure," she bid him.

"Only if you'll join me," he replied with a short, gallant bow.

Raising the ale meant for her father, she touched it to the officer's mug. As she sipped, Mistress Bonnard's words came to mind, as if to rescue her: *In pleasing yourself, you will most please others.*

Anne sipped again, taking strength from the French beguine's wisdom. If her father couldn't be there for her, she would be there for herself.

The officer lowered his mug and smiled at her. She tried to smile back. But the hurt ran too deep.

"Did you hear what happened last night?" Barbe's voice slipped through the quiet of the morning, yanking Anne from her sleep.

"What do you mean?" Like a cat, Anne stretched to hide her interest. Without Jeanne around, Barbe was warming up to her again.

The older girl leaned in, eyes wide. "The Englishman took a ring from Madame's finger."

Anne raised her eyebrows. "A game, perhaps?" From everything she had seen of what went on between Lady Margaret and Charles Brandon, she understood less and less.

"Not a game. He kept it, even though Madame asked for it back."

"But that's unchivalrous," Anne protested.

"Madame called him a *ladrón*, but he didn't understand what she meant."

"I'm sure he planned to return it." Anne sought the English word for *ladrón*. When it came to her, she shivered. 'Thief' was a strong term for her mistress to use, even in courtly banter.

Barbe shook her head. "I don't think so. Madame pleaded, but he didn't give it back."

"Did he offer something in return?" Anne couldn't picture her mistress pleading with anyone. It was beneath her dignity.

"Just sweet words with smooth murmurings." Barbe rolled her eyes.

"How do you know? Were you there?"

"No. She shooed me away. But I heard Lady Elisabeth talking about it this morning."

"She shooed me away, too, when I tried to translate for her," Anne recalled.

"I hope you translated that the king's friend is up to no good," Barbe jested.

"Hardly. But I would have stayed if she hadn't dismissed me."

"She should have dismissed him, too, before he fleeced her out of a diamond ring."

Anne gasped. "A diamond one?"

"The one she wears on her ring finger."

"That's outrageous!" She knew the ring well. It was one of Lady Margaret's favourites. Lady Elisabeth had said it had once belonged to Lady Margaret's mother.

"She seemed to think so, too," Barbe noted.

Anne's ire rose on behalf of her mistress. "Madame will clear things up today."

"She had better, since we leave tomorrow," Barbe noted.

"He spoke of marriage to her," Anne let slip.

"Did he, now? And grabbed a token to let his friends back home know of the high circles he moves in."

"Don't say that! She was so happy last night. I would wish such happiness for her always." Anne glanced away, recalling her mistress's shining eyes the evening before.

"Little fool, don't you see she's caught in the same snare she has warned us against countless times?"

"You're a bigger fool to think so. She's too far above us to fall for a dupe," Anne answered hotly.

"So you say, with all the wisdom of your years," Barbe needled.

"Don't think you are so wise at only a year older than me," Anne retorted.

"I'm old enough to know that all of us fall for a trick sooner or later." With a firm thrust, Barbe pushed her off the couch.

"I'll never do so." Anne reached up and grabbed Barbe's ankle, pulling her down beside her.

"Then you'll never know what it is to lose yourself to love," Barbe proclaimed, tickling Anne until they both dissolved into a giggling heap.

*

On the journey back to Malines, Anne leaned her head against the carriage window. Lady Margaret had taken the first coach with Lady Elisabeth and Madame de Verneuil. The archduke rode with his attendants, leaving Anne and the other demoiselles to follow behind in their own carriage.

"Do you think the archduke is dull?" Agnes de Middelbourg cut through her reverie.

Anne jolted to attention. It was rare that Agnes spoke to her. Whatever she answered was bound to be repeated. "Not dull. Just … different," she said carefully.

Agnes studied her. "Different from your King Henry?"

"King Henry is gay and outward-oriented. The archduke is another sort." Anne wondered what Agnes wanted from her.

"I saw you talking to him the other night. What did he say to you?" Agnes asked, eyes narrowing.

Anne saw her moment to seize the advantage. "He told me not to tell, so I won't," she lied.

The older girl's ice-blue eyes bored into her. "Come now, tell me something of what he said."

"I can't," Anne refused. "He asked for my confidence, and I gave it to him." Charles of Habsburg had dismissed her, making her feel humiliated and incensed. But she wouldn't share that with Agnes.

"Why didn't you dance with him?"

"I didn't care to," Anne replied, reworking the scene to suit her advantage.

"Did he ask you to?" Agnes pressed.

"I told you, he asked for my confidence." It was dawning on Anne that Agnes thought she had something that she didn't. She would keep her guessing.

"It seems strange that you spoke at length yet didn't dance," the older girl probed.

Anne shrugged, turning back to the window to hide her smile. What pleasure it was to hold out on Agnes. It almost made up for the sting of her father leaving without saying goodbye.

Back in Malines Anne noted that her mistress seemed less elated than she had been upon returning from Lille.

"Do you think she's angry over the ring?" Anne asked Barbe.

"I think she's unsettled because she doesn't know the outcome."

"Did she ask for it back?"

"More than once. And he didn't satisfy her request," Barbe recounted.

"Yes, but beyond Viscount Lisle, did she speak to the English ambassador about it?"

"I don't know. But it seems she's waiting for some sort of response and hasn't received it yet."

"Why should she bother?" Anne asked, thinking she would pretend she didn't care at all if she were in a similar position.

"Because she let herself get swept away," Barbe pointed out.

Anne couldn't argue with her companion's reasoning. She had seen it for herself. Her indomitable mistress, capable of standing up to her father the Holy Roman Emperor and her council members representing the Netherlands' seventeen provinces, rejecting Henry Tudor's marriage offer, and telling her nephew what to do daily, had lost her heart to an army officer. It was beyond belief.

"I don't understand how that could happen," she exclaimed.

"I told you, you won't understand until you become a woman. Then you'll understand only too well."

"I'll never let any man overtake my reason."

"You think not, but you'll see," Barbe warned mysteriously.

"What do you know of such goings-on?"

"Not much, but I've observed and heard about them from others," Barbe told her.

"But our mistress is strong and powerful," Anne argued. "She can say yes or no to any who approach her."

"And she said yes to this one, but now that he's gone, he doesn't afford her the chance to say no at the final moment."

Anne crossed her arms. "I shall never say yes to anyone unless the outcome favours me."

Barbe eyed her sceptically. "So say many. But few reap their reward."

"I'll reap my reward before I ever let a man take something from me."

"Oh, you're so sure of yourself," Barbe mocked. "Let's see how sure you are a decade from now."

Anne tilted her chin defiantly. "I'll be sure of myself until the day I die."

"And what if it's that certainty that brings you to ruin?" Barbe asked.

"Then I'll die knowing I stayed true to myself."

"May it comfort you in your final moments. As for me, I'll fall to the man who sings sweet words and offers riches."

"What if he doesn't turn up?"

"My parents will see that he does. And I'll obey them."

"As will mine," Anne said, sure of her parents' ambitions for her. "And I, too, will obey," she added, less sure than before.

"Do you think they'll find you a good match?"

"They'll find me the highest nobleman they can," Anne asserted, her eyes falling upon Agnes de Middelbourg, who had just entered the room. *Then I'll find one even higher.*

FOURTEEN

Waiting in the *petit cabinet* that served as Lady Margaret's study across from her bedroom, Anne wondered why Lady Elisabeth had summoned her. As far as she knew, the *mère des filles* had heard nothing of the stable yard scuffle. But there had been other infractions. As she went down the list, her thoughts roamed to her parents. They would be furious if she was sent home.

She tried hard to fit in with the other demoiselles, but somehow, she didn't. To fit in was the way of a courtier. Her father had told her so time and again. She knew his success depended on being a perfect courtier. Yet at home, he gave as good as he got, matching her mother's sense of superiority with his own soaring ambition. How well Anne understood him.

Struggling to drop her hurt at their unsatisfying exchange in Tournai, she shrugged. One day she would be the one who sent others on important business. What did she care if her father didn't have time for her? She didn't have time for him, either.

The *mère des filles* entered the room and shut the door, leaning back against it.

"What have I done, Madame? Whatever it is, I'm sorry for it," Anne opened. Best to face head-on whatever was to come.

"You must learn to curb your tongue."

Anne swallowed. Now was the moment to show Lady Elisabeth she could. "I try, Madame. Perhaps it is my temperament."

Lady Elisabeth studied her. "You have the temperament of a French woman."

Anne's spirits lifted despite herself. Semmonet had said the same. "What do you mean, Madame?"

The *mère des filles* smiled, but her eyes were stern. "You speak your mind when it pleases you, without waiting to gauge the reaction of others. Do you know what I'm referring to?"

Anne flicked through her list. Had the archduke complained that she had spoken to him out of turn? Or had Lady Elisabeth heard about her scuffles with Barbe and Jeanne?

"I'm not sure, Madame. Could you tell me?"

"You snapped at one of the others in the lecture yesterday."

Heat rushed to Anne's cheeks. She had only corrected the girl's butchery of the passage from Petrarch they were reading. "But she didn't understand what was before her eyes," she argued.

"As you don't understand what's before yours," Lady Elisabeth countered.

Anne stiffened. "I was only correcting her mistake." The nitwit had mispronounced 'to kiss' in French so that it sounded like a bad word that Barbe had flung at a stable boy whose hand had strayed as they had passed by. Certainly not what Petrarch had in mind.

Lady Elisabeth's gaze didn't waver. "It was her mistake to make. Your greater mistake was correcting her in front of the others."

Anne clenched her jaw. "I wanted her to see the error before she made it again."

"That's not your role. At court, one does not correct others in public, no matter the mistake."

"I'm sorry, Madame. Sometimes I speak before I think." The words tasted bitter on her tongue.

"And now that your French is better, we are beginning to see that," Lady Elisabeth noted.

Anne's frustration bubbled up. "I cannot stay silent when something is wrong," she blurted, then realised she had just exhibited what her superior had described.

A silence hung heavy between them. Lady Elisabeth's expression remained unreadable, but Anne could feel her outburst settling like a stone. "That is evident," Lady Elisabeth said quietly. "But you are here to learn how to behave at court, and at court one waits before spilling out what one truly thinks."

Anne's chest tightened. "Yes, Madame. But there are times when I just wish to be myself." She thought of Mistress Bonnard's advice. It was in those moments, when she was most herself, that she stood out. When she blended in, she became invisible, just another demoiselle in a sea of placid, dutiful faces.

"There are times when every one of us just wants to be ourselves. But we save those moments for times alone with our family or a special friend," Lady Elisabeth advised.

Anne furrowed her brow. "A special friend, Madame?"

Lady Elisabeth's eyes glinted with something Anne couldn't place. "Someone who knows you well. And likes you just the way you are, even if you are different from others."

"Am I different from the others, Madame?" Anne's thoughts jumped to Barbe, a special friend just as Lady Elisabeth had described. How was it possible that Barbe had a special friend in Jeanne, too, that pathetic henchman with nothing to offer?

Lady Elisabeth nodded. "Yes, little one."

"Because I am English?" Anne pressed.

Lady Elisabeth shook her head. "Because you are you. A little sharper, a bit more clearly defined than the others."

"Will that change when I get older?"

A soft chuckle escaped Lady Elisabeth's lips. "It will become more pronounced."

Anne's heart thudded. Should she be uneasy? Or proud?

"You must refine that sharpness," Lady Elisabeth continued. "Learn to soften it when necessary. A demoiselle at court must appear pliable, even when she is not."

"How shall I do that, Madame?"

"Watch Lady Margaret. She is soft and pliable on the outside. But she gets what she wants by making others think that they themselves want it."

Anne pondered her words. "Did you not tell me that's how she manages her council?"

Lady Elisabeth threw back her head and laughed. "Madame manages her council the way most of us manage our husbands."

Anne's mouth fell open. "But that's not how my mother manages my father!"

"Perhaps not, but it is the easiest way to get them to bend to our will. You must learn how to handle yourself at court. That is why you are here, and you have the best of all possible examples to follow in Lady Margaret."

"Is this a moment in which I must follow her example, Madame? Or may I speak my mind?" Anne asked, eager to avoid further criticism.

"Speak your mind, *ma chère*. We are alone here with no ears to pry." Lady Elisabeth sat, making herself comfortable.

Anne took a deep breath and plunged ahead. "I don't think that Madame has got what she wanted from the English king's friend."

Lady Elisabeth clicked her tongue. "That is a different matter. In affairs of the heart, all bets are off."

"But when Madame bets, she usually wins." Anne recounted the times she had seen her mistress beat her opponents at cards.

"She will win this one, too, but at some cost to her heart." Lady Elisabeth's smile held sadness in it.

"Why didn't she guard her heart when she counsels us to do so?"

Lady Elisabeth sighed, her eyes distant. "Because none of us can guard our hearts forever. If we could, we wouldn't have hearts at all."

"Madame, I don't understand, although not due to language."

Lady Elisabeth laid a hand on Anne's shoulder. "*Ma fille*, you will not understand until you have lived a while longer."

"It seems a contradiction to rule one's realm yet not rule one's heart."

Lady Elisabeth nodded, her voice quiet. "One of life's greatest contradictions, my dear."

Anne's head spun. "Why is that so?"

"Because the heart rules the head, even when the head knows best."

"But if the heart leads one down a path of unhappiness, why not stick with the head?"

Lady Elisabeth's eyes glistened. "Because the heart rules with passion and the head rules with reason. And passion outweighs reason. It cannot be otherwise."

"I would think some don't let passion overtake their reason." Anne thought of the archduke. She could guess he would rule with his head. He would probably choose a wife with his head, too. Somehow, she didn't think it would be Mary Tudor. "Shouldn't a good ruler use reason to make his decisions?"

"All good rulers use reason most of the time to make their decisions. Until one day comes when they want something so badly that reason flies out the window and they do something rash."

"For example?"

Lady Elisabeth sat back in her chair and rubbed her chin. "For example, Lady Margaret's grandfather wanted Burgundy to be a great kingdom, not just a duchy. He did everything he could to bring it about, including declaring war on all his neighbours."

"Then what happened?"

"He ran out of money, lost the support of his people by overtaxing them, and rushed into attacking the Swiss when everyone knew he couldn't win against them."

"And then what?"

The *mère des filles* sighed, her eyes distant, as if looking into the past. "He lost thousands of his men and finally his own life, ending Burgundy's chance to become a kingdom. Do you want to be known as rash like he was?"

Anne studied Lady Margaret's wooden Indian bust on a side table. His eyes stared severely, accusing her. How was she to stop wanting certain things so badly — her father's attention, the archduke's regard? If they were not forthcoming, she would seek the world's regard, instead.

"Did you know his mother was housekeeper to his father?" Barbe whispered. They stood in the far corner of the Court of Savoy's great hall, awaiting the arrival of their distinguished guest, Erasmus of Rotterdam.

"That's not uncommon," Jeanne sniffed.

Barbe raised an eyebrow. "It is, when the father is a priest."

Jeanne let out a dismissive snort. "That's not so uncommon either."

Barbe's smile was mischievous. "Perhaps that's what he's here to talk about."

"His base birth?" Anne asked, surprised to learn that Europe's most celebrated scholar was the bastard son of a priest.

Barbe shook her head. "No. His criticisms of some not so uncommon Church practices."

"Will he lecture us on not dallying with a priest?" Jeanne jested.

Barbe dug an elbow into Jeanne's side. "There's no fear of any of us doing that. Our parents would have us thrashed."

Pleased that it wasn't her receiving the jab, Anne said, "Why would any woman with sense fall into a priest's arms?"

"For the same reason any woman falls for an unworthy man."

"Do you mean for love?" Anne asked.

Barbe sneered. "Of course not."

Anne's eyes sharpened as realisation dawned. "Is it money, then?"

Barbe tossed her head. "Of course. And that's what his lecture will be about."

Jeanne nodded. "Money is a popular topic."

"I wager he'll talk about sales of indulgences." Barbe's eyes narrowed.

"He's one of Lady Margaret's favourites," Jeanne noted.

"But not Lady Elisabeth's," Barbe added. "Don't praise him in her presence, whatever you do."

"Why doesn't she like him?" Anne asked.

"Too critical of the Church for her taste." Barbe's face smoothed into a courtier's mask as Europe's greatest scholar entered the packed room.

"Lady Margaret has invited me to share my thoughts with you today," Erasmus began, his voice resonant and commanding. He gripped the lectern with long, bony fingers, his keen eyes sweeping over the audience. "But I have thoughts on so many topics that I do not know where to begin."

Anne warmed to his words. She, too, often felt overwhelmed by her thoughts, like a storm ready to burst.

"Therefore, I invite you to offer questions to stir my mind." The craggy-faced master spread out his hands like a priest before his congregation.

Anne's eyes lit up as a hum swept the room. This was a new way to learn, active and engaged rather than sitting and staring dully at one's lecturer. Eyes darted nervously, avoiding the gaze of the scholar who had become a beacon of fresh ideas across Europe.

Finally, Lady Margaret broke the silence. "A question, Sire Erasmus."

"Yes, my lady."

"What do you consider the greatest achievement of our time?"

Erasmus's eyes sparkled. "Undoubtedly, Madame, it is the spread of printing presses so that many can read important works and glean for themselves what truth lies in them."

"A fine answer, Monsieur. Now, who will venture the next question?" Lady Margaret scanned the room as hands shot up, all belonging to members of her household who depended on her patronage for their positions.

"What good are books to those who cannot read?" a steward asked.

"With the spread of books into more hands, reading will become more common. And with it, the understanding of more men and women will lead to enlightenment," Erasmus replied.

"Begging your pardon, Monsieur, but what if it leads to more confusion, instead?" another voice chimed in.

"Do not beg my pardon to raise a good point. It may indeed raise more questions, but God has given every man a degree of free will to find their way to Him."

"Do we not find our way through the Church, Monsieur?"

"We do, but we must make our way through the tangle of Church practices to approach our Lord, and it is through the teachings of Scripture that we can best do so," Erasmus answered.

"And what if some Church practices lack scriptural basis?"

"We must strive to adhere to what is scripturally based and avoid what is not."

"Could you give us an example of Church practices that are not scripturally based?" a brave voice spoke up.

Erasmus's face hardened. "The sale of indulgences, for one. The conscription of children into taking holy orders, for another. The unmarried state of priests, for yet another."

A collective gasp filled the room as the venerable scholar denigrated three time-honoured traditions of the Church in a single sweep.

Anne considered his points. She would not like to be forced into holy orders before she knew what the world had to offer. Yet many were — the younger children of parents too poor to feed them, or those who were natural born, with no social position. Had Erasmus been one of them?

"Monsieur, what if someone doesn't wish to buy an indulgence but faces scorn from those who do?"

"By all means, buy the indulgence if it keeps peace between you and your neighbour. But know that such an act will bring you no closer to salvation than venerating a relic."

Another gasp echoed through the hall as Erasmus disparaged yet another Church tradition. Anne guessed that most in the audience had prayed before relics for God to hear their requests. Did not the donations they offered afterwards go towards feeding the poor and caring for the sick?

"Certain traditions should not be abandoned but rather examined in the light of Scripture," the theologian clarified.

"But Scripture is read by only a few," a voice pointed out.

Erasmus nodded. "Which is why the spread of printing presses is crucial for making Scriptures available to many more."

"But they are in Latin, understood only by scholars."

"Soon they will be translated into the original Greek by scholars who discern what text is original and what is not, and how best to translate it from its original tongue."

"Begging your pardon, but how can you be sure of this, Monsieur?"

"Because I am one of those scholars." Erasmus's tone blended confidence and pride.

A murmur of realisation spread among the audience as they grasped the great man's future plans. Anne wondered what he might say about translating the Bible into the common tongue. From his remarks, it seemed a reasonable conclusion.

"And do you support translating Scripture into the vernacular?" another man asked, as if reading Anne's mind.

"Every man and woman should be able to read the Scriptures in their own tongue," Erasmus proclaimed.

Anne turned to Barbe, her eyebrows raised in silent question. Her companion shrugged, as if to say, *Why not?*

Why not, indeed? Anne thought.

That evening Lady Margaret held a soirée to honour Sire Erasmus. Instead of the usual cards, she sat by the hearth in her *riche cabinet*, the small reception room of her private quarters, sipping hippocras and nibbling on comfits from Antwerp's spice market.

Anne settled on a cushion behind her, cradling Babou to keep him from bothering her mistress. Monsieur Gattinara, Lady Margaret's trusted Savoyard counsellor, joined them, his keen mind and wit evident.

"We benefitted from your talk, Monsieur, but now let us enjoy a quiet moment," Lady Margaret urged.

The scholar's face softened. "As I always do with you, Madame. You are pleasure and comfort itself, within laudable parameters."

Lady Margaret's eyes twinkled. "It is important to set those parameters strictly so that my subjects can rely on me."

Anne hid a smile. Little did Lady Margaret know what she and Barbe got up to when no one was about.

Erasmus's gaze grew thoughtful. "As the Church sets parameters for her children, so that they do not become lost."

"It seems you would widen some of those parameters, Monsieur."

"You know my stance, Madame. Within the Church's boundaries, lest chaos ensue."

Lady Margaret nodded. "I abhor chaos, as it impedes trade."

"Indeed, Madame. England has no better friend than you at the Netherlands' helm."

"And you have been a good friend to England, with all the years you spent there. What caused you to linger so long?"

Erasmus smiled. "I have had the pleasure of the greatest friend a man could have."

"Who might that be?"

"Sir Thomas More, Madame. A member of parliament and recently appointed to the king's privy council. A finer fellow I have never met."

"A great friendship is comforting." Lady Margaret's eyes flickered to the counsellor who had served her for over a decade.

"More wished to be a monk, but his reach is far wider as lawyer, parliamentarian, and father," Erasmus said.

Lady Margaret leaned forward. "As a father?"

"His daughter, who bears your name, is so highly educated in Greek and Latin at age nine that her knowledge surpasses Cambridge scholars."

"Then he is in favour of women's education?" Lady Margaret asked.

"As assuredly as you are with your maids of honour," Erasmus said, making Anne beam at his acknowledgment.

"And what binds you as friends?" Lady Margaret pressed.

"It's as if we share the same heart. He is reasonable and compassionate, always speaking his mind and presenting his arguments so well that others listen and yield."

Monsieur Gattinara looked as if his legal mind was piqued. "It seems this More holds great sway," he put in.

"He is one to watch, Monsieur. Such skills as he possesses are rarely coupled with so good a heart."

Lady Margaret cocked an amused eyebrow. "And this Goodheart is now to guide young Henry as privy counsellor?"

Erasmus nodded. "King Henry will benefit from his guidance."

Monsieur Gattinara leaned in. "And what helm will your hand be on next?"

"I am going to Basel to oversee the printing of some of my works."

"I enjoyed *The Praise of Folly*," Lady Margaret remarked.

Anne had heard of the sharp satire on English society and the Church. Grandmother Boleyn had said it was a good thing it was in Latin, and not English, as a book like that could cause trouble in the wrong hands.

"Madame, I commend your Latin abilities," Erasmus said.

"They are far from good, so I had my confessor translate parts of it into French for me."

The great scholar's smile was knowing. "It must have been a trial for him to see his Church so maligned."

Lady Margaret chuckled. "It gave him a good laugh in parts."

"I'm pleased if my message brings healing rather than hardening hearts."

"I've heard our new Pope Leo enjoyed it," Monsieur Gattinara added.

"Then my book has served its purpose."

"It may serve more of a purpose than you intended," Lady Margaret noted, reaching for a comfit.

Erasmus raised an eyebrow. "In what way, Madame?"

"In ways beyond Church reform."

"How so, my lady?"

"You have questioned authority."

Anne's ears pricked. A warning laced her mistress's tone.

"With humour and satire, of course," Monsieur Gattinara softened.

"It is my way to deliver a message with grace," the scholar replied.

Lady Margaret shifted. "And it has been a success. But it will lead others to question authority. Not all will show the same grace in their displeasure towards the Church."

"The intent of my work is to reform from within."

"Yet with all calls to break from tradition, there will be those who seek change reasonably, and others who seek to overthrow," Lady Margaret cautioned.

"May those who read my works be reasonable and not seek to overthrow the old order."

"But once your works are translated into the common tongue and printed widely, they will reach all classes," Lady Margaret pointed out.

"As I hope they will."

"Ah, then we shall see if reason and moderation prevail over more hot-headed responses."

Erasmus raised his goblet. "You are discerning, as always, Madame."

At that moment, Babou jumped from Anne's arms to Lady Margaret's skirts.

"Take him away," Lady Margaret directed.

Anne captured the dog, guessing he had sensed the chill in his mistress's voice. The conversation had turned a corner. As she fled the room it came to her that not only must Lady Margaret manage seventeen different provinces, including one in revolt — she must also manage the consequences of the New Learning, with its calls to question tradition. Erasmus was foremost of those who questioned. Yet, her mistress had raised the best question of all. What form would the response to Erasmus's criticisms take?

Out in the hallway Anne considered. The path of reform might veer from the venerable scholar's intentions. Did Barbe reach the same conclusions she did from listening to the two men in the stable yard discussing the Church? Did Françoise see the same things as she when they viewed the painting of the Virgin in Lady Margaret's bedchamber?

Already Anne knew that great changes brought unintended consequences. Sent to Burgundy to learn French and polish her manners, she had absorbed far more at the Burgundian-Habsburg court.

Burying her face in Babou's fur, she stifled a snort. Her eyes had been opened to a new way of seeing — one that questioned rather than followed blindly. As for her French? The gap between English and French was vast, not just in language, but in different approaches to life. She squeezed Babou, feeling a thrill of rebellion. Expressing herself in French had encouraged her to embrace pleasure. When she returned home, would her countrymen admire her? Or would they be shocked?

Like a steel blade, Mistress Bonnard's words sliced through her thoughts: *Please yourself, and in such a way you will most please others.*

And if she didn't please others? Anne laughed and gave Babou another squeeze. *Grumble those who may; I will do as I please.*

FIFTEEN

A few weeks later, Sir Richard Wingfield, an ambassador from England, stepped into Lady Margaret's chamber, his boots brushing over the scented rushes on the floor. His broad frame filled the doorway as he offered a formal bow. "My Lady Margaret, thank you for receiving me," he said.

"I am most pleased to do so."

"I come with a letter from my king. And news from the English court." Wingfield held out a pouch with Henry VIII of England's seal on it.

Margaret raised her eyebrows ever so slightly. "Something new that I have not already been informed of?"

Wingfield's throat bobbed. "My sovereign has sent me to ensure you receive the most recent developments."

"Let me read this. Then you may fill me in." She motioned for him to sit as she opened the letter. Moving to the window, she turned her back to him as she read. She did not wish for her face to reveal whatever she thought of its contents. The words before her confirmed what she already suspected. King Henry was growing impatient — no, desperate — to finalise the marriage arrangements between his sister and the archduke.

She turned. "I see that your sovereign is eager to pin down wedding arrangements."

"Yes, Madame. Most eager, as the archduke has now come of age," Wingfield spelled out.

"Fourteen is very young. He is still a year from his majority."

Wingfield shifted in his chair, his eyes never leaving hers. "King Henry has asked me to remind you that the proxy marriage agreement of 1508 stipulates that the marriage is to take place within eight weeks of the archduke's fourteenth birthday." His words hung in the air, a veiled challenge.

Margaret pushed a bowl of comfits in Wingfield's direction. What cheek to bring up some ancient eight-week clause. "Our agreement was with the old king and so long ago," she parried. "I had forgotten about the eight-week clause. Surely your king doesn't wish for his sister to marry my nephew before he comes into his majority." She motioned to her page to pour out refreshment. Taking a goblet from him, she handed it to Wingfield with a smile as dazzling as the jewelled rings on her fingers.

The ambassador accepted the drink, his gaze averted momentarily. "My king is insistent, Madame. He worries the marriage will not take place at all if not completed within the agreed time." He sipped, his eyes betraying a flicker of discomfort.

Margaret also worried. Two large problems stood in her way — her father and her nephew.

Maximilian wouldn't commit to an actual date and had mysteriously stopped mentioning the marriage in recent months. In reply to her recent letters, he had dodged the matter entirely. Instead, he had waxed on about bagging a wild boar outside Innsbruck and asked for details of his grandchildren. As for her nephew? Charles had been blunt. He had told her he was not ready to marry.

Margaret waved an airy hand. "Of course the marriage will take place. But what rush is there if the archduke needs more time to season into a man?"

"I appreciate your wish to grant the archduke more time to grow into adulthood. But we have been waiting for years for this union to take place, and King Henry is not a patient man."

Margaret had seen that for herself in Lille and Tournai. If Henry wanted something done, he wanted it done soon, as any man of twenty-two might. But Charles, a mere fourteen, was far from ready to wed.

As for her father? Enigmatic Maxi presented another hurdle. Either he was angling to extract more money from Henry or making other plans.

"I cannot commit to an exact plan without hearing from the emperor first," Margaret hedged. "But we may start the process, should he agree to this rather … ambitious deadline."

"A good start would be to set a date," Wingfield suggested.

"It would be, wouldn't it?" Margaret agreed, knowing Wingfield would understand that she was unable to do so. Within the affairs of the Netherlands, she ruled without Maximilian's interference. But with a matter as large as a marriage union between England's royal princess and the dynastic heir to the Netherlands, Austria, and Spain, she had not the authority to venture an actual wedding date. Especially with the groom unwilling.

Wingfield offered a conciliatory expression. "Is there anything you can do to reassure my king that we are moving ahead on the matter?"

Margaret's gaze flicked towards the portrait of Margaret of York on the wall. The answer came swiftly from her wise English godmother. "I shall have my scribes prepare writs of safe passage for the princess royal and her entourage to journey here."

Wingfield's eyes narrowed slightly, suspicion lingering. "Within the eight-week deadline, Madame?"

She so wished the ambassador would stop harping on about a deadline. Her father balked whenever deadlines were mentioned. Who did Henry think he was, to hold the Holy

Roman Emperor to a deadline? The English pup had no idea what he was up against in trying to pin down her father. "Yes, of course. I will see to it now." Scribbling a note to her secretary, she handed it to her page then checked Wingfield's expression to gauge his reaction.

The ambassador sipped at his drink, looking somewhat mollified with the crumb she had tossed.

"What news of your court, then?" Margaret asked, eager to steer away from any more marriage talk for the moment.

"King Henry has made some new appointments. One in particular that may interest you."

"Do tell. Has he knighted some stable boy or such?" Margaret jested.

Wingfield choked on his drink. "You are deft, Madame. The king elevated Viscount Lisle to Duke of Suffolk earlier this month."

Margaret straightened the stack of papers on her desk, careful to contain her raging thoughts. "*Is* there a Duke of Suffolk?" she asked. There was the Duke of Buckingham, who had aided in the English victory at Thérouanne and Tournai. And the Duke of Norfolk was Thomas Boleyn's brother-in-law, something Boleyn had dropped into conversation numerous times. But she had not heard of any such title as the Duke of Suffolk.

Wingfield's gaze flickered. "The title has been revived in recognition of Viscount Lisle's service to the king."

"Then he has risen greatly in rank." Margaret kept her tone neutral. Charles Brandon had not provided her with similar good service. He had left her in the lurch, with nary a word as to his intentions. Good riddance to him. She flicked some ashes to the floor from the candelabra on her desk.

"My sovereign thought you might be pleased that he honoured one who holds you in such high esteem," the ambassador continued.

"Thank your sovereign from me." She would not be goaded into offering a congratulatory message to the king's former master of the horse, now catapulted to a dukedom. Certainly, he could have put pen to paper and sent a letter to explain himself or at least offer some flattering words. But he had sent nothing, leaving her to wonder and worry since he had parted from her that past autumn. With her ring, no less.

"And Monsieur Boleyn sends his highest regards and wishes he could offer them in person to his great lady Margaret."

Margaret brightened, relieved to get off the subject of Charles Brandon. "Ah, Monsieur Boleyn. Where is he now?"

Wingfield shifted. "The king has sent him off on a minor mission."

Alarm bells sounded in her head. Had he sent Boleyn to France? She needed her father to commit to this wedding, and fast. If not, England's young and impetuous king might look elsewhere for alliances. With the queen of France dead since January, the French king was on the marriage market. Margaret's stomach twisted at the thought of Henry falling in with the French. She forced a smile, keeping her voice steady. "Tell Boleyn his daughter is a delight and is thriving at my court."

"Ah, yes. He mentioned she was in your service." Wingfield looked as if there was something else he was meant to say.

"Any other news from your court?"

Wingfield's eyes sparked then dimmed. "Nothing of import."

"Oh, come now. Any weddings or scandals?"

A look of modest pride broke out on Wingfield's face. "There was a recent wedding."

"Do tell. Whose?"

"Mine, Madame."

Margaret clapped her hands. "Congratulations, Monsieur. Is your wife with you?"

"No, Madame. But thank you for asking, for I now remember that she bid me send her regards to your young charge, Mistress Boleyn."

Margaret cocked her head. "Does she know her?"

"They were neighbours in Kent."

She motioned to her page. "Summon Mademoiselle *Boullan*."

In moments, Anne appeared, curtseying gracefully.

"Come in, *ma petite*." Margaret watched as the girl moved into the room. She had grown more graceful over the past few months, perfecting the glide of a courtier. "This is Monsieur Wingfield from England. He has a message for you from his wife."

Anne looked surprised.

"Lady Wingfield sends her warm regards to you and says she remembers you from childhood days in Kent."

"I cannot recall a Lady Wingfield, Monsieur," Anne said.

Wingfield smiled at her. "She is now Lady Wingfield, but until recently she was Bridget Wiltshire of Shurland in Kent."

Anne's face lit up. "Mistress Bridget of Stone Castle!"

Wingfield beamed. "The same."

"Oh Monsieur, is Mistress Bridget now your wife?"

"Since last year, my lady."

"How fortunate you are, Monsieur!"

"I am, indeed," Wingfield agreed, the glow on his face matching his words.

"Is she here now?"

"No, Mademoiselle, but I will bring her a message if you have one for me."

"I remember our frolics at Stone Castle, and I am most happy for her to have become a great lady," Anne enthused.

Margaret looked on in amusement as she saw Wingfield's pleasure in receiving her maid of honour's compliment.

"Why, thank you, Mademoiselle. I will pass on your compliments, and I thank you for them, myself."

Margaret motioned her demoiselle out of the room. The *petite Boullan* had accomplished a masterstroke in turning her compliment to esteem both Wingfield and his wife. She was quickly learning the ways of a courtier. Margaret turned to Wingfield. "She doesn't resemble her father, does she?"

"In looks, not so much. But in temperament —"

"She is all her father's daughter, quick-witted with a silver tongue," Margaret finished for him.

"It will serve her well, along with the finest formation a demoiselle can receive," Wingfield added.

"And what formation is that?"

Wingfield dipped his head. "To serve Madame at the Court of Savoy is the highest hope any English parent can have for their daughter."

"Is that so, Monsieur?" Margaret asked, gratified to hear what she already knew.

"It was the Duke of Suffolk who told me so just last week."

Margaret buttoned up her thoughts. "He did mention something like that in Tournai." She had promised to take on his daughter as one of her maids of honour. If she ever turned up, she hoped she would be nothing like her father, either in looks or character.

"He said he was sending his daughter to you to be polished at Europe's finest court."

"I look forward to receiving her." Margaret kept her tone smooth, knowing it would create a sensation back in London if she changed her mind. But her ire rose as her heart took the blow. Charles Brandon had not bothered to communicate with her to confirm the matter before bragging about it to others. She could guess how he had gained his dukedom. Most likely he had won it in a wager with Henry over a joust or a wrestling match. At the thought of wagers, her anger burned hotter. Only weeks earlier, her agent in Aachen had reported that German merchants were laying bets on whether the emperor's daughter would marry King Henry's former master of the horse. It was too much to bear.

"I shall let the duke know upon my return," Wingfield said.

Margaret made no reply. How could she? There was nothing left to say. If there was silence on his end, she would match it. What once was, was no more. Lifting her goblet, she declared a toast. "May your visit here be a success."

"Oh, yes, Madame. And may your happiness be as bountiful as your realm," Wingfield returned.

They clinked glasses as Margaret speculated that neither of them was likely to have their wishes fulfilled for the moment.

SIXTEEN

As spring deepened, fresh tidings arrived from London. Margaret's agent who was posted there, Jacob Jansen, reported that King Henry and the new Duke of Suffolk had teamed up as black and white hermits to compete in a tourney in early May. "Their staves were inscribed with a curious motto," Jansen described.

"Do tell."

"*Who can hold that will away.*"

Margaret examined her fingernails. "And its meaning?"

Jansen hesitated. "Madame, it is being taken to mean that the Duke of Suffolk pines for you."

"Why would anyone think such a thing?" she asked, her tone blithe.

"The duke wore a yellow and blue scarf for Burgundy in his breastplate."

"They are common enough colours," Margaret remarked. What game was Brandon playing?

"Madame, it is but talk. No one really knows, but it is being said at court and in the taverns that the motto refers to you and the Duke of Suffolk." Jansen trained his eyes on the floor.

"How absurd!" Margaret turned her back and moved to the window for air. She must not appear too concerned. If she did, her agent might return to England and sprinkle a rumour that the Duchess of Savoy equally pined for her English duke.

"Yes, Madame." The man bowed, awaiting further instructions.

"Was there anything else?"

"No, Madame."

"Anything at court being said about Princess Mary and my nephew's wedding?"

"No, Madame. Talk of that has died down."

"I see." So, Henry's court was no longer speculating on when the wedding between his sister and her nephew would take place. Instead, it buzzed with rumours of her and the Duke of Suffolk.

"What more shall I find out for you, Madame?"

"Try to learn what King Henry intends for his sister Mary."

"I will do so, Madame. And as for the Duke of Suffolk?"

The corner of Margaret's mouth twitched. "What about him?"

"Shall I find out more about what he intends?"

"No! Why should you?" She sat at her desk with a thump. If Brandon couldn't state his intentions to her directly, she was done with him. If only talk would die down, she could lay the whole entanglement to rest. "Is there anything you would like me to scatter in conversation on your behalf?" Jansen asked.

"Nothing at all." She would take it up with Wingfield, whom she was increasingly coming to like. Distrusting her agent, she could guess that some might be placing coins in his hands back in London to discern what her own thoughts were on the matter of Charles Brandon. Since she could scarcely sort them out herself, she didn't wish to spread any message abroad that might be wrongly construed.

"I am at your service, Madame." The agent bowed.

Margaret opened her desk drawer and pulled some coins from a velvet pouch. Placing them on her desk, she motioned for him to take them then waved him out. The instant the man disappeared she went to the door and bolted it.

Returning to her desk, she rested her head in her hands. Nothing was going as planned. Even her heart wouldn't budge when her reason ordered it to. As for the motto inscribed on her former suitor's stave, what good was his message when he hadn't come to deliver it himself — or to take her in his arms?

Laying her head on her desk, Margaret wept.

In June, unexpected word came from the Danish ambassador. His king wished for a proxy marriage to take place with his intended bride, Margaret's niece, Isabella of Habsburg.

"I am sure something can be arranged in the next few months," Margaret replied, wishing she was arranging the far more important nuptials of the archduke with the English princess.

"It is King Christian's wish, Madame, to hold the proxy wedding on the same day as his coronation in Copenhagen."

"And when is that?" Margaret asked.

"On Trinity Sunday." The ambassador shifted uneasily.

Margaret's hackles rose. "But that is tomorrow!"

"I apologise, Madame. The missive from King Christian arrived just this morning. I came straight to you as soon as I read it."

Margaret shot a glance towards Lady Elisabeth, standing quietly by the window, then back to the ambassador. "Impossible. A ceremony worthy of a Habsburg princess will take weeks to prepare."

The ambassador bowed slightly, as if his deferential angle might soften the blow. "King Christian believes it fitting for his queen to be honoured on the same day as his reign's founding."

Margaret turned her back on him, hiding her frustration behind a mask of poise. Her gaze locked with Lady Elisabeth, eyebrows raised in disbelief. Lady Elisabeth's calm expression remained unchanged, though her eyes held a flicker of agreement.

"Step out for a moment," Margaret ordered.

The ambassador bowed, retreating swiftly, his boots clicking against the stone floor as the door closed behind him.

"What insolence!" she hissed, once he was gone.

Lady Elisabeth nodded. "It is most hasty, but —"

"But what?" Margaret snapped, pacing. Her skirts swished, filling the room with the restless sound of her agitation.

"It is only a proxy ceremony, after all."

Margaret stopped mid-step, hands planted on her hips. "What if I say no?"

"You risk offending the King of Denmark. And the emperor." Lady Elisabeth's eyes met hers.

A bitter laugh escaped Margaret's lips. "Christian has already offended me." Mulling over the consequences of turning down the Danish king's request, she thought of what her father might say. Maximilian wanted the Hanseatic League in the Habsburg fold. Princess Isabella was the means by which this would happen. She groaned inwardly, knowing the answer before she spoke it aloud. "Do you think Madame de Beaumont can get Isabella outfitted in time?"

"I will speak to her within the hour, but I'm sure she can," Lady Elisabeth said.

"We must put together a banquet and dancing."

Lady Elisabeth clapped her hands together. "Oh, Madame, the demoiselles will be overjoyed! I'll tell them to make ready."

"Your husband must alert the men at arms. I'll see to the kitchen and music master. And my nephew — he'll need to escort his sister."

Lady Elisabeth smiled wryly. "He'll be relieved it's not his own wedding."

Margaret's chuckle hid her pain. "Indeed. And there is nothing to be done for it." Perhaps some music and dancing would be just the thing for a June Sunday. She had been in mourning for the past month over the passing of the eight-week deadline with no wedding between the archduke and the English princess in sight. For one other reason, too. *Fortune, misfortune — both strengthen one.* Her favourite motto buoyed her, as it had so many times before. She would make good cheer with the others at tomorrow's proceedings.

"Summon the ambassador," she bade her steward.

In a moment, the Danish ambassador appeared, looking both abashed and expectant.

Margaret straightened. "The ceremony will take place tomorrow at eleven in the grand salon."

Relief flooded the ambassador's face. "I am at your disposal, Madame. And most appreciative." He bowed low.

"Are you to serve as proxy groom?"

"Yes, Madame, if the princess agrees."

Margaret arched a brow. "She will agree." Her voice left no room for doubt. "A banquet will follow, with dancing."

"I look forward to it," he responded with relish.

"Bring your colleagues and we shall make good cheer. And let your sovereign know we require more notice next time."

"I will do so, Madame. And you may be sure he will be well-disposed towards the House of Habsburg when he receives news that his proxy marriage has taken place."

"The emperor will be glad to hear of it." Margaret watched him leave before turning to Lady Elisabeth. "Tell the wine steward to bring up some good vintages. If I must endure this charade, I intend to enjoy it." *And forget my disappointments for a time.*

*

The proxy ceremony went off as planned the following day. Margaret observed Isabella in her lilac-coloured gown, her auburn hair spilling down her back in loose curls. Her second oldest niece was a petite, graceful girl, more sensitive than her older sister Lenore, less hardy than her younger sister Mary. She prayed her niece would hold her own at the court of Denmark, with a husband twenty years older than her, about whom talk had circulated.

Christian of Denmark was said to be ruled by his mistress and her mother. Isabella would be hard put to oust them once she arrived, just as Margaret's childhood friend Louise of Savoy had once been when she had discovered her new husband's mistress installed in the home she came to as a new bride. But Margaret had no intention of sending Isabella to Denmark until a few years had passed. There would be time enough to prepare her for what might lie ahead.

Glancing at her nephew, she saw that he danced with Thomas Boleyn's daughter. There was another graceful bloom, but with a difference. The English demoiselle's face and form were as delicate and small-boned as Isabella's. But her wit was razor-sharp and her manner as confident as she had been at that age. Watching the two together, Margaret noted *la Boullan* managing the much taller archduke with the skill of a grown woman.

"Sir Wingfield has stopped haranguing me about the archduke's wedding," Margaret told Gattinara, seated next to her. She had not invited the English envoy to attend, mostly because preparations had been so rushed. But she was also miffed that the English king had gone silent over the past few months.

"The archduke appears to be enjoying himself," her counsellor replied, dodging her remark.

"He does seem in high spirits, doesn't he?" Margaret thought of how distant her nephew had been with her lately.

"He is in good hands with Mademoiselle Boleyn," Gattinara observed.

Both watched as Charles twirled the English demoiselle in a lively *allemande*. As she reeled in towards him, she turned up her face in a regal pose. With lightning speed, she offered him a smile, then withdrew it just as quickly.

Margaret's heart leaped as she saw the archduke smile in return. "I don't know when I last saw him smile like that." Her dutiful, adoring nephew had escaped her these past few years. At age fourteen he was on his way to manhood, intent on leaving his minders behind.

"Youth has its joys, Madame. He'll return to you in time," Gattinara encouraged.

"May it be sooner, rather than later," Margaret grumbled.

Gattinara shot her a sympathetic look. "It takes time."

"Yet King Henry wanted him married off already." What had happened to the English king's complaints? In the past month his missives had dried up, along with her father's, on the other side of the Rhine. Something was brewing.

Gattinara sipped his wine. "An excellent vintage," he complimented, avoiding the issue.

Margaret sat back and took in the dancers as her mind raced. King Henry had backed off and now she was left to wonder in what direction he was turning. She shuddered. Europe's chessboard had reconfigured since January, with Anne of Brittany's death. France's king was free to marry again. God forbid it would be to the English princess. "Do you sense a shift in tone from the English?" she pressed.

Gattinara looked her in the eye, his answer blunt. "I would guess they have tired of the emperor dodging their requests."

"It is no wonder. But we are in treaty agreement."

"The emperor has already let slip the deadline for its terms," Gattinara observed.

Margaret shook her head, trying to brush off her misgivings. "Something has changed, and I must know what it is."

"Was it not Heraclitus who said the only constant in life is change, my lady?"

"I don't care who said it; I need England to stick to our plan."

"Madame, it is possible that the English king said something similar about your father sticking to their agreement." Gattinara's tone was delicate.

"I am fed up with all these princes changing plans."

"Then at least be proud that you and Princess Isabella have not changed yours."

Margaret tried to smile but didn't succeed. Seeking distraction, she turned again to the dance floor. Charles had switched partners to the Middelbourg girl. Margaret took in her blank, expressionless face. She was without flaw, the most highborn of all her demoiselles. But she did not appear to incite the archduke's interest, nor her own.

As the music changed, Margaret saw her nephew give a slight bow then head to the refreshments table. The *Boullan* girl moved in the same direction. The moment he passed her, she stumbled slightly. Charles put an arm out to catch her. As he did, Anne whispered something in his ear, eliciting a grin.

Silently, Margaret admired the English girl's charm. If only Mary Tudor could wait a few more years, perhaps she could work similar beguilements on Europe's future most powerful leader.

*

"*Ma Boullan*," Lady Margaret called out the following morning.

"Yes, Madame." Anne stopped at the door on her way from her mistress's bedchamber. She held naughty Babou in her arms. He had escaped the ground floor again and had been found on Lady Margaret's bed that morning.

The archduchess sipped her tisane, eyes sharp even in the dim light. "Tomorrow's lecture. You must listen closely."

Anne held Babou tighter. "Why is that, Madame?"

A smile played on Lady Margaret's lips as she lowered her cup. "The topic is important for you."

Anne straightened. "What is it, Madame?"

The dog's ears perked up.

Lady Margaret leaned back, her gaze lingering on Anne for a moment before she spoke. "You will find out soon enough. Just listen carefully. I arranged it with you in mind."

A blend of gratitude and unease crossed Anne's face. "Thank you, Madame."

"Do not thank me yet. "It won't be easy, but you must learn it to reach your full potential."

Anne looked at her with wide eyes. "Oh, Madame, I so wish to do so."

"I know. Your father wishes the same for you, and you have inherited his ambition."

"Is it a bad thing, Madame?" Anne asked.

Lady Margaret's expression shifted slightly. "It is a thing you cannot escape. But you must learn to manage it, lest it rule you. The art of living well is the art of mastering what is within your reach."

"But how do you manage the leaders of all seventeen of your provinces, Madame, without being driven mad?"

Lady Margaret's laugh was deep and genuine. "The trick, *ma chère*, is to make them want to do what I want them to do."

*

The next morning Anne dressed carefully as she mulled over Lady Margaret's cryptic words. Would it be the scholar Erasmus who would give that day's lecture? She doubted it would be Madame Filiberti. She had heard she was in Antwerp, joining her husband for an important art show. Would she wear her ostrich plume for the occasion? Anne giggled, thinking even the finest of Antwerp's portrait artists could not capture the Italian's *sprezzatura*.

Putting on a slim silver necklace below the pearl one Lady Margaret had given her for the new year's gift, Anne admired herself in the Venetian looking glass on the wall. In its reflection, Anne saw Agnes rise from the bed and drift towards her. She stiffened. Was her haughty bedmate about to speak to her? Perhaps Agnes had noted the archduke laughing with her at the wedding festivities the day before. She had used Agnes's tactics on him — a slight delay before answering, a ravishing smile quickly withdrawn. To her astonishment, Charles of Habsburg had smiled back.

"One or the other. Not both," Agnes advised, her eyes fixed on Anne's reflection.

Anne's fingers tightened around the pearls. As usual, Agnes was right. It was just what Madame Filiberti would have said, too, if she were there.

"I was about to take one off," Anne lied, her voice tight.

The older girl sniffed, then turned and walked away.

"Which one should I wear?" Anne called out, regretting it the moment the words left her mouth.

Agnes shrugged, her indifference more cutting than any insult. Jaw clenched, Anne ripped the pearl necklace from her neck, leaving only the silver one. Why should she care what Agnes thought or did? And why did that queenly snob always know what to do in any situation? She guessed what Barbe or Jeanne might say. It would be because Agnes was to the manner born and she wasn't. The thought infuriated her.

Yanking her side of the bedcovers straight, Anne rumpled the side Agnes slept on. Head held high, she swept from the room, ready for the day's court games. She would play to win.

In the lecture hall, excitement buzzed through the air as Lady Elisabeth stepped forward. "Today, we will have a special speaker on a topic of paramount importance."

"Who will it be? What is the topic?" Girls' voices filled the air.

"Calm yourselves, Mesdemoiselles." Lady Elisabeth's tone was brisk. "You will find out soon enough."

Two pages entered the room and took up positions on either side of the doorway. The demoiselles stirred, their chatter dying down as they strained to see who would come through the door.

In a formal entrance, Lady Elisabeth walked into the room then turned and made a deep curtsey to the figure following. To Anne's surprise, Lady Margaret appeared in the doorway. The demoiselles curtseyed in unison as their host and benefactor entered the lecture room.

"Good morning, *mes filles*," she greeted.

"Good morning, Madame," the demoiselles replied from all corners of the room.

The regent settled herself in the massive oak armchair that had been placed on a dais at the front of the room. "I am here today to explain a concept to you that none of your lecturers have dared to take on," she began.

At that, Lady Elisabeth smiled.

Lady Margaret fixed her eyes on her. "Remind me why you refused my topic."

"Madame, there is no one more qualified to speak on today's subject than you," Lady Elisabeth said.

"I see. And I trust my council members might think the same." Lady Margaret leaned forward, sweeping the room with her eyes. "But we must not let them know of this lecture, for what I am to share is for you to take to heart and use with others, as I do with those I manage."

"What is the topic, Madame?" an eager voice called out.

Lady Margaret nodded to Lady Elisabeth. "Tell them."

"Madame the Regent will speak —" Lady Elisabeth paused for effect — "on how to get others to do what you want."

Anne's pulse quickened. Her words echoed the lesson Lady Margaret had hinted at the day before.

"Have any of you ever wished you could get someone to do something you wanted them to do?" Lady Margaret opened.

"Yes, Madame!"

Anne thought of her father. Barbe and Jeanne, too.

Lady Margaret leaned back in her chair, appearing to enjoy the chorus of responses to her opening query. "And how do you think I get my way when I am up against someone with another idea?"

"You tell them that you are the ruler, and they are not," Barbe called out.

Lady Margaret laughed, a confident ease to her tones. "I told my lord the Duke of Guelders that last year, and it did nothing to stop him from raiding my lands."

"Then how did you stop him?" Barbe asked.

"I found a way to make him think it was his idea to stop."

Barbe looked puzzled. "So, you won him over to your side?"

Lady Margaret wagged a finger. "Do not put it that way, *ma fille*. Especially not with powerful men. They must never think that they have been won over by anyone, especially by a woman."

"Then how did you manage him?"

"I sent a letter of thanks for the peace agreement he signed with me years ago. I didn't mention his repeated breaches. Instead, I reminded him that when it was in effect, we had basked in the prosperity of our people." Lady Margaret's eyes twinkled. "With it, I sent a tapestry of his father wearing the collar that my grandfather had given him long ago when he knighted him in the Order of the Golden Fleece."

"And how did he respond?"

"He replied with a note and a brace of quails, suggesting we extend our agreement."

"Did he stop his attacks?"

Lady Margaret's smile broadened. "He did. I drafted an extension of the 1508 agreement and sent it to him, along with a fine bitch from my hound's latest litter."

"Did he sign, Madame?"

Lady Margaret chortled. "He did, indeed." She put a finger to her lips. "But what must remain hidden is that his suggestion was the one I wanted all along."

"Why must it remain hidden, Madame?"

"Because everyone wishes to think they have made their own decision."

"What do you mean?" Barbe pressed.

"All of us strive to get our own way. So, when dealing with someone who crosses you, the trick is to make him want what you want, then praise him when he delivers into your hands the goal you sought all along."

Claude de Saillant waved a hand. "My mother does that with my father when she wants to shop for something on market days and he doesn't wish to wait for her."

Lady Margaret's eyes danced. "Tell us more, *ma chère*."

"She finds out about a bearbaiting or a wrestling contest, or some such event, then mentions it to my father and says, 'If you please, my lord, go and watch it. I'll do a few errands and meet you at the tavern when you're finished.'"

Lady Margaret's mouth pursed. "I'm sure your mother doesn't care to visit taverns."

"No. She wishes to shop. But she knows my father enjoys ending his market day at the tavern, so she wags a double pleasure before him, to which he agrees."

"Your mother is wise."

"Yes, Madame. She gets her way most of the time."

"And she will teach you to do the same," Lady Margaret predicted.

Claude looked pleased. "I hope so, Madame."

"We see from this example that the method to get one's way is to look as if you are giving your opponent his."

"Why must women play such tricks?" Barbe spoke up.

Watching her, Anne sensed she could count on Barbe not to play tricks. She could be devilish, but she was not a trickster.

"'Tis not a trick, but a tactic used by both men and women," Lady Margaret explained. "Clever rulers everywhere use such tactics to achieve their aims without going to war."

"But men like to go to war, do they not?" Jeanne asked.

"Young, rash men can be swept up by the idea of war. But most men who have been to war would rather they never do so again."

"But don't kings often make war?" Jeanne persisted.

"Foolish kings do. Wise ones avoid it."

"What do they do instead?"

"They tie the interests of their enemy to their own. Then they sway those interests to their side. All without revealing their true intent."

"Who has done so, Madame?"

Lady Margaret leaned forward, the demoiselles mirroring her. "Once, there was a king of France," she began.

A hush fell over the room.

"His name was Louis XI, but everyone called him the Spider King," she continued. "He spun a web so strong that none could escape it. And all without shedding a drop of blood."

"Was he liked?" Jeanne asked.

Lady Margaret shook her head. "No, *ma chère*. He was hated by many. But he was powerful and got what he wanted."

"Did you know him, Madame?"

Lady Margaret waved a dismissive hand. "I was caught in his web, and if a greater plum hadn't come along, I would have become wife to his son, the future king of France."

"Would you have been happy?"

Lady Margaret considered. "Perhaps not. I like to rule, not to sit next to one who does." She sat back in her chair, the picture of a satisfied ruler.

Anne tucked her mistress's words away. She liked the sound of them.

"Do you advise us to put a greater opportunity before those who oppose us to sway them to our aim?" Jeanne summed up.

"Precisely. I will let your parents know you've excelled at today's lesson, though I'll keep its details to myself."

Jeanne beamed as Anne considered her question. Her rival's words made good sense, at times. Why then did they always turn into poisoned arrows when shot in her direction?

"Madame, how do you manage when your plan doesn't work?" Françoise asked.

"I bide my time and look for opportunity," Lady Margaret responded.

"What if there is no opportunity in sight?"

Lady Margaret raised a finger. "Sooner or later, opportunity arises. Then you must bend it into the shape your opponent finds most attractive."

"Are your most powerful opponents men, Madame?"

"They are now. But when I was a girl, the one who brought me to France to become its queen was a woman."

"Really, Madame? Do tell!"

"In my youth, a powerful ruler emerged in France." Lady Margaret's tone grew measured, as if reciting an ancient tale. "The Spider King died when I was just three. His daughter, Anne of France, took his place." Her voice dropped. "All referred to her as Madame la Grande."

Laughter bubbled up from the audience. "You're our Madame la Grande!" Claude called out.

"Thank you, *ma chère*, but 'Madame' will do."

"Was she the one whose book you wished us to read?"

"The same. I trust you've all studied it."

A silence fell over the room as the demoiselles avoided Lady Margaret's gaze. Finally, Barbe spoke up. "What was she like?"

"Clever. Like her father."

"In what way?"

"She wove spider webs wherever she could. And when she had woven one around Brittany, she trapped its ruler and brought her to the throne of France."

"To rule, Madame?"

Lady Margaret shook her head. "To be queen to France's king, who was Madame la Grande's younger brother. And in so doing, to bring Brittany into France's fold."

"Did the Breton ruler agree to this?"

"She had no choice. Her duchy was dwarfed by France, and the French had overrun it. She made the best of a bad situation."

"But weren't *you* brought to France to become its queen?"

"Indeed, I was. And the intent of my entire childhood was wiped out in an instant when Madame la Grande ordered her younger brother to marry Anne of Brittany instead of me."

A collective gasp filled the room. Such details of Lady Margaret's past were new to many, and only vaguely known to Anne. Her father's friend, Sir Broughton, had mentioned bits and pieces as he'd escorted her across the Channel, but nothing in great detail. Once they had arrived, he had handed her over to Lady Margaret's courtier, Monsieur Bouton, who had confined his remarks to the weather and passing landscapes as they travelled to Malines.

"How old were you, Madame?" Anne asked.

"I was eleven, not yet a woman."

Anne shivered. She couldn't imagine their commanding leader in such dreadful straits.

"Madame, what did you do?"

"I put on a brave face and soldiered on."

"Oh, Madame, you must have been heartbroken!"

"I was furious. Especially at the woman who had tossed me aside."

"Madame la Grande?"

"Yes, *ma fille*. Anne of France, my mentor and host, turned her favour from me overnight. Yet I was forced to stay in

France for two years more until the return of my dowry could be hammered out."

Lady Margaret waved a hand, and a page appeared with a carafe and goblet. He placed them beside her and poured a glass.

Anne's heart ached for her mistress. She had been duped by the French. No wonder she hated them so. "But Madame, how did you recover from such a blow?" she asked.

"I saw the opportunity in it."

"What opportunity, Madame?"

"The return of my dowry lands meant parts of my own realm of Burgundy were recovered, saved from being swallowed up by France," Lady Margaret explained.

"And now you are its ruler, instead of consort to the ruler of another land," Barbe noted.

Lady Margaret's eyes lit up. "Far more satisfying." She sipped from her goblet, savouring the moment.

The demoiselles buzzed with chatter. Anne marvelled to think that Lady Margaret had been the same age as her at that life-changing moment.

"Now, what more would you like to hear?" Lady Margaret asked, her eyes lively.

"Oh, Madame, we should like more stories about your life!"

"But what about today's lesson?"

"We've learned it, Madame. But your story is far more interesting. Do tell us more!"

Lady Margaret chuckled. "Do you wish to hear about my years in Spain?"

"Yes, Madame! Oh, yes!" a chorus of voices responded.

"Then you shall have to wait until next I find time to address you. I am finished for today," she announced.

"But Madame, we are eager to hear!" Claude pleaded.

"Tales like mine are best savoured in small bites," Lady Margaret said with a smile.

"Then we cannot wait for the next one!" Jeanne said.

"You shall have it. But until then, think on what I have told you today," Lady Margaret counselled.

"That Madame la Grande threw you over?" Barbe asked.

"No, *ma fille*. But rest assured, I will never do such a thing to you, Mesdemoiselles."

A sigh of relief surged through the room.

"What was the lesson again?" Claude asked.

"That you must put it in the head of your opponent to want to do what *you* want him to do. And never let on that you have done so," Lady Margaret reiterated.

"A valuable lesson, Madame!" Jeanne said.

Lady Margaret leaned forward, a finger to her lips. "Keep this between us, *mes filles*."

"We will, Madame," the roomful of demoiselles chorused.

Anne looked around. Her colleagues appeared to be as deeply under Lady Margaret's spell as she was. Their captivating mistress had no equal.

SEVENTEEN

The summer breeze fluttered the edges of Anne's veil as she crossed the stable yard at La Tervuren. The smell of horses and fresh hay filled the air, a familiar scent that always made her restless. Today was no different, but for once, the excitement came not from childish impatience but from something deeper. No longer was she the smallest among the demoiselles. Her slim frame had begun to curve, her height finally catching up. Her courses had begun, too, a strange new mystery she both welcomed and feared. Embracing her budding secrets, she kept more to herself, no longer so dependent on Barbe.

She stood by her palfrey, waiting to mount for an afternoon ride with a few of the others.

"Eh, *Boullan*! Don't shaft me with those pretty eyes," the stable boy whispered as he cupped his hands to give her a boost into the saddle. His eyes lingered on her longer than they had the summer before.

Anne stepped from his hands to gain her seat. After hooking her leg over the pommel, she reached down and cuffed the side of his head.

"Gently, *ma belle*. Remember who's helping you get off this nag," he chided.

Anne kicked the side of her mount, leaving the youth behind in a cloud of dust.

Clear of the stable yards, she pondered his words. No one had spoken to her thus when she arrived at the Court of Savoy as a girl the year before. But now she was a woman.

Glancing over at Agnes de Middelbourg, she wondered how she managed coarse comments from men beneath her station.

And what had Lady Margaret done at her age when a common cur passed a vulgar remark?

Her blood firing, she clucked at her horse and pressed him into a canter, her thoughts straying like the scudding clouds that dotted the azure sky. A few glances at her fellow demoiselles — pink-cheeked and round-bosomed — no longer filled her with envy. She had begun to develop her own battery of charms, ones that had nothing to do with maidenly softness.

Overtaking the others, Anne bounded across the meadows. What joy it was to feel her blood race, her cheeks bloom with roses, and her hair stream out behind, escaping her headdress. She was no longer a girl, but something more — a woman with hidden powers.

At sight of a copse of trees ahead, she reined in her horse. He would be happy to find some leaves to nibble on while she caught her breath. Slowing him to a walk, she entered the thicket of the more forested areas surrounding Lady Margaret's summer retreat, so unlike the flat, open lands around Malines.

A breeze rustled the trees as green and silver leaves shimmered, shot through with shafts of sunlight. With a shiver of pleasure, Anne imagined herself in a fairytale, moving towards an unknown destination.

But all fairytales end. A cry rang out then stopped short. Anne and her mount pricked up their ears. Smoothing her horse's withers to calm him, she rode in the direction of the sound.

Another cry came, a woman's voice. Tightening her grip on her crop, Anne bent low over her mount to escape detection, or an arrow. Were robbers about?

Stealthily, she approached the glade ahead. There, filtered by heavy foliage, a shaft of sunlight rested on a bundle on the ground that moved. And groaned.

Anne caught her breath. It was a man and a maid. What they were doing was easy to guess. She had seen animals at it in the stable yards at home, and in the fields where livestock roamed. Yet this was different. The maid's cries were unlike any Anne had heard before. She couldn't discern if she was willing or not. To Anne's ears, it sounded as if the maid couldn't decide herself.

Unable to tear her gaze away, she watched. Then the maid's eyes flicked open, wide and wild, and met Anne's across the clearing. A furious wave of her hand dismissed Anne.

Anne turned her mount and fled, the scene swirling in her mind. As the stables came into view, she slowed, pondering what she had seen. Lady Margaret always spoke of control, of governing oneself as a ruler governs her realm. But what Anne had witnessed was the opposite of control. The girl in the glade had been swept away by something more powerful than herself.

Anne gripped the reins tighter. Lady Margaret had taught them to be strong, to hold dominion over themselves. No man would have his way with her, unless she was willing.

She flicked her crop through the air. She would not be willing unless it was on her own terms.

Over the next weeks Anne buried the memory of the glade deep within her. Unlike before, she didn't run to Barbe for explanation. Imagining how she would mock such a scene, Anne kept it to herself.

Luxuriating in summer's unfolding, she delighted in its long, lingering days, braiding flower circlets for crowns with the other demoiselles, and enjoying playful glances and whispered flirtations from pages and attendants who accompanied the great lords visiting daily.

Lady Margaret had moved her twice-weekly council meetings to her summer residence. Wherever she went, her government followed, just as her dogs trailed after her from room to room.

Finally, the day arrived when Lady Margaret came again to their morning lessons.

"*Mes filles*, are you ready for the next chapter of my tale?" The rich melody of her voice drew them all nearer.

"Yes, Madame!"

"You may not say so after I've finished," she warned.

The girls settled at her feet, hanging on her every word. Lady Margaret's stories were more than mere lessons — they were windows into another world, one that set them afire. Anne sat among them, silent but watchful, her mind still turning over the scene she had stumbled on in the woods.

"Now, where did I leave off?" Lady Margaret asked.

"In France with Madame la Grande!" Claude cried.

Lady Margaret's laughter bubbled up. "So, you remember."

"How could we forget?" the girl added, breathless with enthusiasm.

"It got more unforgettable once I landed in Spain," Lady Margaret divulged.

"But first, what happened when you left France?" Jeanne asked.

"I returned to Flanders, where my godmother Margaret of Burgundy took me under her wing."

"But where were your parents, Madame?" Agnes asked.

"My mother was dead, my father back in Austria." Her tone even, Lady Margaret looked unconcerned.

A soft murmur ran through the group. "How awful, to lose your mother," Françoise, always gentle, remarked.

Lady Margaret reached out and smoothed the girl's headdress. "I was only two. I remember little."

Anne had always thought of Françoise as weak, but now she wasn't so sure. Maybe tenderness wasn't a weakness; it was just something her family had never encouraged.

"What happened to her, Madame?" Claude asked, her voice hushed.

"She died doing what she loved."

"And what was that, Madame?" Jeanne ventured.

"She was hawking, and her horse threw her."

A gasp arose as Anne remembered the tale Semmonet had told her.

"How terrible!" Françoise cried.

"Terrible for my father, left with two young children and no wife," Lady Margaret said matter-of-factly.

"What did he do?"

"He was in a difficult situation. He had come to Burgundy to marry its duchess, but the nobles didn't like him."

"Did he go back to Austria?" Barbe asked.

"Eventually. But the nobles forced him to leave my brother, Philip, behind to be raised in Brussels."

"Why so?"

"Because Philip was Burgundy's ducal heir," Lady Margaret explained.

"And you?"

"My father wished to bring the Habsburg bloodline to the French throne. So, he negotiated a marriage contract with the king of France to make me his son's wife."

"The Spider King?"

Lady Margaret nodded. "The same. And the Spider King's condition was that I was to be raised in France to prepare to become queen one day."

Françoise leaned in. "Your father must have been sad to lose both his children."

"He was young, twenty-three years old. We were separated by distance but have always been close." Lady Margaret's face softened. "He is a great man."

"If he is your father, he must be a great man, indeed," Françoise remarked.

Anne met Isabelle de Longueval's eyes. How they both longed to feel the same way about their own fathers.

"But how did you end up in Spain?" Jeanne asked.

"Once I returned to Flanders, I was of marriageable age and my father became Holy Roman Emperor. He made brilliant matches for my brother and me."

"Better than the one in France?"

"Much better. I was to become Queen of Spain, with all its wealth from the New World." Lady Margaret sat back, very much the picture of a queen.

The group leaned in, entranced. "Who was he, Madame?"

"Juan, Prince of Asturias," the archduchess related, her voice proud.

"The Prince of Asturias?" Barbe echoed. "I've never heard of him."

"You've heard of his parents." Lady Margaret scanned their faces for understanding. She leaned forward, her voice reverential. "Queen Isabella and King Ferdinand of Spain."

Murmurs filled the room. Everyone knew of the Catholic monarchs; their rule was the stuff of legend. Anne's mind raced with thoughts of Spain, its vast riches, and its powerful rulers. Their daughter now sat on England's throne as its queen.

"Oh, Madame," Claude said, "did you go to Spain to marry him?"

Lady Margaret nodded. "His sister travelled to Brussels to marry my brother. And I sailed to Spain on the same ship she came over on."

"What an adventure!" Isabelle cried.

Lady Margaret's face darkened. "A nightmare. We nearly sank in a storm in the Bay of Biscay."

"How did you get through it?"

"I kept my head and wrote my own epitaph to keep my mind off the storm." Lady Margaret's smile was wry. "It was short and to the point. 'Here lies Margaret, the willing bride, twice married — but a virgin when she died.'"

Laughter erupted, mingled with awe, as the girls took in her courage and sharp wit in the face of death.

"Thank God you were spared," Claude remarked.

"Yes. Because I was greeted by my prince, who was as handsome and refined as any I have ever met." Lady Margaret's gaze softened. "And his mother treated me like a daughter. Warm and welcoming, nothing like Madame la Grande, except that they were both strong rulers."

"And then?" Barbe ventured.

Lady Margaret's eyes dimmed. "I married him in Burgos…"

Anne's insides tightened. Her mistress's face told her there was something darker to this story. "And then what happened?" she asked.

"We spent six months on a joyous wedding trip through Spain." Lady Margaret's tone no longer matched her words.

"You were happy with your prince?"

Lady Margaret gave an intimate smile. "I was overjoyed."

Anne wondered at her mistress's words. Apparently, casting off her virginity had suited her. She wasn't sure if she would feel the same. "And what next?"

"We reached Salamanca, where we were to be fêted in a grand celebration."

"And were you?"

Lady Margaret shook her head, her eyes growing dim. "My prince fell sick."

"Oh no, Madame!"

"Fever gripped him and in three days he was gone."

A gasp filled the air, thick with shock.

"You must have been devastated, Madame."

"I was. But I was also expecting his child."

Another wave of shock swept the room. All knew that Lady Margaret had no children of her own.

Françoise broke the silence. "What happened, Madame?"

"I carried the babe until it was time." Lady Margaret fixed her eyes over the heads of her audience. "But my princess arrived with no breath of life."

Anne's thoughts flew to her mother. She had lost two sons at birth. The room remained still, filled with unspeakable sorrow.

"But I was eighteen and strong," Lady Margaret continued. "I recovered and my mother-in-law cared for me, requesting that I teach French to her youngest daughter."

I know who that is, Anne thought. But this time she didn't blurt out her knowledge.

"Tell them, *ma Boullan*," Lady Margaret directed.

The girls turned to Anne with wide eyes.

"Was she Queen Katherine of England, Madame?" Anne asked.

"Indeed, she was. Catarina was twelve at the time and I was like an older sister to her. We sat in the gardens of the Alhambra, and I taught her French just as Monsieur Semmonet teaches you."

Anne dipped her head to hide her satisfaction at being addressed by Lady Margaret. She was done with fanning the envy of the others. It hadn't got her far. Instead, she thought of her mother, who had confided that Queen Katherine had the most laughable Spanish accent, but that was not to be repeated to anyone. "And then what happened, Madame?" she asked.

"I spent the next year there, recovering and helping Catarina prepare to travel to England to meet Prince Arthur."

"Prince Arthur?" Claude asked.

Lady Margaret motioned to Anne. "Explain."

Anne addressed the group. "Queen Katherine came to England to marry Prince Arthur of England, the older brother of King Henry. But just as befell Lady Margaret, her prince died soon after their marriage. So, she married his younger brother when he became king."

"She had a long wait, too," Lady Margaret remarked.

Anne had heard plenty about it. Her parents had discussed Queen Katherine's early years in England many times. Before the old king had died, the Spanish princess had waited six long years while Henry Tudor pondered what to do with her.

"What do you mean, Madame?" Isabelle asked.

"She had the same problem I had in France," Lady Margaret related. "Her father-in-law didn't wish to return her dowry, so she was stuck in limbo until he died, and she married the new king."

Anne thought of her parents. They had been in rare agreement that Henry Tudor had treated Katherine of Aragon poorly, neglecting to fund her household and withholding her dowry revenues.

"What happened next, Madame?" Jeanne asked.

"I returned to Flanders to Margaret of Burgundy's care," Lady Margaret said.

Anne beamed to think that Margaret of Burgundy was a fellow Englishwoman. But she wouldn't betray her pride by mentioning it to the others. What mattered was that she felt it inside.

"Then what happened, Madame?"

Lady Margaret turned an amused eye on Jeanne. "I was nineteen, sole princess of Burgundy, and dowager princess of Spain. What do you think happened?"

"Your father found another husband for you!" Isabelle called out.

Lady Margaret smiled, a secretive gleam in her eyes. "Exactly. But that, my dears, is a tale for another day."

A chorus of disappointed voices arose. "No, Madame, tell us now!"

"If I find a moment, I will sit down with you again before we return to Malines." Lady Margaret rose and swept from the room like the queen she almost was.

The summer weeks rolled by in a bright haze of picnics, archery competitions, and riding. Anne returned to the copse where she had come across the man and the maid but didn't find them there again. Still troubled by what she had seen, she firmed her resolve — she would not surrender her maidenhood until she was sure it would offer all that she wanted. Never would she give herself to some rash knave in a forest glade.

When Lady Margaret addressed them again, the demoiselles were overjoyed. Vying to be closest to her, they grouped their cushions into a tight circle around where she sat.

"*Mes filles*," Lady Margaret began, her voice a warm hum, "do you recall where I left off?"

"You were back in Flanders, and your father was about to marry you off again," Claude said.

"Ah, yes. My father had found someone new, but I wasn't so keen."

"Why not, Madame?"

"He was only a duke."

Anne's pulse quickened. Her mistress had been betrothed to the French king and married to the heir to the Spanish throne. A duke would indeed seem a comedown.

"But then," Lady Margaret continued, "a most incredible thing happened. Can anyone guess?"

"You fell in love?" Barbe ventured.

"I did. But that was after I met him. What changed my mind before, was that I discovered he and I had been childhood friends."

"But you dislike the French, Madame. Is it not so?" Françoise asked.

Lady Margaret's lips pressed together. "It is. But this prince was not French. He was the Duke of Savoy." She scanned her audience. "Who among you knows where Savoy is?"

Anne racked her brain and came up short. After a moment of chatter, Jeanne asked, "Is it the kingdom between France and Switzerland?"

"Not only between France and Switzerland, but what other realm?"

"Is it Milan, Madame?" Barbe asked.

"Just so, my sage one. A strategic realm, as Savoy controls the pass through the Alps to get to Italy."

Barbe beamed. "Was that why your father wanted you to marry its ruler?"

Lady Margaret slapped the arm of her chair and chuckled. "Of course it was. My father wanted to control the pass to block the French from crossing into Milan." She raised both brows in disdain. "One of their endless attempts to seize it."

Anne pondered the titbit her mistress had dropped. There was much to learn at her court, situated as it was between the Holy Roman Empire and France. Semmonet had told her that Europe's up and coming realms were Spain and Portugal, with their seafaring explorations. And every European prince had his eye on Italy as a ripe plum to pick. Not only was England not at the centre of the world she now lived in, it wasn't even an afterthought.

"But what was the ruler of Savoy doing in France when you were there?" Barbe asked.

"He was a child at the time, the same age as me. His mother was dead and his father busy with a new family. So he sent his son and daughter to France to be raised by his sister, wife to the old king who was known as…" Lady Margaret looked around.

"The Spider King!" several voices cried.

"My dears, you have taken my tale to heart," Lady Margaret approved, a twinkle in her eye.

"Your tale is more interesting than any I've ever heard!" Françoise said.

Anne agreed. It was becoming more interesting with every chapter.

"My intended was my old childhood friend, Philibert of Savoy." Lady Margaret's mouth curved into a wondrous smile, promising far more than childhood friendship.

"Oh, Madame, what was he like?" Isabelle asked.

A glow lit Lady Margaret's face. "He was the best of the boys I played with."

257

"In what way, Madame?"

"He helped me at archery practice. He was patient and encouraging. Not like the others, who couldn't be bothered."

"What else, Madame?"

Lady Margaret's eyes drifted above the demoiselles, brimming with memories. "He had a good heart. And a joyful spirit. He was never glum, always ready to make good cheer and to lift my spirits when I fell into the doldrums."

"But where is he now, Madame?" Claude asked.

"He rests with the angels, *ma chère*. And waits for me there." Lady Margaret turned aside, a hand to her cheek, as if to hide her thoughts.

Anne's heart fluttered.

"Oh, Madame, I am sorry he died, but do tell us about your marriage!" Claude insisted.

"I travelled to Savoy in November and met him on the first of December outside Geneva."

Anne sat breathless, ready for more.

"The snow had begun to fall when his party came into sight. He rode at the head of it and as he came into view, I saw that my long-ago friend had turned into a most handsome prince."

"In what way, Madame?" Agnes asked.

Anne glanced at her, surprised to see that the discussion of handsome princes had piqued her interest.

"He was well-formed and looked as if he were born in the saddle."

"And his face, Madame?"

"His features seemed cut from marble. Strong and chiselled, with a dimple here," Lady Margaret put a finger to her chin. "Irresistible," she sighed.

Giggles arose from the ranks. Anne could scarcely imagine that Lady Margaret would find anyone irresistible. Then she thought of Charles Brandon, whose daughter had recently joined the court. Lady Margaret held depths she couldn't fathom. But now that she was a woman, Anne saw that there were aspects of herself she couldn't fathom, either.

"His hair was light brown, a shade darker than mine," Lady Margaret continued. "He wore it long, in a straight cut with a fringe, and he looked like a prince from a fairytale."

"And how was his manner?" Jeanne asked.

"His manner was the best of all. When my horse came up to his, he dismounted and knelt at my feet."

A sigh went up.

"He looked up at me and said, 'To gain you as a wife is beyond happiness.'"

The collective sigh deepened.

"Then he helped me down from my horse and the scent of him came over me."

"The scent of your horse?" Claude inquired.

Lady Margaret chuckled as the other demoiselles cast scornful glances. "No, *ma petite*, the scent of my manly young prince, with eyes that didn't leave mine for a moment."

A wondrous hush spread over the demoiselles, each imagining, in her own way, such a scene with herself at its centre.

"Oh, Madame, what next?" Isabelle asked.

"What came next is not for your ears, but it was glorious," Lady Margaret divulged, looking far more swept away than she had at mention of Juan of Asturias. "We spent three blissful years in our mountain home in Savoy. My lord hunted and danced and played in all sorts of athletic tournaments, and I — " She paused, her gaze lifting as though seeing those days anew. "I ruled Savoy."

Anne sprang to attention.

"Why did your husband not rule?" Barbe asked.

"He was too busy embracing life to attend to ruling his duchy. But I enjoyed all of its details. After a time, I learned the concerns of each region and took over the meetings he didn't wish to head."

"Did you learn the skills there, Madame, that you put to use here to rule the Netherlands?"

"Just so, *ma chère*. And when I came to the Netherlands, I brought my most trusted counsellors, who have stayed with me ever since."

"Oh, Madame, is that why you named your palace the Court of Savoy?"

"It is, *ma fille*."

"But why did you leave your happy life there?"

"Because even the happiest chapters come to an end." Lady Margaret shifted in her chair, shutting her eyes for a long moment, then opening them. "One day my lord went hunting and drank too deeply from a cold mountain stream."

"Oh, no!" The room rustled with foreboding.

"Oh, yes, *mes filles*. Learn from my tale, for one day you, too, may reach a moment like mine when one chapter ends and another begins."

"What happened, Madame?" the demoiselles clamoured as Anne mulled over chapters in her own life. A new one had begun the day she left England. Another had begun just months earlier, when she had joined the ranks of womanhood. What would the next chapter be?

"My lord's lungs became inflamed." Lady Margaret gazed over the heads of her audience to some faraway place. "He took fever and died."

"Dear God!" Isabelle cried.

"Dear God now holds him in His arms. And I will rest with him again one day in the church I am having built in Savoy."

"But Madame, what if you marry again?" Isabelle asked.

Lady Margaret shook her head. "I shall never marry again. He was my great love, and none can replace him."

A sigh like a breeze rippled across the group and came to rest at Lady Margaret's feet.

Anne thought that no story she had ever heard could be as romantic as the one her mistress had just told.

"Were there no children, Madame?" Barbe asked in her straightforward manner.

"I was his child, and he was mine. We had no need of any more," Lady Margaret said.

Anne mulled over her words, thinking there was more to it than that. Every prince needed an heir, did he not? When Henry Tudor had sued for Lady Margaret's hand, she had refused. Perhaps after her daughter's tragic birth and three childless years with Philibert, Lady Margaret had guessed she was unable to bear more children. It was likely the English king would have wanted a wife who could give him offspring.

"But, Madame, you were so young. Did your father not try to marry you off again?" Barbe asked.

A gossamer laugh floated from the regent's mouth. "He did. But I had got a taste of what pleased me and what didn't. It pleased me to rule, and it did not please me to be sent to another realm where yet another husband might die before his time."

The demoiselles laughed, Anne joining them. Her mistress had been through more in her younger days than any woman she had ever heard of.

"Did you return to Flanders after your lord died?" Jeanne asked.

"Not for several years. Savoy had become my home, and I wished to remain there. But fate intervened."

"What happened, Madame?" Claude asked.

"I will tell you next time."

A groan went up. The archduchess dusted off her gown, as if to shake off her memories. "That is enough for today."

"What can we do to hear the rest?"

"You can attend your lessons, take care of the dogs, and mind that you do not dally with the pages." Lady Margaret's eyes flicked to Agnes de Middelbourg.

It was another ten days before Lady Margaret rejoined the demoiselles in the garden. In the interim Anne kept a close eye on Agnes. The older girl's icy composure appeared to melt when a certain dark-haired page appeared. He served Lady Margaret's important council member, Monsieur Lalaing, and spent an undue amount of time hanging about wherever Agnes was.

Anne marvelled as she watched from a shadowy corner of the loggia near the kitchen pantry. Never had she heard a single laugh escape from the proud demoiselle's mouth. Yet there she stood, giggling and cooing, with her back to the wall and her ardent admirer before her, one hand braced next to her head.

Barbe came up behind Anne. "Think she'll give in?"

"Never." She wished Barbe hadn't appeared. Her mocking observations on whatever they came across had been fun. But Anne was noticing new things that she preferred to weigh without Barbe around to cheapen them.

"So now you're defending the ice maiden? Whose every move you copy?"

"I don't copy her," Anne protested, vowing to no longer do so. Her eyes widened as she watched Agnes allow the page to trail his hand from the wall to her bare shoulder, his fingers grazing her skin.

Barbe's snort was low. "She is on her way, and no one should stop her."

"On her way where?" Anne asked.

"To paradise, my friend."

"What is that supposed to mean? And why should no one stop her? She'll lose her place at court if she goes farther."

"If she does, that will make more room for you to step up." A sly smile crossed Barbe's face as she observed the playful proceedings. The youth now traced the edge of Agnes's bodice.

Anne stared, baffled. Agnes didn't like to be touched. She didn't even like to pick up Lady Margaret's lapdogs. Yet there she was, allowing a page to walk his finger along her neckline. "It makes no sense," she hissed, remembering the scene in the forest glade. The maid's strange cries there hadn't made sense, either.

As the couple moved closer, the girls slipped back into the pantry. "Sense has nothing to do with it." Barbe brought her face close to Anne's. "Wait and see. Your time will come."

Anne backed off. "My time will come only with someone worthy of me."

"That's not how it works," Barbe scoffed.

"That's how I'll make it work." Anne took the cap off a jam jar and sniffed it.

Barbe dipped a finger into the jam, popping it into her mouth. "One day, someone will touch you in a way that excites you until your blood runs wild, and with it, your reason."

"I'll guard my reason, no matter what," Anne retorted. So that was why Lady Elisabeth had told her not to say she was excited about this or that. It seemed that the term had a far more specific meaning in French than in English.

Barbe licked her lips, a knowing smile on her face. "You won't be able to help it."

"I'll never let that happen." The thought of losing control, of surrendering to someone, felt like a betrayal of herself.

Barbe shrugged. "Then join a convent."

"I've no interest in that," Anne huffed.

"That's good, because you would make a poor nun," Barbe needled.

Anne bristled. "Why so?"

Barbe eyed her like a cat toying with a mouse. "Nuns blend in, but you wish to be noticed."

"Maybe I did, but I don't now," Anne said, trying to believe it. In truth, she had wished Barbe hadn't noticed her a moment earlier. But she couldn't tell Barbe that.

"It's not a crime to be who you are. You just don't know how to command attention, instead of demanding it." Barbe's eyes glinted.

The older girl sauntered off as Anne fumed. This time, she couldn't blame Jeanne. It was Barbe who endlessly teased, goading her in predictable ways. Nothing she could do would change it.

Taking a deep breath, she struggled to come up with a solution. Then it came to her. The only thing she could change was her response to attack. It was time to start working on it.

"Who can tell me where I left off?" Lady Margaret's voice floated above the gaggle of demoiselles surrounding her.

Anne stood to one side, avoiding Barbe and Jeanne. She was fed up with the way they made her feel. But the only cure was to stop herself from allowing them to rile her. Until she could master herself, she would keep her distance.

"You were in Savoy, but now you're here, so what happened to make you come home?" Isabelle asked.

Lady Margaret's gaze flickered, the shadow of a memory crossing her face. "Home…" she murmured. "My heart stayed in Savoy when my lord died. But in the autumn of 1506, news came that changed everything."

The girls leaned in. "What was it, Madame?"

Lady Margaret raised a finger, silencing the whispers. "My brother and his wife, Juana, had gone to Spain to claim the throne of Castile. Queen Isabella had left it to her daughter."

"Can women rule in Spain?" Claude asked, wide-eyed.

"In Castile they can. But my brother sought to rule with her, so they went together to claim it as co-rulers. I was at my home in Savoy, deep in plans for building my church, when a messenger arrived." Lady Margaret sighed. "My brother died in Spain, two months after being crowned King of Castile."

"What happened?"

"No one knows, but it is thought he was poisoned. He took ill at dinner one night and was dead within days."

The room quietened, Lady Margaret's grief settling over the girls like a shroud. "Was his wife with him?" Claude asked, breaking the silence.

Lady Margaret's lips formed a thin line. "She was with him, and she remained with him."

"What do you mean?"

"She remained in Spain and didn't return."

Barbe's description of Juana of Castile came to Anne; she had called her Juana the Mad.

"So, you returned to care for his children," Jeanne guessed.

Lady Margaret's eyes sharpened. "Not only that. I came to rule."

"Who ruled at the time?"

Lady Margaret pursed her lips. "My brother did, but while he was in Spain, William de Croy, Lord of Chièvres, served as regent."

"Did you push him out, Madame?" Barbe asked, her arrow flying straight to its mark.

The archduchess cleared her throat. "Let us say I arranged a new position for him." A satisfied smile crossed her face.

The room filled with laughter, but Anne noticed the command in Lady Margaret's demeanour. Power wrapped around her like a cloak, and in that moment, Anne understood why. Lady Margaret had mastered the art of control — not only of others, but of herself.

"Madame, how is it you pushed through so many tragedies to come out on top?" Barbe asked.

"It is where I belong," Lady Margaret said simply. She leaned back in her chair and Babou jumped into her lap.

"The cream rises to the top, does it not, Madame?" Jeanne asked.

Anne glanced at her, seated so close to Barbe that their knees touched. She scoffed to see how hopelessly in thrall Jeanne was. Then, with crushing clarity, Anne saw that she, too, was in thrall.

The archduke Charles picked up his pace, striding across the courtyard and disappearing into the palace as Lady Margaret hurried after him. Anne watched from a distance, noting how deftly he escaped her.

Barbe emerged from the kitchen. "Where do you think he's going?"

"He's trying to get away from Lady Margaret." Why was it that Barbe appeared with greater frequency the more she tried to avoid her?

"An expert on the archduke, are you?" Barbe asked.

"It is obvious, from what I've seen." Turning her back, Anne vowed not to respond to Barbe's prod. If she did, she may as well hand her a sword with which to slash her to shreds.

"As obvious as you are to everyone."

Blood rushed to Anne's head. "What do you mean?" The words tumbled out before she could stifle them. If only she could hold back, Barbe's taunts would belong to Barbe alone. What power that would be — perhaps not over Barbe, but over herself.

"You know well what I mean. You can't hide who you are any more than he can hide that lantern jaw," Barbe jabbed.

"You should stop talking about the archduke that way," Anne said, attempting to steer away from further personal attacks. She conjured up Charles of Habsburg's impassive face. At least he was taking steps to become his own man and move out from under his aunt's sway. Was it not time for her to do the same with Barbe?

"I'm not speaking against him. I'm pointing out what anyone can see, like the way you always need to be noticed."

Anne tried again to shift the focus away from herself. "I thought you were my friend."

"That's the first time you've called me one," Barbe noted.

Anne considered. It was true. She wasn't in the habit of thinking of anyone at court as a friend. Were they not all vying with each other for Lady Margaret's esteem? "If you're my friend, then why are you forever on the attack?"

Barbe looked taken aback. "I only speak the truth."

"You speak out of turn, and I'm done with it." Anne kept her tone calm and low, surprising herself.

"Then so am I." Barbe walked to the doorway and stepped through it.

This time, Anne didn't follow with her eyes. Instead, she went to the door and shut it. Memories of merry times with Barbe would remain. But she had outgrown her.

EIGHTEEN

Margaret sat with Gattinara, enjoying the remains of the day. Sipping on Rhenish wine, they watched the sun's unhurried descent over the North Sea. On her annual summer progress, she was in Zeeland by the beach. Before them, the waves lapped gently, and Margaret smiled to think that England lay just across the waters. What pleasure to contemplate the strong alliance they would forge when her nephew married the English princess. And, finally, the Duke of Guelders had laid down his arms. God knew how long their peace agreement would hold, but nothing lasted forever. At least she found herself in a good moment.

"A messenger to see you, Madame," an attendant murmured, his tone low as if not to break her mood.

"Bring him to me," she bade. God's bones, what did it take to enjoy a few peaceful moments without being interrupted?

She looked around and spotted a man trudging across the sand, his gait weary. He appeared to have travelled in haste with whatever news he brought.

"Lady Margaret, I bear tidings from England." A gust of wind blew his words out to sea as he garbled his message.

"What did you say?" Margaret asked, hoping she had heard wrong.

"The English princess has been promised to the King of France," the messenger repeated.

The stillness of the summer sunset shattered. "Impossible. She is contracted to marry the archduke." With wide eyes, she turned to her counsellor.

"The agreement was signed in Paris on the seventh of August, my lady," the messenger continued.

Margaret's hands tightened on the arms of her chair. "Then it must be stopped."

"It is already done, Madame. The proxy marriage took place in London last week." The finality in the man's voice stabbed like a dagger thrust.

"But how did it come about?" Margaret's stomach churned. It was what she had feared might happen. Spring had passed into summer and no word from England, or her father, had arrived regarding the archduke's marriage to Mary Tudor.

"It is said that King Henry began talks with the French king in late March," the messenger related.

Margaret scowled, sickened to think it had been just after Wingfield had visited. If only she could have pinned down a wedding date. "And when do they deliver the bride?"

"It is said that Princess Mary will travel to France in early October for the wedding."

Her mouth filled with the bitterness of missed opportunities, Margaret swallowed hard. "Go refresh yourself. And do not leave until I give further orders."

After the man disappeared, she pounded her fists on the arms of her chair. "Can you believe this, Monsieur?"

Gattinara let out a heavy sigh. "Such things have happened before and will again."

"That is not the point," she railed. "My nephew has been thrown over. And England is allying with France!"

Her counsellor looked out to sea, his eyes following the sinking sun. "Madame, no alliance between England and France lasts long, so I would not worry overmuch. As for your nephew, he will likely be relieved."

Margaret's anger flared again. "How dare you be so calm?"

"I have seen more summers than you, Madame. Alliances come and go, like the tide on the beach." He shielded his brow and looked out to sea as the flaming red sun hovered over it.

"There sets the sun on our best laid plans," Margaret moaned.

Gattinara shot her a rueful glance. "Other plans will rise with the dawn. Ones that will suit you better."

"Nothing could be worse than England siding with France!"

"Madame, do you not think this is but a momentary union? The French king is ailing and likely will not last much longer. The English princess will be widowed, and your hopes will revive once more."

Her hand slammed against her thigh. "I will never trust Henry again."

"And your father?"

"My father is also to blame for this!"

"Perhaps he hesitated for a good reason," Gattinara suggested.

Disgust washed over her. "There's only one reason he hesitates — he needs more money."

"It would seem the English king offered plenty, but the emperor didn't bite," Gattinara pointed out.

Margaret flung up a hand. "My father has no sense of what he spends."

"It is a tendency shared by many born with the noblest of natures, Madame."

"And now my noble father has missed his moment." Margaret stamped her foot, disturbing her greyhound, who retreated a safe distance away.

"Your father is a phoenix, Madame. He will rise again, as he always does."

"You don't know what I go through with him!"

"I know it well, because I have been at your side all these years, watching you manage both him and your disappointments when he went his own way."

Margaret growled low in her throat. "He is now proving unmanageable."

"Then manage your realm and leave your father to his … pursuits."

She glared at him, but his words rang true. Maximilian had one way to rule, and she had another. His involved mystical moments of knightly allure that convinced his soldiers to fight without pay — but only up to a certain point. Hers involved hard-won trade agreements and keeping the peace to ensure the flow of commerce, both of which won her people's respect.

Raising her glass, she forced a smile. "Let us drink to managing our affairs and not worrying about the way others manage theirs."

Gattinara lifted his cup. "May the sun set on your worries, Madame."

"At least for today, Monsieur."

They looked out to the horizon as the sun sank into the sea. Then they turned to each other and laughed, a cynical edge sharpening their tones.

Once back in Malines, Margaret's gaze fell upon the envelope resting on her desk, its seal from Greenwich unmistakable. Thomas Boleyn's elegant scrawl stared back at her. Picking it up, she thought fondly of the witty man who had graced so many of her evening entertainments. She had missed him, but at least she had his daughter to offer the same high spirits and sharp wit.

Eager to learn if he would be paying a visit, she scanned its contents.

"*By the saints!*" she cried, the letter fluttering to the floor.

Europe's chessboard had reconfigured. Boleyn was requesting an end to his daughter's service. *La petite Boullan* was to take up a new appointment to serve Princess Mary of England in France.

Swallowing her bile, Margaret tried not to take his request personally. Yet the sting of rejection rose within her. The same royal court that had discarded her after she had spent her childhood there would now welcome Mary Tudor of England, attended by the girl whose French Margaret was responsible for perfecting.

La Boullan would be whisked from her service to join the court of her enemies. With pent-up fury, she stomped on the discarded letter. No doubt her bright maid of honour would be delighted to hear of her new appointment.

All eyes were now on France. Louis XII, an ageing king, was to wed the young Mary Tudor. If she bore him a son, the French succession would be secure, dashing the hopes of Margaret's former sister-in-law, Louise of Savoy, and her son, Francis, now Louis' designated heir. The balance of power could tilt in an instant.

A cascade of long-buried memories washed over Margaret. Playing boules with Louise and Philibert on the great lawn at Amboise. Louis, Duke of Orleans, now Louis XII of France, joining them, his handsome face and lean, athletic form matched by flawless manners. He had been invariably kind to her, even after she had been tossed away by Charles VIII in the heartless masterstroke his older sister had forced on him.

Louis had also been thrown over by Anne of France. When the Spider King had died, Louis had expected to become regent during Charles's minority, as his closest male relative. But Anne of France had shouldered him aside, assuming the regency herself as the Spider King's favourite child.

In anger, Louis had fled to Brittany and fought on the side of the Bretons in the Mad War with France. When the Bretons lost, Anne of France had imprisoned him for six years, ageing him before his time.

The sting grew stronger. Not wishing to admit it, Margaret had entertained a moment of hope when her former father-in-law, Ferdinand of Aragon, had suggested a match between her and Louis. But the French would always remain enemies of the House of Habsburg, despite her warm memories of the French king. Besides, she could guess that he had looked for a younger bride to supply him with the male heir he had longed for his entire life.

Tracing the smooth surface of her Indian bust, she mulled over who would gain their heart's desire with the French succession. Would it be Louis, with the birth of a son, or Louise of Savoy, with her son set to inherit the throne? And where did Mary Tudor stand in all this? Was it her wish to be tied to an ailing old man almost three times her age? Or did she count on Louis not lasting long so she could collect her dowager queen's revenues and marry a man of her own choosing?

As she called for her page, an idle thought entered her head. Who might Mary Tudor's own choice be?

Margaret's voice sliced through the air. "Mademoiselle *Boullan* is leaving us," she announced as Lady Elisabeth entered the room.

"Oh no, Madame. Has something happened in her family?"

Margaret's lips thinned. "Not in her family. She's been summoned by the English princess."

"To England?" Lady Elisabeth's brow furrowed.

"No." Margaret's smile didn't reach her eyes. "To France."

Lady Elisabeth gaped. "France? Why France?"

"Mary Tudor is to marry the French king." The words hung heavy between them.

Lady Elisabeth's eyebrows rose almost to her hairline. "Is that so, Madame? I had heard some rumours, but I had thought she was to marry the archduke," she stammered.

Margaret summoned her self-possession, honed by years of training under Anne of France. "A change of plans. The archduke is not ready to marry, and the king of France is."

"The poor girl will be marrying an old man."

Margaret sniffed. "It's not the first time such a thing has happened."

"No, Madame, and it will not be the last. Thankfully for her, he is rich, and she will be Queen of France."

"Yes, it is some compensation. Go and tell *la Boullan* she must prepare, as her time here is coming to an end."

"She'll be devastated," Lady Elisabeth remarked.

Margaret snorted. "She'll be far from devastated once she learns where she's heading. She'll be able to translate all the sweet talk the French king offers his bride."

Lady Elisabeth chuckled. "I doubt that the French king will let any of the English princess's entourage anywhere near their private quarters."

"Her father will send an escort to collect her."

"Are you not sad to see her go?" Lady Elisabeth asked.

"Of course I am. But she is needed elsewhere for another mission. As was I, more than once."

"And look at where you have ended up!" Lady Elisabeth noted, brightening the mood. "At the very centre of the map."

"Let us ensure that its centre doesn't shift to France," Margaret said dryly.

"Of course it won't. How can it, with you in charge of the archduke, who will rule over far greater lands?"

"A refreshing thought. Now, go and give *la Boullan* her news. We will make good cheer and send her off in style."

"On my way, Madame. And may she be grateful for all you have taught her."

Margaret waved her out. One day her promising demoiselle would put to use all she had learned at the Court of Savoy. The little one was cast in her father's mould. If only she could master her headstrong nature, she would go far.

Anne froze. "My father requested me?" The words felt foreign on her lips; a stone weight dropped into her stomach. "Why, Madame? Is my mother unwell?"

Lady Elisabeth smiled. "All is well, little one. You have been chosen by Princess Mary of England to join her in France."

"In France?" Anne trembled. Her heart pounded as images of grand ballrooms and glittering gowns filled her mind. "But why?"

"The princess is marrying the French king."

"But — but will Lady Margaret let me go?" Anne asked, eyeing the garment the *mère des filles* was folding. What gowns would she wear at the French court? And what untold pleasures waited there?

"Of course she will. Your father has written, and an escort will come for you."

"Oh, Madame, so many changes!"

"I know, *ma petite*. Lady Margaret thinks so, too. But such is the way of the world."

Anne's spirits danced. "When do I leave, Madame?"

"As soon as Lady Margaret has made arrangements."

"I'll have time to say goodbye, won't I?" Anne's thoughts ran wild as she pictured joining Mary Tudor's court. Erasmus had called her the most beautiful princess in Europe. She was young. There would be parties and dances, laughter and merriment. What fun it would be!

"You'll have time to say goodbye to all who are fond of you here, so they may wish you the best and see you off." With a sweep of her gown, Lady Elisabeth turned and left the room.

Falling back on her bed, Anne couldn't believe her good fortune. Mary Tudor had chosen her, over others, to serve her in France! Disappointments with her father scattered like dandelion puffs in the breeze. Whatever he hadn't done, he must have sung her praises to the king's sister to achieve this appointment. As for all who were fond of her at the Court of Savoy, she wasn't sure there were many. Semmonet would miss her, and Barbe would have one less sparring partner. As for the others, some would be jealous, others indifferent.

Rolling onto her stomach, Anne laughed with joy. To think she would put to good use all she had learned here. It was an opportunity beyond comparison. Armed with a command of French, she was ready.

"What's all the giggling about?" a voice called.

Anne turned to see Barbe approach. "You will not believe what has happened," she said, bubbling over.

"Let me guess. You have been chosen to marry the archduke since he has been jilted by the English princess."

Anne gasped. "You knew about that?"

"Lady Margaret's page just spilled the news. Everyone is talking about it in the kitchen."

"No. Even better than that!" Anne cried, unable to resist heightening the drama.

"Agnes has been discovered to be with child and sent home in disgrace, giving you her entire bed!" Barbe plopped down next to her, rumpling the bedcover on Agnes's side.

"No, guess again!"

"You are to marry the King of England and must leave immediately to prepare," Barbe jested.

"He's already married, but you're on the right track," Anne teased. "Princess Mary is marrying the King of France and I'm called to serve at her court!"

Barbe sat up, eyeing her critically. "I suppose all those lessons with Semmonet paid off."

Anne felt a twinge of sadness. Despite their differences, she would miss Barbe. But in her heart, she had already left her. "What will I do without you, *ma Barbe*?"

"You will do just fine, *ma Boullan*." Barbe lobbed a pillow at Anne as they both dissolved into laughter.

Margaret was nettled. She wouldn't rush to accommodate Thomas Boleyn's request.

"You will tell him his daughter won't be ready until next month," she ordered. Boleyn would know her displeasure the moment he opened the letter and saw she had not penned it herself.

Her secretary, Marnix, dipped his quill into the inkwell. "But does he not wish for her to return home so that she may accompany the English princess to France?"

Margaret stared at him, wishing it was Boleyn she was staring down instead. "It does not matter. I can't spare her until October. Tell him to make arrangements accordingly."

"Certainly, Madame. But … he may not be pleased."

"Good," Margaret snapped. "Let him be displeased. It is nothing compared to what I feel."

Marnix gazed at her in admiration. "You will make your point, Madame, by delaying the demoiselle's departure."

"That is my intention," Margaret replied with a sniff.

Her secretary spoke as he scribbled. "Who would have thought that the archduke's intended bride would be offered to the French king instead, my lady?"

"It is a betrayal of our agreement," Margaret stormed, "and I will never trust the English king again." *Nor his duplicitous close friend.* It remained to be seen whether she could trust Charles Brandon's daughter. But she would not dismiss the young girl for the sins of her father.

"Rightly so, Madame. But the situation may soon change, if reports of the French king's failing health are to be believed."

Margaret whirled towards the window, glaring at the horizon. "Indeed, it will change, as everything does. But I'll not let this insult to the House of Habsburg go unanswered."

Marnix spoke carefully. "Should the French king die, the princess will be on the market again. And by then the archduke may be more ready for marriage."

Margaret raised her chin. "Should Mary Tudor be available again, my nephew won't have her. She and her father have broken their promise to us, and we will not treat with them again on her account."

"Understood, Madame. I will finish this letter and bring it to you to sign."

"Finish it now, so I can sign and be done with it."

"Shall I include the usual valedictions?"

"No. Boleyn must know I am not happy about this. No valediction, no best wishes, and no congratulations to be sent on to the bride." Margaret paced as her secretary wrote. In a moment he was finished. She leaned over the short letter and scribbled her name, then pushed it back to Marnix.

"Very good, Madame. I will send this off now."

"I can imagine his face when he opens it. He'll see I'm angered, and he'll choke on thoughts of all the times we've enjoyed together."

Marnix looked curious. "Did you not tell me that Monsieur Boleyn is an ambitious man, Madame?"

"I did. And he is. Let him feel my sting. He needs to know my displeasure so he can report on it to that red-faced pup, his king."

A grin spread across Marnix's features. "Well stated, Madame." With a bow, he left the room, calling for a messenger on his way out.

Margaret pounded the top of the head of her Indian bust. She wished it was King Henry's red-blond head instead. He could go to hell with his new plans to ally with France.

The only alliance worth making in Europe was on the horizon, when her nephew came of age. Then all the rulers of Europe could come bowing and scraping to Charles of Habsburg's door. She would be the one to open it. Or not.

NINETEEN

September swept by like a windblown leaf, the activity of the harvest filling the fields around Malines. Hay bales lay stacked in tidy rolls, their golden hues a stark contrast to the dark, rich earth. Grapes glistened in the sunlight, their sweet aroma mingling with the scent of apples freshly plucked from the branches. Once October was upon them, Anne delighted in the newly crisp autumn air, signalling her own new adventures soon to come.

The day before her escort was to arrive, she tried to pay attention to her lessons, but her mind was far away, leaping ahead to glories unknown. With each passing day she felt herself drift farther towards France's embrace, shedding her childhood and approaching the mysteries of adulthood.

Lady Elisabeth's voice cut through her thoughts, its message sounding much like Madame de Verneuil's. "Above all, you must remember not to speak before thinking."

"Will it get me in more trouble in France than it did here?" Anne asked, her spirits high.

The *mère des filles* wagged a finger, her tone laced with experience. "It will get you in more trouble the older you are."

Anne wrinkled her nose. "But there are times when I just want to say what I think." Now that she was leaving, she had nothing to lose. What fun to tell Lady Elisabeth how she really felt.

"Then be careful about when and with whom you do so."

"I will tell my future husband everything. And no one else," Anne declared, a hint of defiance in her voice.

Lady Elisabeth shook her head, her eyes glinting with hidden truths. "It is never wise to tell one's husband everything."

Anne's brow furrowed. "But don't you?"

"No, little one, I don't. When you get older, you will find that men can be weak in the area of what others think of them. Especially powerful men. If you are married to one, you must shield him from the full truth about himself, even from your own lips."

Anne dug in her heels. No longer would she play the courtier, at least not until she arrived in France. "If I am married to a powerful man, I will tell him what others fear to say, so he knows he can rely on me to be honest."

Lady Elisabeth frowned. "Your role as a wife will be to comfort and support, not to deliver truths that could harm."

"But how can the truth be harmful if it's meant to help someone?" Anne's eyes lit with fervour.

Lady Elisabeth sighed. "*Ma chère*, you speak with the fire of youth. But once age has trimmed your flame, you will see that it's best to hold your tongue when failing to do so may cause more harm than good."

Anne balked. "If I see error in someone's ways, I will let them know." Erasmus's impassioned lectures had fired her, yet she wrestled with his reluctance to criticise the Pope.

"You mustn't go too far," Lady Elisabeth warned.

"I will speak if correction should be made."

Lady Elisabeth tutted. "You will regret it, if you do."

"I'll regret it if I don't live as I believe." Anne thought of the Pope, of such fearsome authority that went unchallenged, and felt a surge of courage. She would not live her life like a timid mouse.

"'Tis not the way of the court," Lady Elisabeth advised.

Anne's eyes flashed. "'Tis my way."

"Then you will need to be head of your own court, for if you serve at someone else's, you must follow their lead, no matter what you privately think."

"Lady Margaret is head of her own court and does what she pleases," Anne pointed out.

"Lady Margaret appears to do as she pleases, but she weighs her words carefully and acts with prudence," Lady Elisabeth amended.

Anne thought of her mistress's weeks of abandon with Charles Brandon one year earlier but said nothing. For the most part, Lady Margaret kept an admirable rein on herself. "Lady Margaret is true to herself. I will follow her example, as she has taught me."

"I would hope she has taught you to be prudent and circumspect in all things."

Anne's mind wandered to other lessons Lady Margaret had imparted. "She has shown me how she wields power."

"Then may you use similar skills of your own to do the same one day," Lady Elisabeth encouraged.

A vision of Lady Margaret's assured demeanour sparked Anne's reply. "They may not be similar, but they will be my own."

"I don't doubt it, little one. If you school your impulses, you will go far."

"I cannot wait!" Anne crowed, dancing around the room.

"Then go and join the others," the *mère des filles* bade. "And show me you have learned something from our conversation."

"I will, Madame!" Anne shot out through the French doors into the garden, on fire to embrace her future.

"I enjoyed overhearing that," Margaret remarked, gliding into the room.

Lady Elisabeth started then sank into a hasty curtsey. "Oh, Madame, I didn't see you there!"

"*Ma Boullan* is full of pepper and spice. She will go far,but—"

"But what, Madame?" Lady Elisabeth asked.

Margaret's gaze was knowing. "You may fill in the rest."

Lady Elisabeth paused, as if hesitant to voice her thoughts. "But will she go too far?"

"Precisely." Margaret locked eyes with her lady-in-waiting.

"I hope not, Madame. She has great aptitude."

"And a great temper, too, I hear."

"Oh, Madame, what have you heard?"

"Only that she had to be pulled from two others in a scuffle in the stable yard."

Lady Elisabeth chuckled. "They were both larger than her, too. The men were impressed."

"I slapped my brother's face more than once in my day," Margaret reminisced, her eyes twinkling.

Lady Elisabeth's hand flew to her mouth. "Oh, Madame, who could believe it?"

"I was the only one who dared to," Margaret recalled. How infuriating Philip had been at times, with his godlike beauty and blithe, cutting manner, especially towards his wife.

"Like you, she is daring. With a bold spirit."

"Not to be broken, as it is part of her charm," Margaret mused, watching Anne through the French doors.

"But it must be curbed, Madame. You are the best example of that," Lady Elisabeth qualified.

Margaret's gaze was distant. "When I was her age, I was no longer wanted in France and waiting to return to a homeland I had never known."

"Oh, Madame, how did you endure those dark days?"

"I hid my feelings and concealed my thoughts." Margaret flicked a speck from her sleeve, along with the memory of those two grim years.

"You are a master at that."

Margaret gave a wry smile. "I had practice." How well Anne of France had taught her the art of dissembling, then used it against her. "And I learned such skills by age thirteen, as our little *Boullan* has not."

Lady Elisabeth shook her head slowly. "No."

"But perhaps she will use her own set of skills," Margaret speculated.

Lady Elisabeth frowned. "Let us hope so."

"May she shine at other courts as she has shone here," Margaret proclaimed, heading for the door. She had done her best with Thomas Boleyn's girl. No one could turn a spirited courser into a plodding palfrey.

Anne's escort arrived just as the leaves on the trees in the courtyard of the Court of Savoy turned gold. Her prospects were turning gold, too, glittering with untold adventures ahead. With her trunks packed and Lady Elisabeth fussing over her travel cape, she was ready to embark on her journey.

"You will do well at the French court, *ma Boullan*. As you have done here." Lady Elisabeth's tone was both warm and cautionary. "But remember not to stand out too much. It is never wise at court."

"I will do my best, Madame." Anne's eyes danced. *I will do my best to stand out gloriously, one day*, she thought.

"I will take you to Madame so you may say your farewells." Lady Elisabeth gestured for Anne to follow her. "Come now, before she goes into council."

Anne hurried along behind, bidding silent goodbyes to her favourite paintings on the walls of the rooms she passed through. The red-orange corals in Lady Margaret's collection cabinet seemed to wave farewell, their spiky branches offering a tender blessing. Outside Lady Margaret's study, Anne paused, her heart heavy with the weight of parting. Lady Margaret was in conference, giving orders to Lady Elisabeth's husband, Monsieur Lalaing, for the seating at that day's council meeting.

His page loitered in the hallway across from Anne, the same youth that had dallied with Agnes de Middelbourg a few months earlier in Tervuren. The moment Lady Elisabeth passed through the door, he looked Anne up and down.

"You will keep your eyes in your head," she hissed. No longer was she the child who had arrived at the Court of Savoy. She was now a woman on her way to the French Court, armed to navigate its intricacies.

"*Entrez!*" Lady Margaret's voice rang out from within.

The door swung open. From behind Lady Margaret's desk, Babou bounded to greet Anne, burying his nose in her gown until she wrested him away. The reality of leaving washed over her, and the thought of never holding him again tugged at her heart.

Lady Margaret looked up from her papers. "Why so sad, *ma Boullan?*"

Anne's voice trembled. "Forgive me, Madame. But I may never see you again."

"Nonsense, little one. We will cross paths again. And if not, you will carry me in your heart." Lady Margaret rose from her desk and came close.

"'Tis true, Madame. I will hold you in my heart for all time. And your mottoes, too."

Lady Margaret's laughter danced through the air, warm and confident. "Which one is your favourite?"

"I most admire '*Groigne qui groigne, vive Bourgogne*', Madame. 'Tis a bold challenge," Anne exclaimed, thinking 'grumble those who may, long live Burgundy' suited a woman as powerful as Lady Margaret perfectly.

"I enjoy its meaning, too, little one."

Anne tilted her head. "But what of your other motto?"

Lady Margaret's eyebrows arched. "Which one, *ma chère*?"

"The one that reads, '*Fortune, infortune, forte une.*'"

A shadow of contemplation crossed the regent's face. "It means that both fortune and misfortune strengthen one."

"Strengthen a woman, Madame? Or strengthen anyone, man or woman?"

Lady Margaret's gaze grew distant. "Facing both fortifies anyone, *ma petite*. But it particularly strengthens a woman."

Anne searched her face. "Why so, Madame?"

Lady Margaret's eyes sparkled with a knowing light. "You will find out for yourself. And may you hold fast to my mottoes for the strength they will bring you."

Anne nodded, her voice earnest. "I pray for strength for the years ahead."

"You shall have it, for those who ask God for strength receive it from Him."

"Did you?"

Lady Margaret's smile wrapped around her like a warm Flemish cloak spun from English wool. "What do you think?"

"I think you are the strongest woman I have ever known," Anne exclaimed as the great lady opened her arms. Anne fell into them, all too aware that she might never feel them again.

The future beckoned, glittering and sharp. Lady Margaret's mottoes would gird her to face whatever lay ahead.

In the courtyard, the coach stood ready, men bustling about, tightening straps and securing trunks. In the crisp autumn air, the clatter of hooves mingled with the murmur of preparations. Barbe detached herself from the cluster of demoiselles that stood to one side, their cloaks wrapped snugly around them. "Ready for your journey?"

Anne's voice was thick. "I will miss you."

Barbe raised an eyebrow. "You will forget me the moment you cross into France."

A swirl of emotions rose inside Anne. "I'll never forget you."

Barbe smirked as she tweaked Anne's headdress. "I know you too well, *ma Boullan*. Go with God and be happy."

Anne sang out her response. "I'll be most happy, and so will you."

"May it be so," Barbe agreed. Embracing Anne, she gave her two quick, fond kisses.

Françoise de Bréderode, Claude de Saillant, and Veronique de Hallewijn said their goodbyes, their faces a mix of curiosity and farewell.

Jeanne de Rosimbos lingered, her gaze uncertain. Moving towards her, an irresistible urge overcame Anne. Opening her arms, she offered an angelic smile. As Jeanne's jaw dropped, Anne planted a kiss on her cheek. "She's all yours," she murmured.

Jeanne's eyes narrowed as she pulled back. "She always was," she hissed.

No longer bothered, Anne didn't respond.

Isabelle de Longueval stepped up, two ribbons in her hand, one yellow, one blue. "*Tiens*, don't forget the colours of Burgundy."

Taking the ribbons, Anne leaned in. "And don't forget — we can't change our fathers, but we can change ourselves."

"I won't forget," Isabelle whispered back, her eyes gleaming.

Anne cast one last look at the Court of Savoy's entrance. Agnes de Middelbourg stood in the doorway. As their eyes met, she gave a half-hearted wave then disappeared inside. Anne chuckled. She had learned much from Agnes. But what joy it was to leave her behind.

Madame de Verneuil glided over, folding her into an embrace. "Go with God," she murmured.

Semmonet approached, his bow deep. He kissed Anne's hand as if she were a grown woman. "I wish I could come with you to watch your progress."

"I wish you could, too," Anne lied. She was eager to present herself at the French court alone, without minders to clip her wings.

At last, Lady Elisabeth stepped forward, her gaze steady. "Do not forget what you have learned here," she said, kissing Anne on both cheeks with deep affection.

Anne fought back tears, her voice resolute. "Never, Madame."

"Time to go," her escort called out.

Anne climbed into the carriage as cries of '*au revoir*' rang out. She returned them, but in her heart, she knew it was '*adieu*'. Too much beckoned for her to return.

With a smart flick of the horses' reins, the journey commenced. As the carriage rumbled down the Keizerstraat, Anne spotted a falcon high in the pale blue sky.

Circling overhead, it straightened its path and flew in the direction of France. Anne's time at Margaret of Austria's court was over.

A NOTE TO THE READER

Dear Reader,

The inspiration for *Maid of Honour* came to me when I was researching my book on Margaret of Austria. I was surprised to learn that Anne Boleyn had spent over a year as a maid of honour at Margaret's court in the Burgundian-Habsburg Netherlands from 1513-1514. The more I researched, the more I realised that very little has been written about this chapter in Anne's life.

No one knows Anne Boleyn's exact birth date. Some scholars argue 1501. Others say 1507. It is my considered opinion that it was 1501, in alignment with the conclusions of two preeminent historians and Anne Boleyn scholars, Alison Weir and Eric Ives.

Deciphering the enigma that was Anne Boleyn is like trying to catch the wind. My intent is to leave readers with a lingering impression of what influences England's most controversial queen came under as she moved from girlhood to womanhood at Margaret of Austria's Burgundian-Habsburg imperial court.

Anne Boleyn was larger than life — more vivacious, more witty, more impassioned, more headstrong, more ambitious, more vengeful, more determined than most of the rest of us. All of which led her to England's throne as Henry VIII's queen, and then to the scaffold, transforming her into a legend.

Margaret of Austria was early sixteenth-century Europe's most powerful female leader. She governed the Burgundian-Habsburg Netherlands from 1507-1515 and again from 1517-1530. Her Court of Savoy in Mechelen (referred to in this work by its French name of Malines, as French was the language of

Margaret's court) was an incubator for the Italian Renaissance to thrive and seep into the sensibilities of Northern Europe.

The *sprezzatura*, or effortless grace, that Anne absorbed at Margaret's court is a central theme of Baldassare Castiglione's 1528 master work, *The Art of the Courtier*. This watershed book lays out the attributes of the ideal Renaissance courtier. Its 1507 setting indicates that the term *sprezzatura* had come into parlance in Italy just as Margaret came into power as ruler of the Burgundian-Habsburg Netherlands.

It can be assumed that Margaret was familiar with the concept of *sprezzatura*, as she exercised it brilliantly, ruling the Netherlands with a natural authority and respected and admired by those she commanded.

I would argue that the superb grace that set Anne Boleyn head and shoulders above others at the 1520s English court was first learned not in France, as is widely believed, but at the hands of Margaret of Austria, one of the towering figures of early sixteenth-century Europe.

If you enjoyed reading *Maid of Honour*, I would be grateful if you would help others discover this book by posting a review on **Amazon** or **Goodreads**. Readers can also connect with me via **my website** or on **Facebook**.

I hope you will continue with the Anne Boleyn Chronicles and join me in France in Book Two of the series as we uncover more of the early influences that shaped the dazzling and enigmatic Anne Boleyn.

Rozsa Gaston

Sapere Books is an exciting new publisher of brilliant fiction and popular history.

To find out more about our latest releases and our monthly bargain books visit our website:
saperebooks.com